Inspector Ghote
Caught in Meshes

INSPECTOR GHOTE
Caught in Meshes

H.R.F. KEATING

Academy
Chicago
Publishers

AUTHOR'S NOTE

*The nature of this story has made it necessary to venture
here and there into fantasy. There is no such thing as the
Special Investigations Agency (though there is a Federal
Bureau of Investigation, but that is in another country).
There is no India First Group, and the secret that it
protects is equally imaginary. There is certainly no such
person as my Inspector Phadke and his behaviour is
dictated entirely by the demands of the story. There is
not even a Queen's Imperial Grand Hotel.*

H.R.F.K.

Published in 1985 by

Academy Chicago Publishers
425 N. Michigan Ave.
Chicago, Illinois 60611

Copyright © 1967 by
H.R.F. Keating

Printed and bound in the U.S.A.

Library of Congress Cataloging-in-Publication Data
Keating, H. R. F. (Henry Reymond Fitzwalter), 1926–.
    Inspector Ghote caught in meshes.

    Reprint. Originally published: London : Published for
the Crime Club by Collins, 1967.
    I. Title.
PR6061.E26I38   1985   823'.914   85-15831
ISBN 0-89733-178-8

PROLOGUE

THE THREE MEN had been sprawled there in the shade of the big Flame of the Forest for nearly two hours, but although it was very hot and almost intolerably muggy they had not slept. There was a feeling of tension behind their air of easy-going relaxedness. It showed in the way every now and again one of them would check over his gun.

The Sikh in the orange turban had an American self-loading Garand rifle and the other two had revolvers, one a British Army officer's issue Webley and the other a much abused Smith and Wesson dating from the early years of the century. This last was hardly reliable at a range over five yards, but none of the three expected to use it at even this distance.

The people of the village just below the slight hill on which the solitary Flame of the Forest stood had taken some time to get used to their visitors, but an hour after their arrival they were left almost completely to themselves. The old women squatting outside the huts gossiped away as they pounded the corn and hardly so much as glanced across at the three of them in the shade of the big tree. The little children tumbled and played unconcernedly in the dirt. Over in the fields, still muddy from the monsoon rains which had hardly yet finished, the men, naked all but for a cloth round their waists, and the women, with their harsh red and green saris tucked between their legs, bent low over their work as they had done all their lives and would go on doing. Afterwards.

: :   : :

Nor did any of the villagers pay much attention to the bullock cart that had lumbered past about the same time that the three strangers had settled down under the Flame of the Forest. It came from the next village south and its driver was known to them all, a notorious ne'er-do-well,

5

Bholu, much gossiped about because once a year or so he would make his way right up to Poona, toiling over the sharp ascent of the great Ghats, and there he would lose every anna he had been able to lay his hands on in whatever gambling games he could find.

With a man like Bholu it was not in the least surprising that he should drive his lumbering beasts through the village, going this time north away from Poona on the road which led eventually to the distant, teeming city of Bombay, and then abruptly seem to lose interest and stop. He had halted in the shade of a small banyan tree by the roadside. He had had at least that much sense. And there he had stayed, letting his great, heavy-horned beasts lower their heads and tug discontentedly at the few tufts of grass growing there.

A hundred yards or so down the road a gang of men, some of them recruited from the village, were at work mending the embankment where it had fallen away during the first heavy monsoon rains. But Bholu paid them no attention. Instead he sat on the boards of his big, awkwardly-constructed cart and looked backwards to where under the wide-spreading Flame of the Forest tree the Sikh stranger's orange turban shone like a gaudy jewel.

If anyone spared Bholu a thought they would have believed he was sleeping away the heat of the day. But he was not. In spite of everything he was awake, wide awake.

: :   : :

The three men waiting under the Flame of the Forest had already passed through the village earlier in the day. They had come from the direction of Poona in a battered old Buick painted for the most part a bright blue. But they had not stopped and no one had taken any notice of them. Dozens of vehicles went rattling by along the road between Poona and Bombay at every hour of the day.

In the car then there had been five of them. They had driven past, negotiated the place where there was single-lane traffic only by the roadworks and had gone on to a village about ten miles away. Here two of the party had been let out of the car, rather unceremoniously. No sooner had the battered blue Buick swirled round and left again, heading back in the Poona direction now, than the pair had begun conducting a search of the immediate area. Whatever it was they were looking for they appeared not to find, because after a little a short and rather angry consultation had taken place between them. Then they had approached the villagers.

With a good deal of truculence they had asked for fuel to build a fire, and when they paid they had done so too generously, which did nothing to appease the feelings of resentment they had aroused. The blacksmith, from whom they had bought a can of kerosene at a grossly inflated price, was most vocal in expressing this general annoyance. As a man of substance, the possessor of a petrol pump strategically situated at a point where the straight road from Bombay made a small unaccountable twist and traffic conveniently slowed up, he naturally exercised certain rights of leadership. He was expected to set the tone in questions both moral and practical. And he enjoyed exercising this right to the full.

So he was the first to express open doubts about the intentions of the two interlopers. Why did they want to build a fire? They had brought nothing to cook. And even when the fire was ready, a neat heap of dried dung-cakes and pieces of brushwood, they had done nothing about lighting it.

The blacksmith did not actually put these doubts to the two men sitting beside the unlit fire taking advantage of the shade made by the road embankment. Every time anyone had asked them a friendly question they had bristled aggressively. It was quite likely that if they were pressed too far they would start an ugly incident of some sort. But in the shelter of his tumbledown little shop the blacksmith put the case against them in no uncertain terms.

"And why do they jump up to look at every car coming from Bombay direction?" he demanded in conclusion. "They are cars only. There is nothing to look."

His hearers nodded gravely. That clinched the matter.

: :   : :

The elegant, dark green, hired Chevrolet, not long out of Bombay, was moving fast down the straight length of the trunk road to distant Poona. Already it was covered with dust, although there was nothing like so much of it on the surface of the concrete as there would be later in the year. But then the car was being driven a good deal faster than it should be.

Leaving the city not long before it had acquired a long black scratch on the rear nearside wing where the driver, a tall, beige-suited young American with a crest of extraordinary, flaming red hair and an equally unmistakable streak of flaming red beard, had grazed a lamp standard. But this experience had apparently done nothing to warn him to take it less hectically. The car, headed firmly south now, was shooting along the road every bit as fast as it was safe to go, and faster.

: :   : :

The two truculent men beside the unlit fire leapt to their feet for the twentieth time. The car coming towards them slowed. The driver, a harassed Mysore civil servant taking his family back to Belgaum after a wedding, negotiated the double bend by the blacksmith's petrol pump with care. The two men craning over the top of the embankment slumped down again and sat waiting.

: :   : :

Bholu, the bullock driver, sitting in his cart in the shade of the small banyan by the roadside, shook himself to make sure he had not dropped off. Above him the sky was brazen with heavily massing clouds.

: :   : :

Under the Flame of the Forest on its gently moulded hillock the Sikh pulled two cigarettes from a packet of Cavander's and tossed them over to his companions. Then he pushed himself up from the rope bed they had hired from the people in the village. It was not a very good bed. The wooden end-bars were too thin and in consequence the long cords were slacker than the cross ones. The Sikh had been contemptuous when it had first been carried over to them, but a chorus of voices had sworn that it was the best in the village. He had paid less to borrow it than had been hoped.

With his face crinkled to protect his eyes from the glare he looked away north in the direction of Bombay. The road stretched straight and long into the far distance cutting through the patterned squares and strips of the caramel-coloured fields. Here and there a tree broke the straightness of the line for a moment, like the little banyan in the shade of which the bullock cart still rested. Farther on the line was more effectively interrupted by the gang at work on the fallen embankment. Piles of stones lay half across the concrete, and ant-like figures could be seen moving slowly from one heap to the next or clambering painfully down the side of the embankment itself.

Beneath the wide sweep of the metallic sky, with the sun almost directly above them now, the sounds of the gang's labours were too faint to be heard. The Sikh slumped down on the creaky bed and picked up the Garand rifle once again.

When they had first arrived, parking their battered blue Buick in the shade of a straw-rick and facing it carefully towards Poona, their weapons had evoked a flurry of questions from the curious villagers. Eventually and grudgingly the Sikh had said that they had come to shoot "some mad dogs." The reply had appeased the villagers, more or less. It was the most informative answer they could persuade the party to make on any subject, and so they had been shruggingly abandoned as a source of entertainment. Back at their laborious daily round, nobody thought to wonder why it was that the strangers never made any attempt to find mad dogs to shoot.

::   ::

The red-haired, red-bearded American was still pushing the elegant green hired Chevrolet along for all it was worth. Penetrating dust had settled everywhere round him and his taut features were covered with a fine layer of it, streaked once or twice where a path had been traced by a heavy drop of perspiration.

Suddenly on the long, straight road ahead he spotted a man in a check shirt and jeans standing beside a small, over-loaded family car waving energetically. The little car, a Fiat, was halted far enough out on the road to make it necessary to slow down drastically.

The red-bearded American was unable to avoid looking the stranded driver full in the face. The appeal made to him was blatant.

He braked abruptly.

" Hell," he said.

The man in the check shirt hurried over.

" Gee," he said, " you from the States too?"

" Guess so."

" That's just great. You see what's happened to us? Back axle gone."

He turned and glanced at his car. Back-axle trouble might have been expected. From its heaped-up roof rack to its cluttered floor the little vehicle was almost all load. Spare tyres, a push-chair and rolls of bulging bedding made up the roof baggage. In the open boot there was a Primus stove, petrol cans, a formidable tool-kit, two buckets and a shovel. In the back three T-shirted children sat cross-legged on top of a mound of suitcases. Each spare space held a box of Kleenex. A determinedly cheerful young mother wearing a faded Aertex shirt sat in front nursing an enormous string-bag of fruit. She looked very, very hot.

The father of the family had become even more cheerful.

" This is great," he said again. " We saw a kinda garage about ten miles back. I think someone from there could fix this. They're pretty good at breakdowns, the Indians."

The red-bearded driver of the big, hired Chevrolet looked at him in silence.

" So if you could just give me a lift back there," he went on, unabashed, " then maybe they could come out here with some kind of a mechanic."

He looked expectantly at his compatriot.

"Ten miles back," the red-bearded man said. "I saw that place. It's fifteen miles there if it's a yard. I'm sorry but I have to get to Poona and quick."

He looked at the watch strapped to the inside of his dust-covered wrist.

"Hell," he said, "I've wasted too much time as it is."

"But—but, gee. I can't ask just anybody to go back, and if I have to walk all that way in this heat . . ."

The young family man looked up into the brazen dome of the sky. But already his fellow countryman was jerking the hired Chevrolet savagely into gear.

: :   : :

It took the blacksmith a good while to stir up his fellow villagers to the point of action. But at last they moved in a body out of the comforting shade at the back of the shop. The blacksmith followed them. He had picked up a rusted length of iron drain-pipe that had been lying in a corner for years waiting for a use to be found for it.

Three or four of the stouter-hearted villagers looked around for other weapons. It took them a few minutes to find anything suitable. But at last they were ready, one armed with a length of chain, another with a big vegetable-chopping knife, a third with a long piece of bamboo which had been half holding up a corner of the blacksmith's veranda.

"We'll teach them," the blacksmith said. "Coming here like that."

There was a satisfying, angry mutter of agreement.

"Get them running," the blacksmith shouted.

They advanced in a knot to the edge of the road opposite the point where the two interlopers had built their unlit fire. The sound of a car approaching fast from the Bombay direction caused the posse to halt. They might perhaps have got across the road before it arrived, but they were prudent men and they waited.

The car slowed with a squeal of brakes at the unexpected

kink where the petrol pump was. On the far side the faces
of the two intruders appeared on the top of the embankment
like two dusty boulders with wide, white staring eyes.

They both registered the fact that the driver of the car
was red-haired and red-bearded at exactly the same instant.
Simultaneously they let go their holds and slithered down
the slope of the embankment. As if carrying out a well-
practised routine, one seized the kerosene tin, screwed off its
cap in a series of swift jerks and upended it. The liquid
golloped out on to the little pile of sticks and dung-cakes.
The other watcher had already opened a box of matches.
With shaking fingers he pulled one out and, without closing
the box, attempted to strike it.

The dark green Chevrolet pulled smoothly away. The
blacksmith and his men took heart from the suddenness
with which the intruders had vanished the moment they
themselves had appeared at the other side of the road. They
set out to cross now with new resoluteness.

The fumbler dropped his match.

From the top of the embankment the blacksmith and his
men looked down.

" What do you want here?" the blacksmith shouted.
" You have no right. Do you think you own the place?"

The man who had poured the kerosene grabbed the
match-box.

The blacksmith's supporters were applauding.

This time the new match was struck without trouble. In
the silence that had followed the blacksmith's speech the
tiny spluttering sound as the flame burst could be distinctly
heard. The man holding the match stooped swiftly.

From the heap of sticks and dung-cakes a twirl of thick,
sooty black smoke went up.

The two interlopers turned at once and ran. With a
ragged cheer the villagers set out after them. None of them
paid the least attention to the fire. But its smoke, despite
its coming into being so haphazardly, rose steadily into the
sullen stillness of the midday air.

: :   : :

Under the shade of the big Flame of the Forest the Sikh leapt up from the creaky bed. He grabbed hold of the arm of the man nearer him and pointed.

To the north perhaps some ten miles away a thin, soft black streak of smoke was slowly mounting into the brazen sky.

Quickly the Sikh unknotted the grimy white sweat cloth from round his neck. He took a couple of paces forward out into the sunlight. He lifted his right arm and slowly waved the dirty cloth. It spread out and fluttered a little. The others, intent on giving their guns one last, unnecessary check, paid no attention.

Down by the banyan tree Bholu, who had succeeded in staying awake for all the oppressiveness of the heat, staggered to his feet. He shook his head a little to gather himself together and, standing astride the clumsy frame of the cart, waved his bare arm once or twice in the air. Then he turned, scrambled to his place on the butt-end of the cart's heavy shaft, and leaning down first to the right then to the left, he seized the tails of his great, lanky bullocks and gave each a vicious twist. The huge animals, jerked out of a heat-induced doze, started suddenly forward. The cumbersome wooden wheels of the cart grated sharply out. Heavily it progressed down the road in the direction of the single-lane section where the embankment labourers were sleeping through the worst of the heat.

: :   : :

The man in the dark green hired Chevrolet was pushing the car along at maximum pace once more. Irritatedly he glanced down at his watch, then took a new grip of the wheel and tensed forward in his seat. Ahead of him the dusty concrete lay in an unbroken ribbon. Never for an instant did he take his eyes off it.

: :   : :

The lumbering bullock cart ceased to move just as it reached the roadworks. The squeaking of its wheels had caused two of the sleeping labourers down at the foot of the half-reconstructed embankment to stir. But when the sound stopped they went back to sleep again without having moved.

The huge cart was still in place a few minutes later when the dark green dust-covered car came up. The driver was in plenty of time to halt when his insistently-sounded horn failed to clear the way.

At the far end of the single lane he leant his flaming red-bearded head out of the car window.

" Will you get the hell out of the way?" he shouted.

Bholu, perched on the heavy shaft between his two whitish beasts, looked at him blankly.

" Hell, I don't speak your damned language, whatever it is," the red-headed American yelled.

He opened the car door and got out. He marched along towards Bholu pointing with great forcefulness in the direction he wanted to go. He glared at the bullock cart. He made it utterly plain that with its two great, pointed-horned animals it was blocking his way.

He hardly noticed the three figures who stepped out from the shade of the banyan a little farther along the road and advanced towards him. In the soft dust their flapping sandals made scarcely any sound. The Sikh pushed the safety catch off on the Garand rifle with his thumb.

The bullock on Bholu's left lowered its green-tinted horns with the little glinting brass tips and the bobbing coloured thread balls round them. Softly he pawed at the ground. A long trail of heavy saliva dripped slowly down his loose dewlap. Both beasts steadily flailed their much-twisted tails, stirring the flies to motion on their dirty white flanks.

When the American noticed the three advancing men he did not appear to take in the fact that the Sikh carried a rifle and the other two had revolvers, one a British Army issue Webley and the other an extremely old Smith and Wesson.

" Hey, you fellows," he called. " You speak English? Can you tell this sonofabitch to get his stinking, crummy wagon out of my way?"

The three men did speak a certain amount of English.

But they did not reply to the American's request. Instead they walked steadily and silently forward.

The sound of the strident New World voice caused a good many of the labourers at the foot of the embankment to stir in their sleep. But not one of them thought it worthwhile to get to his feet and investigate. For a few moments the mid-day quiet returned.

Then came the sound of shots in the hot stillness.

CHAPTER I

INSPECTOR Ganesh Ghote sighed for his native land. Things had come to a pretty pass. A visiting American shot down in the crudest sort of highway robbery. A dacoity taking place within fifty miles of Bombay, on a main trunk road. And that this should happen to the brother of a world figure like Professor Gregory Strongbow. Here was the world's foremost hydrodynamics expert, a man who had conferred immense benefits on the human race, on holiday in India and his brother is brutally murdered.

It did not bear thinking about.

The blue Dodge police truck went thundering along the dusty Poona road. The pattern of the fields whirled past, broken only by the occasional deeply-cut, wandering nullah or the clustered huts of a village. Ghote looked steadily ahead.

It should not be far now. And the moment he arrived he must get his teeth into the case. It would not be an easy affair. Dacoits were notoriously difficult to track down. No doubt these had carried out their robbery quite openly and had relied as usual on going into hiding until the trouble had blown over. But for once they had miscalculated. They had contrived to pick on someone too important, and they had killed him. At least for once there would be maximum backing at all levels.

Ghote vowed not to rest till he had identified the culprits

and step by step had tracked them down. He owed that much to the national reputation.

They approached a fantastically overloaded little Fiat which had broken down by the roadside. An American family by the look of it, the children in bright T-shirts, both father and mother in jeans. Luckily there was a mechanic lying on his back under the vehicle. This was no time to have to stop and offer assistance.

And now a momentary slow-down where the road took a sudden twist round a blacksmith's shop and its rusty old petrol pump, and it should be about another ten miles.

Yes, the deputy superintendent had said the dacoity had occurred where the traffic was held up by roadworks and there ahead was a place where the embankment had crumbled away. And yes, there was a dark green car stopped in the full glare of the heat. That should be it.

His driver brought the over-heated Dodge to a screaming halt worthy of the best traditions of the Bombay Police. Ghote jumped lightly down and took in the scene with a quick glance.

A harassed and sweaty but stolid-looking constable was keeping back a small crowd of gaping villagers and workers from the road-mending gang. The empty car, a Chevrolet, unusually enough, stood at the point where the road narrowed to one lane. At the other end of the single lane there was a bullock-cart. Its two bullocks with their coloured horns down were dragging at the last remains of some roadside tufts of grass. A couple of paces from the car there was crudely traced in the dust the outline of a man's body. Beside it the surface of the concrete had been darkened by a dried-up pool of blood over which buzzed some fat flies.

Ghote went over towards the constable to get his report.

And was suddenly startled to hear a loud shout from a little way down the road.

" Hey, you."

He turned. But immediately regretted having done so.

The shout might not have been directed at him. It should not have been directed at him, an inspector of the Maharashtra State Police.

Only he knew perfectly well that it was.

There was no doubt either about who the shouter was. Striding along the dust-layered surface of the road was a tall, broad-shouldered Westerner. Everything from the well-hung cut of his crisp, beige-coloured suit to his broad-brimmed straw hat with the coloured band round the crown proclaimed him an American.

"You," he called again, as he strode forward. "You, are you the inspector from the police they said was coming from Bombay?"

Ghote squared his thin shoulders.

"I am inspector in charge of case, certainly," he said.

"Well, I'm glad to see you finally got here," the American replied.

The thought flashed into Ghote's mind that this was a pressman. He found the notion a little daunting. Indian journalists he could cope with, though he never much liked even their brashness. But an American reporter. A tough, remorseless conductor of special investigations. How had this one got on to the murder so quickly? It was typical of them. And what would he not make of it? The sort of reports he would file would knock crores of rupees off tourist revenue.

Ghote licked his upper lip.

He would be asked all sorts of details about his personal affairs. There would be uncomplimentary physical descriptions of himself in each day's story, of his lack of height and his thinness. He had heard about American-style papers. They would want to mention his wife, his child. Perhaps they would say that Protima spoke English badly, that she distrusted Western furniture and clothes.

"Now, I'd like to know right away just what you intend doing," the American said.

Ghote looked up at him. He seemed to be in his late

forties, broad and still slim. He had a markedly handsome face with a long, straight nose, and a crisp darkening of beard-shadow along the sides of the wide jaw. Undoubtedly he was tough. And there was an angry glint in his eyes.

"I have no time for Press affairs now," Ghote said loudly. "I have a great deal of work ahead in the conduct of the investigation. Kindly wait until afterwards."

"Press affairs?" the big American said. "What the hell do you mean, Press affairs?"

He glared down at Ghote.

"Look," he said, "it's my brother who's been murdered here. My brother. And I want to know just what you're going to do to pin down the men responsible."

A hugely unsettling wave of astonishment swept over Ghote. Was this really Professor Gregory Strongbow, the world-famous scientist? If the man himself had not said so, it would have been almost impossible to believe. He did not look old enough. He looked much too active. Why didn't he stoop? And the tously hair under that hat with the bright, coloured band, that was hardly academic. Then there was the way he had shot out those questions in that reporter's style. But perhaps this was due to the shock of his brother's death.

"Professor Strongbow," Ghote stammered. "I beg your pardon. Please accept my profound regrets. Allow me to introduce myself. Yes. Yes, of course. I am Inspector Ghote, of Bombay C.I.D. Specially detailed to investigate this case. Yes, Ghote. My name is Ghote."

In an onrush of desire to make up to Professor Strongbow for his original attitude, Ghote wondered whether he ought perhaps to tell him more about himself. To bring out his wife's name and his boy's, to state his own qualifications in full, even to explain that although he was married to someone who did not speak English well she was still an intelligent and characterful woman.

But the professor gave him no opportunity.

He shot out a broad, tanned hand for Ghote to shake. His grip was impressively firm.

"Glad to meet you," he said. "I guess I may have been a little abrupt. To tell you the truth, I'm pretty on edge."

Ghote's eye went involuntarily to the crudely traced outline in the dust. He saw too for the first time that in the door panel of the dark green Chevrolet there was a dented round hole where it must have been struck by a bullet.

"Perhaps we should go over to the shade to talk the matter," he said.

Professor Strongbow seemed glad to fall in with the suggestion. He turned quickly away and took out a handkerchief to wipe his face.

"It certainly is hot," he said. "And humid."

They set off towards the shade of a small banyan tree between the roadworks and the village. Ghote saw that a small car was parked under it.

"You were not with your brother?" he asked the professor. "You were travelling in another car?"

"No, I wasn't with him. I was staying overnight at Poona, visiting the hydraulics laboratory there. I'm in that line myself."

"But you are the foremost world authority," Ghote said. "When I was given my instructions for the case this was specifically stated."

The professor smiled slightly. Ghote noticed that in spite of the determined line of his jaw and the uncompromising straightness of his nose the eyes were deep-set and understanding. He wondered suddenly whether he had embarrassed him.

"But why was your brother not with you in Poona?" he said quickly.

Almost at once he regretted the question. He should not be drawing the bereaved man's attention to such things in such a tactless manner.

But the professor seemed only too anxious to explain.

"It's like this," he said. "My brother and I decided to come to India together. I had some vacation due and I thought he ought to get away for a bit. But we don't have all that many interests in common. We didn't have, that is."

He took a few paces in silence, and then resumed with a jerk.

"Yes, that's how it was. We split up. We decided to split up for a while. He went out yesterday to see some things that primarily interested him, and I went over to Poona to see the hydraulics lab there. A pretty fine set-up too."

"Thank you," said Ghote, "thank you."

He coughed a little.

"And you had arranged to meet to-day in Poona?" he asked.

"No," said the professor.

A trace of a frown appeared on his wide forehead.

"No, to tell you the truth, I wasn't exactly expecting Hector to come on to Poona. The arrangement was I would see him to-morrow when I got back to Bombay."

"But he changed his mind?"

For a little Professor Strongbow did not answer.

"I guess he must have," he said at last. "Hector was somewhat impulsive, you know."

He fell silent again.

From something in his tone Ghote deduced that impulsiveness was not part of the professor's make-up. And the professor himself seemed to realise the implications of what he had said almost at once.

"Not that impulsiveness isn't a fine thing," he added. "I sometimes think a good many of us are liable to think so long we finally don't act at all."

"There is a great deal to be said on both sides," Ghote observed, feeling torn between supporting the professor in his eulogy of his dead brother and not appearing to criticise the man himself.

The professor grunted.

"Your tourist people in Poona were certainly very nice to me when the news came through," he went on. "They put this girl, this Miss Brown, in touch with me right away. And she fixed up a car and got us out here."

Ghote noticed that in the car parked in the shade of the

banyan a girl was sitting. She appeared to be wearing a sari.

"Miss Brown?" he asked.

"Yes," said the professor. "I guess she must be some kind of a Eurasian, though she looks pretty British and talks that way. But she told me her first name was something Indian."

He laid a hand on Ghote's elbow and halted him a moment.

"As a matter of fact," he said, "I didn't exactly catch what she said when she told me. It sounded like Shack—something. Is that possible?"

"Was it perhaps Shakuntala?" Ghote suggested.

"Yes. Yes, that's it. Shakuntala, you say? Thanks, Inspector. I didn't want to have to hurt the girl's feelings by calling her Miss Brown all the time."

Sitting sedately at the wheel of the little grey Hindustan she had provided for the professor, Shakuntala Brown smiled a little when she saw the two of them approach. Ghote noticed that, in spite of her sari, her hair was a light brown and her complexion distinctly pink and white. He wondered for a moment where she could come from. But he had no time for much speculation. As soon as the professor had introduced them, bringing out the Shakuntala with noticeable clarity, he felt obliged to start putting all the right questions. It was important to give this foreigner the correct impression of Indian policework.

"Please tell," he said, "something of your brother's habits. Was he for example a great free spender? Was he accustomed to pull out his wallet and offer to pay in notes for the least service?"

The professor considered gravely for a moment.

"No," he answered. "No, I don't think you could say that about Hector. He might have got excited some place and waved a lot of money about, but he certainly didn't give the impression of being loaded."

He gave Ghote a quick, appraising look.

" You're wondering why anyone should have picked on him to rob?" he asked. "Did you know that those guys had been waiting over there by that tree all morning?"

"All morning? Waiting?" Ghote said, with a sharp frown.

"That's what your patrolman told me," said the professor.

He looked steadily at Ghote.

"Is that what you'd have expected?" he asked.

But, unexpectedly, it was Shakuntala Brown who answered.

"Mr. Strongbow," she said, "you will have to get used to the idea that India is a very different country from the United States. People have a different time-scale here. They are prepared to wait hours for the very slightest of reasons. You couldn't be expected to understand that."

She spoke with vehemence. Ghote once more wondered about her. Was this her usual manner? Or did this unexplained behaviour on the part of the killers cause her to feel furious for some reason?

But there was no time for side-issues. He turned back to the American.

"The car your brother was driving," he said. "It is an expensive model and unusual. Had you bought it for the length of your stay in India?"

"No," Professor Strongbow answered thoughtfully. "No, I don't know anything about the car. I guess Hector must have rented it just to-day."

"To go to Poona to see you?"

"That I can't say for a fact."

"But it is likely? He was driving on the Poona road. You were in Poona."

"It looks like a reasonable assumption certainly."

"But you told you did not know why exactly he should come to meet you?"

Ghote noticed a sudden blankness in the cool eyes opposite him.

" No, I don't know that," the professor said. " I guess he suddenly wanted company or something."

Ghote shrugged his shoulders slightly.

" Perhaps he told someone in Bombay," he said. " You are staying at the Taj Mahal, or perhaps you prefer the Nataraj?"

" No," said the professor. " As a matter of fact we settled for a place called the Queen's Imperial Grand."

" Surely that is a very old-fashioned hotel for Americans?" Ghote said.

Professor Strongbow smiled just a little.

" That's more or less the point," he said. " We weren't all that anxious to find ourselves with a crowd of people from the States."

Ghote, who was beginning to think of the next stage in his inquiry, added one more question out of mere politeness.

" You preferred to see more of our country?"

Busy with his thoughts it was an instant or two before he realised that the professor had not answered. He looked across at him.

After a moment the American spoke.

" The truth of the matter is," he said, " that Hector had become somewhat notorious just recently back home. He had expressed certain vigorous political views, and had been forced out of his post at the university we both teach in. So I persuaded him to keep out of the limelight for a while."

It was plain that he was reluctant to say this of a brother so recently killed. Ghote stepped quickly out of the shade of the little banyan and signalled to the constable.

The man, who had been waiting patiently just out of earshot, came over at a trot and crashed thunderingly to attention.

" Inspector sahib?"

" You were the man who reported the dacoity?" Ghote asked.

" Yes, Inspector sahib. I am stationed five miles away only. As soon as one of the men from road repair gang informed I proceeded here by bicycle immediately."

" Good man. The body was still where it fell then?"

" Yes, Inspector sahib. But owing to the great number of flies and the presence of vultures I ordered it to be taken under shelter, having first made outline in road dust."

" Excellent. And what signs of dacoity did you observe?"

" The body had been robbed, Inspector sahib. But the thieves had failed to notice passport in back trouser pocket. It was through this that I made preliminary identification. When the burra sahib here arrived he carried out confirmation."

The constable dipped his head respectfully towards Professor Strongbow.

" Yes," said the American. " It was Hector all right. And the men who killed him must be found."

The angry glint had come back into his eyes. Ghote hurried on with his interrogation of the constable.

" I hear the men in question waited all morning up there under that Flame of the Forest tree," he said. " Is that correct?"

" It is what the villagers say, Inspector sahib."

" How many men were there?"

" Three, Inspector."

" And you obtained full descriptions?"

The constable sighed.

" These village people," he said. " They see nothing. They make no methodical observations. They told only that one was a Sikh and that they smoked a great many cigarettes."

" I will question myself later, but you seem to have done well."

" They were right about quantity of cigarettes smoked, Inspector," the constable said. " I examined ground under tree myself. There were forty-eight stubs present. Cavander's brand."

" Common enough," Ghote said, " but good work all the same."

He felt some pleasure that the constable was giving a good impression to the American. Certainly the latter was missing nothing. His eyes never lost their grave alertness for an instant.

" How did the men get here?" Ghote asked the constable next.

" They came by car, Inspector."

" Did any of the village people take its number?"

" None who saw it can read, Inspector sahib. They said it was a blue car and old only."

Ghote grimaced. But it was the sort of thing that might be expected.

The American beside him took half a pace forward.

" Inspector," he said, " I'd like to know something."

" Certainly," said Ghote.

" Now that you've established those guys waited all day just till Hector's car came along, does that alter your opinion at all of the nature of the crime?"

" That it was a dacoity?" Ghote said.

" If that means highway robbery, yes."

" A dacoity is technically a robbery carried out by five or more persons," Ghote said.

" All right, allowing for the fact that there seem to have been only three in this case, do you still think it is just a matter of straight robbery?"

" It is unusual for dacoits to wait so long," Ghote agreed.

He saw a look of acute interest flick into the American's eyes, to be replaced at once by his habitual cautious watch-fulness.

" It is unusual," Ghote repeated, " but no more. It is probable that your brother's car was the first to stop at the roadworks. You see that the bullock-cart there blocked the way."

He turned to the constable.

" The cart was there at the time of the accident?" he asked.

"Yes, Inspector sahib. I gave orders for no one to move."

"Good man."

"There is one thing, Inspector, also."

"Yes?"

"Some of the village women report having seen a small fire of black smoke start from a point down the road shortly before the dacoits left their waiting place. They believe it was a signal fire, Inspector."

Ghote heard the American catch his breath beside him.

"These women," he asked the constable, "are they to be trusted? Or are they foolish gossips only?"

"I think they may be right, Inspector. Certainly, it is strange for anyone to start a fire like that. But I could not leave the scene of the crime to carry out investigation."

"No," said Ghote. "But I will investigate just as soon as I have finished here."

"Then you think this may not be a simple robbery?" the American said eagerly.

Ghote turned to him.

"Please," he said. "There are certain things which appear a little unusual. But it is people we are dealing with, even though they are criminals. You cannot expect people always to do things according to the pattern of the text-books."

"So you are going to claim this was just robbery?" Professor Strongbow said.

He sounded disappointed.

Ghote looked up at him squarely.

"Professor," he said, "it is perhaps hard for you to understand that someone as close to you as your brother has been killed in a most ordinary way. But this is almost certainly what has happened. He has been victim of accident, if you like. The accident of these men choosing this day to commit dacoity. It is natural to look for signs of something special. But it is a mistake to try to read special meaning into the slight differences this case has from one to-morrow."

For some moments the American did not reply. Then he sighed deeply.

" You could be right," he said.

Ghote looked round more briskly.

" It is necessary now for me to examine the body," he said. " I imagine you would prefer to stay here by the car with Miss Brown?"

" No," said the American, " I'll come with you."

" But it is not necessary for me to hear your identification," Ghote said.

" All the same I'd like to come."

" As you wish."

They walked back along the road to the village in silence. The constable marched just ahead of them to show Ghote the way to the hut where he had had the body carried. His feet thumped steadily and evenly on the dusty surface of the road and then squelched through the mire of the shady village.

They stooped and entered the hut.

Already there was a sharp, unpleasant smell and the flies were buzzing hard. Ghote looked down at the rather thin figure in the beige, silk suit with the ugly rips in the chest and the dark, dried stains of blood. The face bore only the slightest resemblance to the professor's by the hut entrance. Above all, the crest of flaming red hair and the streak of beard of the same intense colour made the dead man look different.

Behind him the American spoke.

" He was not the sort of man you could mistake," he said.

" No," Ghote said. " A fine man, Professor."

" A distinctive man," the professor answered.

Ghote felt that the comment was hardly the proper one in the circumstances. It was not what ought to have been said about a brother so recently killed. It was not a correct tribute.

But after all the professor was an American, and perhaps they were different about such things.

To change the subject a little he pointed to a small

black and white metal disc the dead man had in the button-
hole of his left lapel.

"What is this, please?" he said. "It is some sort of
badge?"

"Yes," Professor Strongbow answered. "It's a badge all
right. A CND button. The Campaign for Nuclear Dis-
armament. Hector was a great one for that. As a matter of
fact it was that that caused all the trouble back home, the
reason why I persuaded him to come over here really."

He watched silently as Ghote continued with his examination.

"Yes," he said after a little, "I persuaded him to come.
To keep him out of trouble."

He gave a short, unmirthful laugh.

Ghote finished doing what he had to do and straightened
up.

"There's one thing," the American said. "That button.
Can I take it?"

Ghote knew it was not strictly allowable.

"Please to have it," he said.

The American bent forward, twisted the button out of its
place on the lapel of the beige-coloured suit and slipped
it into his pocket. They went out in the oppressive
heat.

Ghote was relieved to be able to walk briskly back to the
scene of the shooting, and as soon as they arrived he fired a
stream of questions at the patient constable, who dutifully
pointed out the few material factors there were to show.
Ghote checked the name of the car-hire firm that owned the
dark green Chevrolet. He inspected the vague scuffled
patches in the dust where the killers must have stood. He
gauged the distance between the car and the bullock-cart at
the far end of the roadworks.

The police breakdown truck coming to haul away the
Chevrolet for examination arrived in a great swirl of dust.
It stopped with a howl from its brakes, slewing dramatically
across the road. Ghote bit his lip in vexation. Behaviour of
that sort did not really give an impression of efficiency. It

simply made the Police Department look like a lot of children.

A cheerful head constable jumped out of the truck swinging a driving-wheel fitted with clamps to go over that of the car to be fingerprinted.

"Okay to take, Inspector?" he shouted.

Ghote noticed that the American had turned and was walking slowly back towards Shakuntala Brown under the little banyan. He turned back to the head constable.

"You be damned careful with that car," he snapped.

The head constable executed a pantomime of being extremely chastened. He approached the dark green Chevrolet on tiptoe.

Ghote hoped that the professor had not seen this display. It was difficult to make out.

"Inspector sahib," the local constable said respectfully at his elbow.

He turned to him with relief. At least here was somebody who did what he had to do sensibly and properly.

"Yes?"

"If the car is going, Inspector, shall I tell this bullock cart wallah to be on his way?"

Ghote looked across at the squatting figure of the driver on the big, unwieldy cart.

"No," he said, "you will not tell him to go. That man set up a fine road block at just the right time. I want to know why."

CHAPTER II

INSPECTOR GHOTE strode determinedly towards the patient, squatting figure of the bare-backed bullock-cart driver. If there was anything more to the attack on the red-haired American than a simple dacoity, then this was in all probability going to be his chance to find out.

But something in the sharp forcefulness of his stride

must have signalled a warning to the man perched on the clumsy shaft of the big cart. Because with a sudden leap into the air he flung himself down on to the road, staggered once and hared off along the dusty concrete surface with his long, bare legs scissoring out like a champion runner's.

Ghote went after him in an instant.

The constable was scarcely slower off the mark. But both of them had to negotiate the bulk of the heavy cart and by the time they had a clear run the bullock driver was well ahead. His skinny body looked as if it ought not to have the stamina to keep going at this pace for more than twenty yards, but plainly his looks were deceptive. It was all Ghote could do not to fall behind, and the constable, pounding along in his heavy boots, seemed to be even less well able to keep in the chase.

Ghote swore to himself. The fellow would not have to go far before he got some chance to get out of sight. And once he had done that he could disappear into the vast stretch of the countryside with its hundreds and hundreds of anonymous, almost unidentifiable people and be lost perhaps for ever more. There were thousands of homeless men wandering up and down the length of India, and it was beyond the scope of the possible to check on more than a handful of them.

Already the almost naked runner ahead of them was nearing the professor, slowly making his way towards the banyan tree. A hundred yards or so further on and the village would be reached. And there in a dodging game among the cluster of huts their quarry would be almost certain to get away.

And then the man stumbled. Perhaps in passing the tall form of the American he had taken his eyes off the road at his feet for an instant. But whatever the cause, he had stumbled badly. And Ghote and the constable had their chance. Within moments Ghote had closed up to the point where he was ready to fling himself forward in a final lunge.

He felt a sense of pounding joy as he took a deep breath and launched himself into the air.

Something heavy struck him a tremendous blow on the left shoulder, sending him sprawling away off target. His reaching fingers almost touched the bullock driver's earth-stained loincloth but the impact of the blow was too strong. With a jarring crash he landed flat on his face on the hard concrete.

It was the big American. He had taken it into his head to hurl himself at the bullock driver at just the instant Ghote had launched himself forward. And he too had landed every bit as awkwardly in the dust. Above them the constable came to a teetering halt, his way totally blocked by their outstretched bodies.

Ahead, the fugitive gave one quick glance round and then turned, leapt helter-skelter down the road embankment and was off across the wide spread of the fields.

" Damnation," said Ghote.

The American heaved himself up till he was on all fours on the dusty road.

" Inspector, I'm sorry," he said. " I've let him get away."

He pushed himself upright.

" I don't know what came over me," he said. " I don't usually act like that. I guess it was just that I suddenly realised that here was someone who could lead us to the men who killed my brother. I guess I suddenly thought I could avenge Hector that way."

He looked at the figure of the bullock driver, already getting smaller as he headed stubbornly across the pattern of the little fields. A long way behind, the constable, who had in his turn jumped down the embankment, was toiling conscientiously on.

" And all I did was to make sure the guy got away," the professor said.

Ghote reflected that this was probably true.

" Kindly do not worry," he said. " It was good of you to try to stop the fellow."

And suddenly he saw that all was not yet lost.

He turned to the professor.

" Your car," he said, " can I use same?"

" Sure thing."

The American swung round at once and began running towards the little grey Hindustan by the banyan. Following, Ghote noted that he ran well, taking long economical strides over the dusty surface of the road.

And he thought fast too, for all his generally cautious approach to things. Already he was shouting to Shakuntala Brown at the wheel of the little car to move over.

By the time Ghote had got there she was in the front passenger seat. The professor scrambled into the back. Ghote jumped in, banged the door to and tugged at the starter. The engine broke into life and Ghote swung the little vehicle round and set off along the road in a storm of fresh dust.

Within a minute they had reached the narrow cart-track which Ghote had suddenly spotted as they had watched the fugitive gradually getting smaller and smaller as he ran from field to field. Ghote swung the little Hindustan off the road and set it bucketing and swaying down the narrow, crumbly track as fast as he dared.

" You know," said Professor Strongbow from the back, " with any luck we're going to cut the guy off."

He leant forward with an elbow on the top of each seat. And suddenly the little car gave a violent lurch to the right as its front offside wheel dipped into a deep rut and its engine stopped dead.

They were hanging perilously over the banked edge of the path, with below them in the shade a miry patch of caramel-coloured earth waiting for their fall. The professor flung himself back with a groan.

" I just should never have said that."

And the shift in weight did the trick. The little car rose an inch or two in the front, Ghote leant backwards as much as he could and restarted the engine. Cautiously he slipped into reverse and put in the clutch. The car crept back on to the path again.

Half a minute later they were off once more. And within

INSPECTOR GHOTE CAUGHT IN MESHES 33

another two minutes Ghote and the professor were sliding down the bank from the path into the fields. Ahead of them, not fifty yards away, the bullock driver plunged on unaware of his danger.

"This time I'll leave him to you," the American said as they set off across the soft earth of the recently flooded fields.

He dropped back a yard or two and left Ghote to make the running. Quite soon the bullock driver heard them. He looked up startled almost out of his wits, and began to go off in a new direction. But it was too late. A pace or two more and Ghote was within striking distance again.

This time, with his quarry plainly exhausted to dropping point, he did not attempt to fling himself forward. He ran on a little, closing the gap between them with every stride. Then he reached forward and grabbed.

The hunt was up.

Ghote swung his captive round to face him. And found that he had misjudged his man. A sharp, well-pointed blow hit him hard in the pit of the stomach and he sat down abruptly in the soft earth, cursing himself all the way. The bullock driver appeared to be filled with new life at this success. He tore off again while Ghote, feeling sick, looked round.

It was hardly possible that the constable would catch him. He had stopped when he saw the fugitive had been cut off and was now much too far behind. Ghote heaved himself to his feet. He felt totally winded. It looked as if he had lost his quarry after all.

But he had reckoned without the professor. He came past at that moment, going like the wind. Somewhere in the chase he had slipped off his jacket and the hat with the gay, coloured band had been snatched off long before. Now his shirt was puffing out behind him and a heavy lock of his dark hair was biffing and battering at his eyes. But nothing was putting him off, and in a moment he shot himself forward in a low tackle that brought the bullock driver down with such a thump that the crows in every field around rose up in the air cawing like a whole congregation of startled old ladies.

Ghote quickly stumbled over and caught hold of his thin wrist before he had a chance to lash out a second time.

" Thank you very much," he said to the professor.

" I was the one who nearly let him get away in the beginning," the American said.

" You certainly made up for it," said Ghote. " I hope this fellow will turn out to be worth all the chasing."

: :   : :

Ghote waited to begin questioning his prisoner till they were all back at the scene of the killing. With the driver of his own truck, who had made it clear that his business was driving and not chasing people over fields, and the stolid local constable each holding the man by one arm, Ghote stood in front of him looking him straight in the face. He was rather gaunt in appearance with a wide moustache covering the whole of his upper lip and defeated, down-ward-looking eyes.

" Well," Ghote snapped, " what is your name?"

No answer.

" Your name?"

" Bholu."

Very sulkily delivered, without looking up.

" All right, Bholu," Ghote said, " you blocked the road with your cart so that those dacoits could rob the car when it stopped. But your friends made the mistake of killing the driver. You were helping them. That means you are as guilty of murder as they are. So you would certainly be hanged."

He waited for this to sink in.

Bholu could not have looked any more miserable. But Ghote assumed that after perhaps half a minute the full unpleasantness of his position would have become quite clear to him.

" Now," he went on, " there is just one chance for you. If you give me every bit of help you can, then I would see if something can be done. But it is see only, you understand."

Bholu gave a short moan.

"Come on," Ghote shouted suddenly, "talk."

Bholu stole a glance to the ground at his side but said not a word.

"Very well," Ghote said, turning away, "put him in the truck. We will take to Bombay, charge him straight away, and in no time at all we will have him hanged."

He noticed Professor Strongbow, standing a little way apart, begin a movement of protest. Quickly he walked off before the American could say anything.

Bholu broke into a sudden clamour of speech.

"Sahib, sahib. I cannot tell. Sahib, if I tell they would shoot me. Sahib, I know it. They would shoot me, sahib."

Ghote turned round comfortably.

"And if you do not tell," he said, "we would hang you."

Bholu darted quick glances from side to side. The constable at his back gave his right arm a sharp twist.

Then, in a very quiet voice which Ghote had to lean forward to hear, Bholu began to talk.

"Sahib, they are not dacoits at all," he said. "It was not to rob the American that they made me stop his car. It was for them to kill him. Sahib, they were paid to do that. They were paid a great sum to kill the American with the red hair and the red beard."

Professor Strongbow stepped quickly forward. He gave Ghote a long, questioning look.

Ghote concentrated on the bullock driver.

"These men who were paid all this," he said, "who are they?"

"Oh, sahib, I do not know."

"Yes, you know. How could they come to you for help if you did not know? Who are they?"

"Sahib, sahib, I owed one of them money. I had great losses, sahib."

"Who did you owe? Why did you owe him?"

" It was the cards, sahib. Sahib, I could not help. I had to do what they told, sahib. So much money I am owing."

" Who did you owe the money to?" Ghote said. " I want the name."

" To Lal Mahsi, sahib."

" Lal Mahsi? What Lal Mahsi is this?"

" Lal Mahsi who keeps a house for playing cards at Poona, sahib."

" Ah, him," Ghote said, though the gamblers of Poona were altogether unknown to him. " You went to which house to lose so much money at cards?"

" To the one in the Sadashiv Peth, sahib."

The gaunt-faced bullock driver gave a dry sob.

" The number of the house?" Ghote said.

He knew Poona well enough to remember that the houses in the crowded old city were numbered right through each quarter, with figures running up to thousands.

" What number in the Sadashiv Peth?" he asked.

And Bholu told him.

" All right," Ghote snapped. " And the others? The names of the other men with Lal Mahsi?"

" Sahib, I had never seen before. It is true, sahib."

" But they came here to kill an American with red hair?"

" Yes, sahib, yes. They knew when he would be coming, sahib. By a signal."

Bholu's eyes were blank with misery.

" Look, Inspector," Professor Strongbow said, " I told you before I wasn't sure my brother was killed during a straight robbery, didn't I?"

" Yes," said Ghote, " several things are beginning to fit into place now."

The American looked at him speculatively.

But before he had decided to say anything more Shakuntala Brown, who had been listening with disturbing intentness to every word that had been spoken, intervened.

" All the same, Professor," she said, with more urgency than seemed called for, " I'm sure the inspector will tell you that people in this country will invent any story to get themselves out of trouble. Don't forget, on the face of it it still looks most likely that your brother was killed in an ordinary dacoity. He was robbed, remember."

The American said nothing. But he looked at Ghote.

" Thank you, Miss Brown," Ghote said. " But what Professor Strongbow has noticed is enough to make me have damnable doubts about this being simple dacoity. Damnable doubts."

: :   : :

" One thing there can be no doubt about at all," Deputy Superintendent Samant barked, " is that what you have got to deal with, Inspector, is the nastiest case of dacoity we have had for years."

" But, DSP," Ghote said, " I think it is possible that——"

" Yes," said DSP Samant sharply, " the fact that the victim was the brother of a very distinguished foreign visitor does not really alter the nature of the crime at all. Dacoity, Inspector, pure and simple dacoity within fifty miles of Bombay."

Oppressed by the severe neatness of the DSP's office with its walls covered in many-coloured charts each completely up-to-date to that morning's entry, Ghote sat wondering when and how he was going to say what he had to. Because, cost what it might, respect for his own deductions coupled with a strong feeling that he must not let his new American acquaintance down, were going to make him contradict every word the Deputy Superintendent was saying.

He listened respectfully while the DSP vented his irritation that such an event should happen within his jurisdiction, and worse on his duty-day.

Then at last there came a pause.

" Sir," Ghote said, " I beg to state I am not convinced this is a case of dacoity. Sir, I believe it was assassination."

" Nonsense, man, just because the victim was important,

don't get it into your head that the crime has to be something special too. Dacoity, man, plain dacoity. Now, what are you going to do about it?"

"But, sir, the red-haired American's arrival at the point where he was ambushed was clearly signalled by means of a fire. I questioned the people at the village where it was lit, DSP. And they had no doubts that the fire was a signal."

The DSP's hands gripped the arms of his heavy cane-seated chair decisively.

"Just because some stranger chooses to light a fire in their village a lot of ignorant country people get all excited," he said. "But that doesn't mean that one of my officers has to fall in with them. I want to hear no more about it, Inspector."

"DSP," said Ghote with a trace of desperation, "Professor Strongbow, who is most determined his brother's murderers shall be brought to book, himself supports my view."

The DSP sighed. Sharply, like a little shunting locomotive.

"Inspector, Professor Strongbow is a most distinguished scientist. He is the brother of the murdered man. He is a guest in our country. But none of these things means that you are obliged to adopt his every passing opinion and slavishly copy it. Pull yourself together, man."

"Yes, DSP. But there is the question of why the killers waited all morning near the place in question, sir."

"All right, Inspector, let me hear you out to the bitter end. Now, just why does Professor Strongbow think his brother should have been assassinated? Assassinated."

The DSP gave a laugh that sounded much more like a bark.

"Sir, he would not say. He simply stated, sir, that the circumstances seemed to him to indicate his brother had not been killed in the course of a robbery only."

"He would not say?"

"No, sir. I pressed him as far as I could, sir. But he is a distinguished visitor, sir."

" And he would not say?"

" No, sir."

DSP Samant's greyish Mahratta eyes glared.

" But you, Inspector, you feel obliged none the less——"

The telephone, which had begun to ring a few moments earlier, brought his tirade to a stop. He picked up the receiver.

" Samant. What is it? What is it? Mehta? Mehta? Never heard——"

A sharp voice uttered two syllables at the far end of the line.

The DSP coughed.

" Colonel Mehta," he said, " good evening, sir."

The voice at the other end of the line began a long discourse of sharply broken up phrases. The DSP listened.

Ghote, standing to attention in front of the big desk with its neatly ranged wire baskets, tried not to listen. He concentrated his attention on the wall behind the DSP where a large street map of Bombay hung. He set out to trace the route between the office and his home.

" But, Colonel, if Mr. Strongbow was on an official——"

The distant voice cut in sharply.

But the word Strongbow had caught Ghote's attention. He considered himself absolved from the duty of being only physically present in the DSP's office. If this conversation was anything to do with his case, he owed it to himself to hear every word he could.

But he tried to keep the expression on his face as distant and respectful as it had been before.

" Yes, yes, I see, Colonel," the DSP said, " that puts quite a different complexion on the matter. An unofficial visit is definitely snooping. Definitely. And Trombay is the Atomic Energy Establishment. We cannot tolerate snooping there."

The voice at the other end of the line made a brisk observation.

" Yes, I see, Colonel. But all the same, surely he could not have learnt very much. After all——"

A very short pause.

" Oh, I did not realise that, Colonel. He is—— He was a physicist, eh? Nasty business."

Ghote thought he caught something about Colonel Mehta knowing it was a nasty business. But he could not be sure that he had heard properly. There was something else too which he did not catch at all.

Whatever it was it made the DSP start glancing here, there and everywhere round the room as if he was looking for something with the utmost urgency. Ghote, handicapped by not knowing what this object was, began looking too.

" Briefcase, man, briefcase," snapped the DSP.

A cold feeling swept through Ghote's mind. The briefcase was on the DSP's desk. It had been almost under his nose. If he pointed this out, it would make his superior officer look a fool. On the other hand, he obviously wanted his briefcase, and quick. He was looking plainly frantic, holding the telephone receiver at the full length of the wire, uttering placatory noises and trying to peer round the corner of the desk at the floor in front of it.

Taking advantage of this, Ghote nipped forward, grabbed the initial-stamped case, and proffered it in silence.

The DSP dropped the receiver, yanked furiously at the straps of the case, opened it at last, dragged out the evening paper of the day before and began wildly threshing it apart.

He grabbed up the receiver again.

" Yes, Colonel, I have it now. Damn' fool hid my briefcase. Gossip column, third item. Yes. I see it."

He began to read, muttering out a word or two every few seconds to indicate to Colonel Mehta on the far end of the line that he was still with him. Ghote, leaning fractionally forward to get a better view, was able to see that the item the DSP was reading was accompanied by a small, blurred-looking photograph surrounded by sharp black lines. After a few seconds he connected it with the dead body he had looked down at in the foul-smelling hut out on the Poona road.

The voice at the far end of the telephone line crackled impatiently.

"Yes, Colonel, I have read it now," the Deputy Superintendent said. "But it seems to me, you know, that the fellow was some sort of a crank. All this nonsense about joining the ' Hands Off Cuba ' movement and leaving his job over nuclear tests. Whatever any of us may feel about whether this country should make a Bomb, I hardly think one is called on to leave one's job over it."

The DSP spoke with a certain easy blandness. Colonel Mehta, whoever he was, replied with a plain crackle of fury.

"Oh, yes, yes," the DSP said quickly. "Yes, indeed, Colonel, I do see that. A convinced nuclear disarmer and a qualified physicist. The combination, exactly, Colonel."

Another burst of jabbered words.

"Yes. Well, thank you, Colonel. I will do as you suggest. It will be most helpful. But one more thing, Colonel."

Squawk.

"It would be most useful if you could tell me just what it is that Mr. Hector Strongbow could have discovered out at the Atomic Energy place at Trombay."

The telephone receiver in the DSP's hand crackled and spat so violently that he was forced to hold the earpiece a few inches away from his head. Ghote distinctly heard the words "ridiculous and impertinent curiosity." But he decided to erase them for ever from his memory.

The DSP put his ear back to the receiver again and listened attentively.

"Yes, Colonel," he said at last. "I give you my personal undertaking. Except for the inspector in charge of the case and myself not one word about the matter will be mentioned here. Not one single word."

A final fierce crackle from the far end and the DSP replaced the receiver in its cradle with a long whistle of a sigh.

"Inspector Ghote," he said, "it seems that your dead man visited the Trombay Atomic Energy Establishment the

day before his death. That is a fact you are to keep completely to yourself."

"Yes, sir, I would——"

"And, Inspector."

"Yes, DSP?"

"It further appears that this case is no longer a matter for
this department."

"Oh. Then I revert to roster duties as heretofore, sir?"

"No, Inspector, you do not. You report at once to
Colonel Mehta of Special Investigations Agency. You continue your activities working alongside him. And heaven
help you, Inspector."

CHAPTER III

THE ADDRESS Ghote was given for the Special Investigations Agency proved to be that of an enormous and ancient
office block in the Fort area. The big, many-pinnacled,
hundred-year-old building, redolent of the days when
mighty British interests built alien, aggressive citadels in
Bombay to remind themselves of distant, different and im-
pregnable castles, was not at all the sort of place the
inspector had imagined as the headquarters of the mys-
terious body that had intervened so unexpectedly in his
affairs.

If ever the block had been devoted to one particular
purpose those days had long gone. Now it was divided and
sub-divided into a hundred little sets of different offices
fitting complexly together inside the great dark red honey-
comb of a building. The Special Investigations Agency
must be only one among them. In the tall entrance hall
with its high walls broken into long rectangular panels by
long rows of projecting pillars, Ghote found a huge black
notice board split up into dozens of tiny compartments.
Each had a name on it written in white paint yellowed to a

lesser or greater degree according to the age of the firm in
question.

It took Ghote a long time to spot at the top right-hand
corner of this massive directory, in letters still almost completely white, the simple words "Special Investigations
Agency."

He had hoped at first that the board might give him
some indication of the nature of the agency. The larger
firms in the building had several compartments of the
notice board to themselves and indicated where their various
branches were located and sometimes even announced the
names of heads of departments. But the Special Investigations Agency provided no such clues. The only fact to be
deduced about it was that it occupied one of the offices at
the very top of the building.

He set out to climb flight after flight of stairs to see what
more was to be discovered.

He did not feel at all happy. Not only was he venturing
into unknown territory where all his familiar and trusted
links with his fellow policemen would no longer hold, but
the whole business of Hector Strongbow's death had now
taken on dimensions entirely beyond him. DSP Samant had
not helped. Beyond giving Ghote the address he was to go
to, he had done no more than extend a vague assurance of
providing any help needed. When Ghote had ventured a
question he had told him that he would find out all he
needed to know from Colonel Mehta.

Ghote paused for a moment at the turn of the stairs
and wondered how long it would be before he even got up
to where the colonel was supposed to work. Resignedly he
set off again. Ten stairs up, turn, ten stairs up, another
turn.

His feelings of dissatisfaction crystallised into the thought
that he was going somehow to be prevented from probing
the American's death to the bottom. This business of his
having paid that unofficial visit to the Atomic Energy
Establishment out at Trombay smelt plainly nasty. Was it
all going to end with an order to let the case simply drop?

When someone was murdered he wanted to know who had done it and to get them firmly behind bars just as quickly as possible. That was what he was for. It was his job. And now it might be pulled from under his feet.

The walls beside him grew progressively shabbier as he climbed. The patches where the distemper had peeled away got larger. The stains where passers-by had spat out bright red betel juice grew older and dustier. His doubts about what lay ahead increased.

What sort of an organisation could possibly have its offices in such sad and petty surroundings?

And at last, right at the top of the interminable stairs, there was the door he was looking for. It did nothing to relieve his pessimism. Its last coat of paint had been applied long ago. A layer of dust lay undisturbed along the bottom of each of its panels. The only thing that indicated life of any sort was a small black-painted board on which the words " Special Investigations Agency " had been super-imposed on the half-obliterated traces of innumerable former tenants.

Ghote stepped up to the door and briskly knocked.

" Come," a voice called.

Cautiously the inspector opened the dusty door. He found himself in a small outer office. It was totally bare. A large, smooth-surfaced, faceless safe was embedded in one of the walls, but otherwise there was no furniture of any sort. Even the ubiquitous trade calendars, which have to be hung somewhere, were entirely absent. There was only another door facing him, every bit as dusty as the first and standing slightly ajar.

" Inspector Ghote," the sharp voice said from behind it. " Come in, man, when you're told."

Ghote felt a sudden inward sinking. His name already known. His arrival expected.

He pushed at the second door. The office that he now found himself in was furnished to some extent. Bang in the middle of the bare floor there was a table with a telephone on it. Placed at it was a small, hard chair. Sitting in a slightly larger chair on the far side of the table was a man of about forty-five, whom Ghote supposed must be Colonel Mehta. But otherwise the room was as bare as the outer office. Not a cupboard, not a filing cabinet, not even a scrap of paper.

"At ease, Inspector, at ease," said Colonel Mehta. "Take a pew."

With a brief economical gesture he indicated the hard chair in front of his table. Ghote pulled it out and sat down with his knees neatly together.

He looked at Colonel Mehta.

The soldier in mufti. It was written all over him : his neat, discreetly checked suit and firmly knotted striped tie; the hard-trimmed, vigorously bristling moustache above the stern line of an unsmiling mouth; the square set of the shoulders and the habitual, utter straightness of the back.

Ghote prickled. Soldiers were people he had had little to do with, creatures from an alien, different world with other and different standards.

"Well, Inspector," the colonel said, "no doubt you're wondering just what the bloody set-up is."

"DSP Samant said you would inform, sir."

"Did he indeed? Well, don't you be too sure. The less anyone knows about me and my work the better I'm pleased. Never forget that."

He glanced sharply round the bare room.

"That's why I sit in a place like this all day," he went on. "I don't surround myself with clerks and orderlies and all the rest of it. I don't go filling in yards and yards of bumpf. Too many people are full of an appalling urge to make out reports on everything in sight. And what happens next, eh? They have to stick by what they've written. Slows 'em up, bogs 'em down. Damn' bad idea."

"Yes, sir," Ghote said shortly.

"Ha," said Colonel Mehta. "All this isn't telling you what the Special Investigations Agency is, is it?"

" No, sir."

" Yes. Saw you thinking just that. Not all that much gets past me, you know."

" No, sir."

" All right then. What shall we say about Special Investigations?"

Abruptly the colonel got to his feet and began pacing up and down the bare floor of his cramped office.

" In every modern country, Inspector," he said, " whether it likes it or not there has to be an organisation like mine. Every country has secrets. And when you've got secrets you have to have someone to make damn' sure they stay secret."

He swung round and stared hard at Ghote, sitting neatly on his hard chair.

" Now I know there are all sorts of bloody organisations that might be called on to deal with protecting secrets," he went on. " There's the Intelligence Bureau up in Delhi for organised, major crime. Or there's the Special Police Establishment wallahs. They might have a finger in the pie if corruption was involved, as it almost always is. But people like that are too big. They're open to pressure. They're in danger from leaks. No, what you've got to have is a small, highly efficient outfit that reports straight to the top and keeps itself pretty much to itself. Well, you can give it what name you like. We happen to call ourselves Special Investigations Agency."

He stood for a moment tautly considering whether he had said all he had meant to.

" Let me tell you one thing more," he added at last. " And that's this : the Special Investigations Agency has never lacked work."

He strode abruptly back to his bare table, pulled out his chair and sat down.

" Now," he said, " about this particular matter."

Ghote leant forward.

" You may have thought, Inspector, that you were dealing with nothing more than a piece of damned dacoity. Let me assure you that you couldn't be more wrong. Hector Strongbow was shot dead as a deliberate act. And I can tell you precisely who ordered that act."

A fierce jet of satisfaction went through Ghote. So he was going to find out after all who had killed the American.

"I can tell you who ordered the death," Colonel Mehta said. "But I cannot give you one single name."

With an effort Ghote kept his face impassive. But his thoughts were bitter. He was going to be cheated. He was going to be prevented from doing the thing he existed for.

"I said just now that my outfit was kept pretty busy," Colonel Mehta went on. "Well, a good many of our activities are concerned with one organisation. They're a body you won't ever have heard of. And yet one day, if things go their way, every man jack of them will have their names in the papers week in week out as rulers of this country."

For an instant Ghote wondered whether the trim figure sitting in front of him, elbows on the table, might not be someone he was dreaming about. Every word seemed to be leading more and more rapidly away from reality.

"Inspector."

Colonel Mehta barked it out like an order.

"Inspector, you think all this is a lot of ruddy fantasy, don't you?"

"No, sir. That is, sir—— Sir, it is hard to believe."

"Yes, Inspector, it's hard to believe. Though I should have thought the body of Hector Strongbow would have convinced you. That was real enough, wasn't it?"

"Yes, sir, it was real. But all the same, a group that may one day rule this country and yet no one has heard of it . . ."

"Exactly, Inspector. That's precisely its strength. It has a name but scarcely anything else that you can lay your hands on. It's called 'India First' and it consists of one small group of leaders plus a considerable number of agents. Now, hardly one of those agents knows more than two of the others, just the chap he gets his orders from and the chap he passes orders to. So there's nowhere you can get at them. And yet, when India First thinks its time has come, it will spring into life and, in a couple of hours even, you won't be able to move an inch without bumping up against one of its men."

He leant back a little in his heavy chair.

"You know what I sometimes call India First, Inspector? I call it a revolution in embryo. It's there. It's tiny. But given the right conditions it will change overnight from a little group of outcasts into the lawful government of this country. And who'll be the traitors then, eh?"

He sat looking at the inspector in silence. It was a good while before Ghote ventured to speak.

"And it is India First that you suspect of killing Mr. Hector Strongbow?" he said.

"I bloody well don't suspect them. I know. It's stamped with their hallmark, sheer bloody efficiency. I've thought for a long time that they had a man inside at Trombay. With the boys there producing plutonium as all the world knows they do, they were bound to try to infiltrate. You can see what happened. This chappie spotted Hector Strongbow sneaking round, realised a little later from the bloody paper that he was a trained physicist and a nuclear disarming fanatic and put in a report, pretty sharp. Then his masters acted."

The colonel paused to let Ghote absorb this train of events. But a very different thought had entered the inspector's head. He sat rigidly on his hard chair and voiced it.

"Sir," he said, "if Mr. Hector Strongbow had found out something at Trombay that was meant to be secret, was it not just as much in the interests of Special Investigations Agency that he should not broadcast it to all the world?"

Colonel Mehta's neat eyebrows rose.

"Yes, Inspector," he said, "it was. Our interests are identical. India First wants India's secrets to stay secret just as much as we do."

"Sir," Ghote said, "I read the newspapers. I know what goes on in other countries. In some places, sir, if a

foreigner came across a secret to do with atomic energy their
Secret Service would not let him live."

Colonel Mehta grunted.

"You're quite right, Inspector," he said. "I can't pretend I'm crying any tears for Mr. Strongbow. But there are
strict orders for a case like that. We have to bring the
chappie in for trial. For trial in camera if necessary, but
fair and honest trial."

"Sir, if you are not crying tears for Mr. Strongbow, I
am. He was killed, Colonel. You say it was on the orders of
the leaders of India First. Very well, it becomes my duty
to find those men and charge them with conspiracy to
murder."

Colonel Mehta laughed.

"If they ever let us catch them alive," he said, "we'll
charge them with a sight more than the murder of one
American tourist. But your brief is rather different,
Inspector. It isn't concerned with Hector Strongbow. It's
concerned with his brother."

"His brother? With Professor Gregory Strongbow?"

"Yes, Inspector. You see, the situation there is rather
tricky. According to my information, the professor had left
for a visit to Poona before his brother got back from Trombay. It looks as if Hector was hurrying over to Poona to
consult his brother when he was killed. But the question
arises: had he in the twenty-four hours between his visit
to Trombay and his death managed to give his brother just
a hint of what he knew?"

"You mean he might have telephoned him?" Ghote
asked.

"Telephoned? Don't be a bloody fool, man. You don't
put information like that on an open telephone wire in any
circumstances. Even Hector would want to keep it strictly
to himself till he blew the gaff. That's just first principles."

Ghote sat in silence. The colonel's reasoning, now he
came to look at it, was perfectly correct. In this new world
he had stumbled into, a world of distrust in every direction,
everyday reactions no longer applied.

But he would have preferred not to have been called a bloody fool to his face.

"Right," said the colonel. "Now if it turns out that Professor Strongbow did get a message of some sort from his brother, India First is going to get to know. You can bet your boots they're working full out on that this very minute."

Ghote risked a question.

"How would they do this, sir?"

"Oh, a dozen ways. They'll have men making casual inquiries at his hotel. I dare say they'll contrive to search his baggage. It wouldn't be too difficult."

"No, sir."

"They won't want to kill a second American visitor unless they have to. But if they do find out he knows something, they'll risk raising double hell all right to stop him talking. And double hell they'll get. I hear your professor saw the American Consul this afternoon. If there's a second death, we'll be forced to kick up such a shindy nothing else will matter. So, if only for that, I need to know just what the situation is before India First does. And that's where you come in."

"Me, sir?"

"You, Inspector. If the professor does know something, he'll very likely decide to play his cards pretty close to his chest till he gets back to America. So it's up to you to gain his confidence. You'll have every opportunity. You can go on carrying out your investigation, outwardly. But remember, your real objective is quite different. You're there for one thing : to find out just how much Professor Strongbow knows."

: :   : :

Inspector Ghote approached the Queen's Imperial Grand Hotel in a state of inner tempestuousness echoed ironically by the churning anger of the sea in the great sweep of the bay on to which the hotel looked. A strong wind, which had sprung up with the suddenness usual at this time of year, was sweeping across the broad boulevard of Marine Drive.

Even in the darkness of early evening the crashing of the waves beyond was disturbingly evident.

The inspector felt his worst forebodings had been fulfilled. He had been violently uprooted from the familiar network of his everyday activities. He had been deprived of the sense of support they gave him in whatever difficulties he might encounter. And he had been abruptly left to float in a stormy darkness.

A task had been imposed on him which he knew he had to carry out however much it went against the grain. He had to discover from this American in the hour of his bereavement whether his brother had succeeded in confiding anything to him before he had been killed, and what it was that had been said. And one thing was plain. The American would not be ready to tell him. If he had been the sort of person to pour out his troubles to any sympathetic listener, everything would have come out already.

But now confidences would have to be prised out of him. It was a hateful duty. In the short time he had known Gregory Strongbow he had come to have a strong feeling of respect for him. And together they had joined in the chase of the bullock driver and had brought it to a successful conclusion. They had shared that and it had made them, if only a little, friends.

And now it had become a duty to use that friendship to extract from the American something he would prefer to keep secret. Worse, he would have to pass on what he had learnt without letting the American know he was doing it.

It might not have been so bad, if he was not feeling so strongly the tug of his proper calling. He ought not to be tricking secrets out of innocent foreigners. He ought to be finding out who had killed Hector Strongbow. And, to add to it, he had been ordered to pretend he was doing exactly this. He would have to carry out all the stages of a murder investigation, and yet stop himself thinking of it as the thing he was doing. The temptation would be there all the time. The familiar procedures would have to be merely gone through, a series of meaningless rituals. And at every moment they would tempt him to give them his full allegiance.

But he would not succumb. If worming a secret out of Gregory Strongbow was to be his task, he would do it.

He climbed the spread of marble steps, traced over by a web of black cracks, and entered the huge, ultra-decorated pile of the hotel.

He was not, however, to have his unwanted meeting with Gregory Strongbow as soon as he had expected.

In the hotel foyer, a deserted area of chequered tiles where four or five isolated groups of wicker chairs clustered round stumpy, dust-covered palms in squat wooden tubs, a tall figure hastened towards him. He wore a dark, flapping, European-style suit, much creased and ink-stained, and walked with curious, erratic, over-long strides. Ghote had recognised him at once. He was a journalist, writer of a daily column, a man called Dharmadhikar, known to every-body by his initials, V.V.

"Inspector, Inspector."

V.V. began to speak, in a loud, insistent voice, well before he had reached his target. Although the big foyer was temporarily deserted except for the hotel receptionist distantly at work behind her big counter, Ghote experienced a violent desire to put a finger to his lips and shush down this strident noise.

"Inspector Ghote, the very fellow I was wanting to see."

"Good evening," Ghote said. "But I regret I have important business."

V.V. caught hold of his elbow with a large, bony hand.

"Ah ha," he said. "It is no doubt business with Pro-fessor Gregory Strongbow?"

Ghote had half-admitted it before his sense of discretion caught up with him.

"It is police matters," he eventually said with a jerk of stiffness.

"Yes, yes, indeed," V.V. replied. "Police matters, of course. The killing of Hector Strongbow is a police matter most certainly. But, Inspector Ghote, ask yourself whether it is not more. Ask yourself whether it is not a public matter also."

" I did not say it was the murder of Mr. Strongbow."

" You did not, Inspector Ghote. But that is the business I have to talk with you. The murder of Mr. Hector Strongbow, brother of a most distinguished foreign visitor, whom I have had the honour this moment to see."

" Professor Strongbow?" Ghote said. " Where is he, please?"

The gangling journalist's eyelids drooped for a moment over his prominent eyes.

" I make note that it is Professor Strongbow you are wishing to see," he said.

" Well, what if it is so? His brother has been killed. Is it so extraordinary that someone from the police should wish to talk with him?"

V.V.'s eyes were wide open now.

" But what will Professor Gregory Strongbow say?" he asked. " Will he wish to state complaints about the conduct of investigation, Inspector Ghote?"

Ghote was filled suddenly with the thought that Gregory Strongbow would be quite right to complain. The investigation was taking place only as a front for something quite different.

" I cannot discuss," he said.

" But, Inspector, the public has a right to know that this investigation is being conducted full steam ahead. That is something you must agree, isn't it?"

" I have no time for Press questioning now," Ghote replied.

" Then you do not agree? You consider this is a matter to hush up? Remember, Inspector Ghote, please, that there have been other attempts to hush up cases considered inconvenient by the police department."

" It is not question of hushing up."

V.V. leant his bony face down over Ghote's.

" Then be so kind as to give me main outline of police activity to date," he said.

Brusquely Ghote tugged his elbow from the journalist's grip.

"I regret," he said, "I have urgent business."

Business, he thought to himself, which I would much rather put off and put off till at last it is all forgotten.

"Very well, Inspector Ghote, then may I say that the inspector in charge of the Strongbow case refused to comment when asked whether the police were not totally baffled?"

Ghote felt as if a huge, leather-winged insect was battering and buzzing at him without prospect of abatement. With a spasm of pure irritation he plunged out of the journalist's reach. Only when he was at the far end of the big chequer-tiled foyer did he turn round defiantly.

"You may say nothing, nothing," he shouted.

Coldly furious, he set out to find Professor Strongbow. It took him some time, but at last he ran him to earth in the hotel's Bulbul Permit Room. The remains of his anger flared in a last bitter thought. He should have guessed, he said to himself, that an American would be found in the sole place in the building where it was permitted to consume alcohol in public.

And then the bitterness evaporated. He went across the room to the high-backed cane sofa where the unacademic-looking Professor Strongbow was sitting, feeling that he was calm enough to set about his unpleasant task with some subtlety. He noticed with relief that Shakuntala Brown was not there. Perhaps after all the professor would be willing to say more about his brother when he was sure of not being interrupted.

But the moment the big, broad-shouldered American spotted Ghote he leapt to his feet.

"Ah, it's you, Inspector," he said. "At last."

To Ghote's complete surprise there was an unmistakable note of anger in his voice.

CHAPTER IV

GHOTE FELT a sense of painful shock. Of all the things that might happen he had not expected that Gregory Strongbow would turn on him. And the American had made no attempt to keep his voice low. At the sound of his biting words the barman had looked up from behind his high, dark-wood barricade and the knot of bearers standing in a far corner had moved as one man to stare in his direction.

"Yes, at last," the American repeated, no less angrily and no less noisily. "I'm delighted to find that someone's going to bother to tell me something after all. I thought I was going to be left here for ever hearing not a damned thing. It's only my brother who's been killed, you know."

"Professor, please," Ghote said. "I have been doing my best."

"Naturally you've been doing your best. Damn it, that's your pure duty."

"But what more can I do?"

"I'll tell you what more you can do. You can come out with the truth. I've been doing some thinking since we got back to Bombay. And I'm not sure that I haven't been soft-soaped all the way along the line."

"Sir, I assure you——"

And abruptly Ghote realised that if the American had not been soft-soaped up till now, the process was about to begin. He himself had come into the permit room, with its new wall-paintings of lovers, nightingales and wine-bibbers all around, with just that intention. He found he could not go on.

He hung his head.

When Gregory Strongbow started speaking again, Ghote did not at first even listen. Then suddenly he awoke to the

55

fact that the American's voice was no longer rasping and angry. He paid attention.

" Believe me," the American was saying, " I don't ordinarily behave like that. But I guess I'm all to pieces. Look at it my way. I'm kind of disorientated. It's partly that it's all so different out here, but I just don't know any longer what's the truth and what isn't."

Ghote felt a flood of sympathy for the big American, looking at this moment so very foreign with a lock of brown, curly hair flopping down on to his forehead and the blue eyes underneath clouded and pained.

He sat down opposite him on the edge of a big, low armchair and leant forward. Only to realise that he was not able to say the things that had sprung to his mind. He would have liked to have burst out that he shared the American's sense of having his familiar ties suddenly sheared away. He would have liked to have told him that the two of them were in the same situation. And instead he was going to have to sever yet one more link that the American had with reality. He was going to have to give him, in place of the reassurance he was entitled to, a string of half-truths about his brother's death and its investigation.

" Professor Strongbow," he said cautiously, " I do not think you need to have these feelings. I was about to assure you that police methods in this country are not so different from police methods anywhere else. We are devoting full resources to our inquiries."

He saw in the American's handsome face the effect his words were having. There was a closing-up, a withdrawal. It was unmistakably plain.

" Okay, so you're doing fine," the American said. " But you still aren't telling me too much about it."

" That has been simply due to lack of proper opportunity," Ghote replied. " But I would tell you now. There is, to begin with, a most thorough search going on in Poona for the men whom Bholu, the bullock driver, betrayed."

" A good many hours have passed since you got that

information out of Bholu," Gregory Strongbow said mulishly.

"Of course. But kindly do not think those men will be seated at home awaiting arrival of police. It would take a great deal of time to establish where they may be in concealment."

"And that is all being left to the Poona police?"

"Naturally I am putting faith in the men on the spot," Ghote answered. "In due course if results fail to eventuate I would go to Poona myself. But in the meantime I am trusting them to do their work in a proper manner."

"But what if they don't do their work in a proper manner? My brother's killers get clear away, I suppose. Well, I don't intend to let that happen. I brought Hector over here, and I mean to see the whole matter of his death finally cleared up."

"Be certain the police department is not lacking in efficiency," Ghote replied. "But are you yourself even giving full co-operation? Already it seems to me that you have been unwilling to tell all you could about your brother."

The American, who had just picked up his glass of faintly sizzling whisky and soda, set it down sharply on the dark, polished table with the big brass ashtray dead in its centre.

"Just what do you mean by that?" he snapped.

Ghote was a little surprised at the vigour of his reaction. But, having at last brought the conversation to the point he had been manœuvring towards, he decided he must press forward.

"I mean for example," he said, "that you have never told where your brother went when you each decided to make a different expedition yesterday morning."

Watching the American closely, he saw a new wariness come into the blue eyes.

"Well, if I didn't tell you that, it was pure oversight," Gregory Strongbow answered after a moment. "Hector went over to Trombay, to the Atomic Energy place. That was his field, you know."

" It was an official visit?" Ghote asked.

The American shrugged with noticeable carelessness.

" I don't think so. Hector just said he'd take off for Trombay when I told him I wanted to see the hydraulics labs out at Poona. I guess he hoped they'd show him around if he just checked in there."

" I see. And is this what happened?"

" I don't exactly know. He spent the whole morning away, so I guess he must at least have gotten inside the place."

" But, since you did not see him again after this visit, you naturally do not know about it?" Ghote asked.

" That's not exactly so," the American replied. " If we're going to put so much emphasis on me telling you everything, then I'd better dot all the i's and cross all the t's. I did as a matter of fact see Hector after he'd been to Trombay."

Ghote felt his heart pounding. He knew he had to be icily careful at this point. He leant even further forward. The faint bitterish smell of the American's whisky impinged on his nostrils.

" And now please," he said, " I want you to think very carefully. Did your brother say anything to you, when you saw, to give a clue as to why he should go out to Poona?"

But Gregory Strongbow answered sharply.

" I already said I have no idea why Hector was going out to Poona. I just suppose he changed his mind and thought he'd join me."

" What was it he said to you when he met you after going to Trombay then?"

" He didn't say very much about anything," the American answered.

" But, please, he may have said something which would give a clue to help investigation."

" I tell you he did not. We just happened to meet for a

few minutes, a few seconds even, outside this Victoria Terminus you have. I had my train to catch. I just saw him and called to him and we exchanged a few words."

" This was outside V.T. Station? You did not go to a restaurant for a cup of tea, perhaps?"

" Certainly we did not. I already said: it was just a few words spoken right there on the sidewalk with half a million people milling all around."

" I beg your pardon then."

Gregory Strongbow looked a little mollified.

" These few words," Ghote went on. " Can you remember exactly what your brother said?"

And abruptly the American's anger returned.

" No, I cannot," he said. " And if I could, I don't think I would repeat them to you. We had a short, private conversation between two brothers. That's all."

" But it would be of great practical value to know what was in your brother's mind at that point."

" No, it would not."

" Please, I think you are obstructing my investigation with this attitude. You seem totally unwilling to tell things I need to know. And yet you are free enough with giving out Press interviews."

" I have not given out Press interviews."

" Excuse me, I met a journalist as I entered the hotel who told he had come from seeing you only that moment."

And suddenly Professor Strongbow grinned.

" I've done it again," he said. " I've let myself get all worked up. You're perfectly right: I did give a Press interview. Or at least when this guy came up and said he'd written a piece about Hector in his column I just told him that I hadn't really anything to add. He asked me a couple more questions and I simply replied 'No comment.' I certainly told him nothing I haven't told you."

And Ghote decided he would have to leave it at that. It was more than obvious that Gregory Strongbow had not the least intention of telling him what the talk with his brother

outside V.T. Station had been about. Or at least not at this
time. He would simply have to report what he had found
out to Colonel Mehta and try again later.

The thought was not pleasant.

:: ::

Within an hour Ghote was back at the Queen's Imperial
Grand Hotel. The hour had been every bit as hateful as he
had expected. Colonel Mehta, sitting as upright as ever in
his scoured bare room, had done nothing to conceal his
anger that his orders had been baulked. This, his expression
implied as clearly as if he had written it out under Ghote's
very nose, this is what comes of working with damned
inefficient civilian police.

Ghote left feeling that he had let down the whole force
from the commissioner to the newest constable. And his
outlook was not improved by the thought that the task in
which he had partially failed was not what he should have
been doing in any case. He ought to be at this moment
sitting in his office urging on the people at Poona, and
instead he was going back to Professor Strongbow to see
how quickly he could persuade him to change his mind and
tell him in full what his brother had said on the crowded
pavement outside V.T. Station.

All the way to the hotel he scolded the driver of his truck
for not going fast enough. And the driver, a dried-up,
nutty-faced long-service constable whose whole life lay in
nurturing this particular blue Dodge, had dourly listened
and had got through the jostling traffic at exactly his usual
speed.

At the Queen's Imperial Grand Ghote went straight back
to the Bulbul Permit Room. But Gregory Strongbow was
no longer there. A quick tour of the public rooms failed to
produce either the American or even his Tourist Department guide, Miss Shakuntala Brown. Ghote went back to
the big chequer-tiled foyer and over to the reception desk.

Behind its glossy teak rampart the receptionist he had
noticed earlier on was still sitting, perched on a heavy, high

stool and busy sorting through a pile of cards from a wooden index file behind her. Ghote saw now that she was a Parsee. She appeared to be about forty-five or so, though it was difficult to tell as she plainly spent a lot of time contriving the sprightlier manner of someone ten or more years younger. But tell-tale lines of anxiety round her eyes betrayed her and her cheeks were a little hollower than they should have been.

On the narrow top of the teak counter, around which there ran a little brass rail giving it a faintly nautical touch, there was a fretwork stand about six inches high bearing a strip of white card on which there was written in purple ink the words " Miss Mira Jehangir." Evidently the Queen's Imperial Grand did what it could to emulate the practices of the glossy new Nataraj and the newer Shalimar.

" Miss Jehangir?" Ghote inquired.

It had occurred to him that it was more than likely that the person behind the desk would not correspond to the name on the notice. But his pessimism was unfounded. The receptionist swiftly spread a thin, bejewelled hand across the cards she was sorting over and looked up.

" Can I help you?" she said.

" I am looking for Professor Gregory Strongbow."

" What name is it, please?" Mira Jehangir asked.

Ghote was a little surprised to receive this counter-question but he gave his name without demur.

Mira Jehangir picked up a pencil from the shelf beneath the gleaming deck of the mildly nautical counter and carefully wrote Ghote's name down.

" And the nature of your business?" she inquired blandly.

" Professor Strongbow is expecting me," Ghote replied stiffly.

" I see. Then I shall have to find out whether we have a Professor Strongbow on our register."

" But he is guest at the hotel. I am wishing to know simply whether he is in or not."

But Mira Jehangir slipped down from her tall, heavy

stool and without another word turned to the wooden index on the wall behind her. She began opening and shutting the drawers with a great parade of business efficiency.

"Yes," she said, after some little while, "I can put you in touch with Professor Strongbow."

"He is in his room? What number please? I will go up."

"He is most probably in the Bulbul Permit Room," Mira Jehangir replied, turning back to the inspector. "Like many foreign guests he spends much of his time there."

Ghote noted calmly that only an instant before she had denied knowing whether Professor Strongbow was staying at the hotel at all.

"I have just come from the permit room," he said sharply. "I know very well Professor Strongbow is not there. Is he in his room, please?"

"I will make inquiries," Mira Jehangir replied.

Her eyes flitted round the big foyer as if she hoped that something would happen to prevent her taking this unequivocal step. But evidently she found nothing. She moved along to a house telephone, of a pattern obsolete enough not to belie her desk's air of belonging to the early age of steam navigation.

She asked for the professor. A voice at the other end spoke, but Ghote was unable to hear what it said. Miss Jehangir replied with a guarded "Yes" and listened again. At last she put the ridged tube of the receiver back on its curling hooks.

"Professor Strongbow is not able to receive visitors," she said.

Ghote frowned.

"You did not tell who was asking for him," he said. "Inspector Ghote."

"I have your name," Mira Jehangir replied, tapping her note-pad with a long, pointed, deep pink nail.

A suspicion came into Ghote's mind.

"You spoke with Professor Strongbow in person?" he demanded.

" Professor Strongbow is not in his room."

" But you told you had rung him."

" I think there must have been a misunderstanding. I rang only the bearers outside the professor's suite. They informed me that he was not there."

" And you do not know where he is ?"

Ghote stood in front of the elegant, evasive Parsee and put his question with force.

" I cannot help you," she replied, her eyes flicking into the background.

Ghote turned away. He felt furious. He ought to have made arrangements to keep in touch with the professor. He might be gone for hours now and there would be no chance of making any progress with his distasteful task and perhaps getting back to his proper work.

He stood disconsolately beside one of the five potted palms islanded in the cold sea of the foyer.

Suddenly a voice whispered from the other side of the dusty, drooping spines of leaves.

" Excuse, sahib."

Ghote swung round.

Standing discreetly behind the palm so as to be almost invisible from the reception desk was one of the hotel bearers, an elderly man with sad eyes wearing a much-darned white uniform. When Ghote looked at him he salaamed deeply.

" Sahib, you ask for Strongbow sahib ?" the man said.

" Yes," Ghote said. " Yes, yes, I did."

" I am Strongbow sahib's room bearer, sahib."

" Do you know where he is ?"

" No, sahib."

" Then what——?"

" But, sahib, he ask me if he shall take coat to wait for friend out in Marine Drive. And, sahib, I told most definitely coat would be necessary. I told immense great waves at this time of year. Sahib might get very badly wetted to the skin. Most definitely coat, I told."

" Quite right, quite right," Ghote said heartily. " But did

Strongbow sahib say where in Marine Drive he was going to wait for his friend?"

" Oh, no, sahib. If Strongbow sahib want to wait there, I would not be asking anything about that. Only telling coat is most definitely necessary."

"Yes, yes. A coat would be very necessary," Ghote agreed, cursing inwardly that the bearer's devotion did not extend beyond recommending appropriate clothing for the prevailing weather.

He gave the man a small tip and hurried out.

What he had learnt was disquieting. Why should a respectable American visitor choose to meet someone in the open air on a night like this? The wind was whipping across the broad span of Marine Drive outside and down in the sea the waves were crashing and thundering against the sea-wall.

Going down the sweeping marble steps of the old hotel he could not prevent himself breaking into a trot, though it was hardly the dignified behaviour the police force might expect from one of its officers. Luckily, his driver had not deserted the truck. He had its bonnet-flap back and was wiping the top of the engine with a small piece of greasy rag.

" Good man," Ghote said. " Now listen, I want to see if I can find someone waiting somewhere along Marine Drive. He should not be too hard to spot, a tall American. He would be wearing a coat."

The driver gave his engine one more careful wipe.

" Yes," he said, " he would need coat. Along there waves have been breaking right across road."

He pointed into the middle distance like a conscientious guide showing a visitor a cherished view.

" Hurry, man, hurry," Ghote snapped. " We will not find him by standing here talking about waves."

" Very good, very good, Inspector sahib," the driver replied patiently.

He gave one final, obsessional flick at his engine with the rag, clamped down the bonnet and climbed into his seat.

"Which way, Inspector? Left towards Colaba first?"

He nosed the truck to the edge of the long sweep of the boulevard and waited.

"No," Ghote said perversely, "go the other way, right, up towards Chaupati."

The driver shrugged and swung out into the broad road.

It had begun to rain and there was scarcely anybody about. Away ahead of them an earnest citizen was marching along with an umbrella held almost horizontally to one side in an effort to keep at least a quarter of himself dry. As they drew up to him a sharp cross-gust turned the umbrella almost instantaneously inside-out. Ghote saw him gather the spiky remains together and stride away bare-headed and resigned.

But this was the only sign of life. Hard though Ghote peered into the squally darkness, he could not see the least trace of a tall, coated American waiting in this unlikely place for an unknown friend. Certainly the sea side of the road was totally bare. No one in their senses would walk there, exposed to the wild swirls of spray that were flung at intervals over the protecting wall as the great waves hurled themselves against it.

Even such traffic as there was went at speed. Driving slowly along on the sea side as they made their way up to Chaupati, it was easy to understand why everyone else was hurrying. The biggest of the waves looked as if they were bound to crash over the narrow top of the sea-wall, and each looked powerful enough to catch the truck up and sweep it into the wind-tossed hedge dividing the two carriageways.

"Switch on the headlights," Ghote said.

The alternate glare and shadow from the big blocks of flats made peering into the darkness doubly difficult.

The driver obeyed, and with this help it was more possible to be sure that even on the far side of the road, in the comparative shelter, no one was lingering about.

They reached the tall statue of Lokmanya Tilak presiding forlornly over the deserted stretch of Chaupati Beach where in less happy times he had exhorted great crowds to rebellion. And still there was not the least sign of the big American.

" We had better go the other way," Ghote said grumpily.

He realised that it would have been much more sensible to have taken that direction first. A rendezvous was plainly more likely down near the busy streets of the Fort than up at this end of Marine Drive, with its respectable, pastel-coloured blocks of expensive flats.

" Get a move on," he muttered half to himself as the truck swung across the road in a wide U-turn.

" Better not go too fast, Inspector sahib," the driver said. " It is hard to see, and we may have missed him already."

In deference to the fact that the man had been right about which direction they ought to have taken in the first place Ghote let this pass in silence.

The truck headed back along the wide sweep of the bay, its headlights picking out every now and again a heavy plume of white spray whirling far across the road.

" My wife's cousin's son was drowned just here four or five years ago," the driver said. " He was out playing just at the end of the monsoon like this, and a wave swept him right over the wall. In one second he was gone."

Ghote refused to let himself take this remark at more than its face value. But he edged forward on the worn seat of the truck and peered even harder into the tricky darkness surrounding them.

CHAPTER V

THE HEADLIGHTS of the slowly moving police truck picked out the high, looming walls of the Brabourne Stadium nearly at the far end of the long sweep of Marine Drive. Inspector Ghote sighed.

" If Professor Strongbow was ever here at all," he said, " we have certainly missed——"

His driver must have caught sight of what had stopped him in mid-sentence at the same instant as he had. Jammed-hard brakes sent the truck skewing wildly round on the wave-wetted surface of the wide road. Before it had come to rest Ghote was out and running forward with every ounce of his strength.

" Stop," he shouted. " Stop. Police."

His cry must have reached the group of struggling figures on the far side of the road close up against the low top of the sea-wall. Three of them turned for an instant and looked over in his direction. But it was for an instant only. Then they swung back to the fourth figure, the tall man in the light coat already down on the ground. With one concerted heave they raised him like a log above their shoulder level.

" Stop," Ghote shouted again.

But he knew it was useless. Long before he could reach them the three attackers with a last lunge would send the prone figure in the flapping coat swinging over the low top of the sea-wall. And with the great waves hurling themselves eagerly forward he would have no chance after that.

The three dark shapes ducked a little as they gathered themselves for the throw.

And with total suddenness there came the huge roar of a giant wave swinging high over the top of the wall. The solid block of water hit the struggling group and swept all four figures tumbling before it.

Ghote stopped and stood with staring eyes.

Several moments passed before he was able at all to make out what had happened. But when he did so he saw the scene with extraordinary clarity. The huge wave had collapsed into a mere sheet of swirling water as it spread across the wide road, and behind it the four figures it had tumbled down were outlined like statues. The three attackers, having been on their feet, had been hurled farther into the roadway than their victim. As Ghote watched they crouched or knelt in the rushing sea-water, their faces still turned towards the point where they had intended to hurl their victim to his death.

It was clear that they must have dropped Gregory Strongbow the moment the wave hit them. He was a good deal nearer the low sea-wall, already on his feet and staring wildly round as if looking for some new danger.

After the screaming roar of the wave at its highest there was now by comparison almost complete silence. In this point of lull even the swirling water on the road seemed still.

And then Ghote heard something new.

He swung round towards the sea. A second wave, out-topping the first, like a full-grown brother overshadowing the stripling, was progressing towards them with a silent speed that belied its size.

The three attackers must have seen the mass of dark water at the same moment. They put their heads down into their arms and braced themselves for the impact. The American, looking in their direction, had not yet realised what was happening.

Ghote put his head down and pelted forward.

He reached the American before the water hit the sea-wall beneath them. He seized him round the chest and actually lifted him off his feet with the force of his dash forward.

Then the water came over the wall. For a long minute everything was chaos. Breath-crushing, choking salt sea was everywhere, first hurling itself forward, then whirling back in an undertow almost as powerful.

And, after what seemed a time too long to measure, at last there came something approaching peace.

From the foot of the inner side of the sea-wall where he had calculated that a narrow strip of safety might lie Ganesh Ghote struggled to his feet. Beside him the big American groaned loudly in the darkness. Ghote reached out to him.

" Can you run?" he said.

" Yes. Yes, I can."

" This way."

He took the American by the hand and together they dashed across the wide area of the road in the direction of the police truck. Water, inches deep still, tugged at their feet.

But it seemed that there was to be no third wave. The sequence had altered. Away in the distance Ghote heard a comparatively puny mass of water break harmlessly to pieces against the protective concrete blocks in the darkness below. And equally, it appeared, the human danger had vanished. Hardly had they reached the truck when the driver hurried up.

" Inspector, you are okay?"

" Yes, yes. We managed to get into the shelter of the top of the wall."

" The others have gone, Inspector. When the water had gone I saw them running. I tried to chase. But it was no good."

" All right," Ghote said. " It does not matter. But we must take Professor Strongbow back to his hotel. He is soaked to the skin at least."

He was no drier himself. The two of them sat in the back of the truck with the cold sea water seeping down on to the floor all round.

After a little Ghote put a question.

" What happened, Professor, please?"

The American lifted his head.

" I got a call at the hotel," he said. " It was someone who said they could tell me more about Hector if I met them on my own. He said to wait on Marine Drive by this Brabourne Stadium. Is that the name?"

" Yes, yes. But who was this person?"

The American groaned a little.

" He wouldn't give his name," he answered. " Or at least that's what Shakuntala said. She took the call."

" I see. Then you went to the place indicated?"

" Yeah. I waited around a while, and then these guys came up. I expected there would be only one, but it didn't seem to matter. They seemed to want me to go over to the far side of the street with them. I thought it was to go where there was no one around. So we crossed over. And then they went for me. I did what I could, but it was three against one."

He looked out into the darkness as the truck hummed its way steadily along the wide sweep of the boulevard. The waves were beating rhythmically against the masonry of the sea-wall sending high towers of spray flaunting into night air. He shivered and turned to Ghote as if for reassurance.

But Ghote was lost in thought. And for all the rest of the short trip back to the hotel he remained silent. Silent and worried.

The American put no questions. It seemed he too had plenty to think about.

: :   : :

Ghote had stayed in Gregory Strongbow's suite at the hotel only long enough to make sure he was comfortable and to extract a promise from him not to go out again in any circumstances. Then, wet and cold though he was, he had hurried down to the hotel foyer where he remembered having seen a public telephone.

Quickly he slid the heavy door of the booth to behind him and rang the number Colonel Mehta had given him. It was supposed to reach him at any hour of the day or night. Listening to the sound of ringing at the far end, Ghote hoped that for once one of the colonel's arrangements might have broken down.

But abruptly the ringing ceased and a voice he recognised at once as Colonel Mehta's asked sharply who was calling. Briefly Ghote gave him the bare facts about the attack on Gregory Strongbow.

" I suppose you didn't catch any of the damned fellows."

Ghote felt obliged to defend himself. After all, for a mere policeman he had done well enough.

" No, Colonel, we did not catch. My driver gave chase

but they had too much start. Otherwise we might have got it out of one of them who ordered this attack."

What reply Colonel Mehta made to this counter-thrust Ghote never knew. His voice suddenly receded so far into the distance that it was impossible to make out even one word.

"Colonel. I am sorry, Colonel, but you have gone very faint."

At the far end Ghote could make out that the colonel was shouting.

"Something seems to have gone wrong with the line, Colonel," he said.

"Listen, man, listen."

"Yes, Colonel."

Ghote listened with fierce intentness. He saw that his damp clothes were making a small puddle on the floor of the telephone booth.

"You will not get far along those lines, Inspector."

"You believe this attack was not connected with the killing of Mr. Hector Strongbow?" Ghote asked.

"Don't shout, man, don't shout. I can hear you perfectly well. And of course our friends are out to get the professor now. But they're too bloody clever to let you catch them through one of their strong-arm men. Chaps like that just work for money and no questions asked."

"Yes, Colonel, but——"

The far, far, tinny voice at the other end broke in. Ghote stopped and strained to hear.

"No, Inspector, what you forget is that you're up against some very good chaps. Don't you believe all this nonsense about the Indian inability to carry out any plan with a modicum of simple efficiency. It just isn't bloody well true. I know. I knew it in the Army. We didn't stand for inefficiency there, I can tell you."

In Ghote's right ear, sensitised now to a high point, picking out the faint crackle of this lecture, there came suddenly a single click. The noise was as effective as a pistol shot.

Ghote involuntarily jerked the receiver away from his head. When he gingerly listened again the colonel was still talking, but his voice had returned to normal strength. Ghote decided to pretend he had missed nothing.

"The finest fighting force in the world," the colonel was saying. "You can't beat the simple Indian jaiwan as a fighting man, Inspector, and don't you forget it. It may have pleased certain people at certain times to make out that nothing Indian was any good. But that doesn't accord with the bloody facts. Who was the first man to discover the laws of gravity, eh?"

Ghote realised with a hot flush of embarrassment that this was a question he was expected to answer. An enamel-bright recollection of himself at the age of eleven sitting in a long desk cramped against half a dozen school mates came into his mind. He could see, as if it was this moment, Mr. Merrywether, their implacable Anglo-Indian teacher, standing in front of the dusty whitish blackboard and rapping out the story of Newton and the apple.

But he knew that, of all the answers to give, the name Isaac Newton would be the least acceptable.

"I don't know his name," Colonel Mehta snapped out at the other end of the line. "But I can tell you this much, man. He was an Indian, an Indian. And atomic theory. What about that? All buttoned up by Indian sages hundreds of years ago. And we even had a perfectly adequate flying machine in those days, so they tell me. And cotton cloth. Where was the earliest known sample in the world found? In the Sind Desert, man. In the Sind Desert."

Ghote's eyes focused on a short message some vandal had scratched on the sacred dark wood of one of the panels at the back of the booth. "I love Gracie," it stated. He wondered how long ago the desecration had taken place. No doubt the lover had long since transferred his affections to some other Betty, Milly or Rosie.

With a start he realised that the voice at the far end of the line had ceased to speak.

"Yes, sir," he said hastily. "But this is what I have

been wondering, sir. Can I now cease attempts to find out what the professor heard from his brother? It seems India First has decided he learnt something, does it not, sir?"

"No, Inspector, you cannot cease your attempts."

Ghote thought for a few seconds.

"Please," he said at last, "I would like to know why."

"Because orders are orders, man."

"Sir, I am not Army officer."

"I don't care what you are, or who you are. You're under my command now and you do what you're bloody well told."

"Sir, can I go to higher authority?"

"No, Inspector, you cannot. Understand this: there is no higher authority for you to go to. You've been entrusted with State secrets. Secrets no one under Prime Minister level has any right to know. So you keep them right under your hat. Now and for ever. Do you get that?"

"Yes, Colonel," Ghote said.

It was an admission of defeat. What the colonel had said was, after all, perfectly true. In this world of darkness into which he had been plunged there were no lifelines.

"And you definitely wish me to continue to seek the professor's confidence, sir?" he said bleakly into the telephone mouthpiece.

"I most certainly do, Inspector. I have to find out what the leakage point is at Trombay. Just remember that."

"Yes, sir. But then, sir, may I tell the professor about the existence of the India First group? Sir, already he suspects his brother's death is not simple dacoity. So I will never gain his trust if I continue to pretend the death in question was a straightforward matter, sir."

There was a long pause at the other end. Ghote began to think he had lost the connection. But at last the colonel answered.

"Very well. You may tell him India First exists. But not one single word about us, do you understand? As far as Professor Gregory Strongbow is concerned there is no such thing as the Special Investigations Agency."

" Yes, sir. And thank you."

" You may tell him that you have been charged with his personal safety, Inspector. That's so as to give you everything you need to stick close to him. And if you can't learn about that conversation outside V.T. Station under those conditions, then you'll be making a pretty poor show of things, Inspector."

This time there was no mistaking that the phone had clicked dead. With a feeling of dull heaviness Ghote pushed open the sliding door of the dark booth.

:   :   :   :

Gregory Strongbow was alone in his suite when the inspector knocked. He came to the door, led Ghote through the curious ante-room devoted to housing a single heavy ironing-board for the use of the visitor's bearer, and on into the sitting-room. This was a vast, airy chamber with a number of pieces of heavy furniture all grouped round a rather small wicker table placed in the exact centre of the big, somewhat threadbare Kashmir carpet. Dominating the whole was a tall decorated mirror fixed to the wall opposite the windows. As a looking-glass the mirror had disadvantages. The chief of them was that under the glass there had been ingeniously inserted a full-length coloured picture of George, King-Emperor of India. But large areas of tarnish also detracted not a little from the mirror's usefulness.

The professor appeared to have got used to its looming presence and no longer paid it any attention. Ghote found himself constantly turning back to it.

But he made himself pay attention to business.

" Miss Brown?" he asked first. " Is she here in your suite?"

Shakuntala Brown had been causing him a good deal of anxiety. On the way up from his conversation with Colonel Mehta he had begun thinking about the close knowledge India First seemed to have of the professor's whereabouts. And he had come to the conclusion at once that it was more than likely they had a spy close at hand. Shakuntala Brown filled the bill. He had had to admit that she was not the only possibility. Two others were clearly suspect. There was V. V. Dharmadhikar for one. He certainly seemed to be taking a very keen interest in all the professor did. And then there was Miss Mira Jehangir at the reception desk downstairs. There could hardly have been a less satisfactory encounter than his brush with her earlier on.

Nevertheless Shakuntala Brown remained the most likely candidate.

" Shakuntala ?" Gregory Strongbow answered. " No, she isn't here. She was. But she went out. She'll be back though. Did you want her for something ?"

" I would need to see her," Ghote said. " I need to hear about the telephone call she took."

" Yes, I guess you would. Have you any idea who that caller could have been ?"

" Yes," said Ghote, " I have."

Gregory Strongbow looked startled.

" Already ?" he said.

" There is something I ought to have told you before," Ghote replied.

He saw the look of hope growing in the American's face and quickly continued.

" I believe you already think there is more to your brother's death than a simple killing. Well, I can tell you now that I think this also. Your brother was victim of a terrorist group, a group called India First."

Gregory Strongbow frowned.

" A terrorist group ?"

" What else ?"

The American kept silent. Then he took a pace towards Ghote and looked down at him almost angrily.

" I'll tell you who else," he said. " By the Indian Government, or some outfit of theirs. Damn it, Trombay is an Indian Government affair, isn't it ? So if Hector was killed because he went there, it stands to reason he was put out of the way by Indian Government agents."

" But it is not so," Ghote almost shouted.

He felt a sense of outrage that anyone should make such suggestions about his country.

And the feeling must have communicated itself to the big American. At once his aggressive look softened. He put out a hand and vaguely waved Ghote down into one of the sprawling armchairs surrounding the pathetic little central wicker table, and then squatted on the edge of the next chair in the circle.

" Listen," he said, " I'm not claiming that India is the only country in the world that would do a thing like that. Hell, if you'd asked me three days ago I'd have said India was one of the few countries that wouldn't. But my brother is dead. I brought him over here and he's dead. Look, I'm not saying that there aren't guys working for the U.S. who wouldn't kill someone to stop a security leak."

" Please," Ghote said, " I assure you in India it is not so. It must not be so. There are orders not to deal with things in that way. I can reveal that much to you. And kindly consider this : there is such an organisation as India First. It exists to make India seize an important place in the world. I assure you of this on authority I trust."

" All right, all right," Gregory Strongbow said.

A look of hurt was crinkling the lines round his eyes.

" Then if such an organisation exists," Ghote argued, " is it not more likely that they killed your brother?"

Gregory Strongbow leapt to his feet.

" Okay," he said, " I hand it to you. It is more likely. We'll go on that——"

Someone knocked at the door.

For a moment Ghote and the professor looked at each other as if this was the first move in a concerted attack. Then the American smiled.

" Relax," he said. " It'll be Shakuntala."

He went to the door and opened it. Shakuntala Brown was there.

Ghote looked at her with care. She had changed her sari since the afternoon. Indeed, she looked so fresh now that this was probably where she had been while he had been talking to Gregory Strongbow. The sari she was wearing now was silk, a deep red patterned with cream circle shapes. For a moment Ghote thought it would look well on his wife, but then he decided that it was a little too restrained to reflect her personality properly. But it suited this girl's fair complexion.

" I think the inspector here wants to ask you a few questions," the professor said to her.

She crossed the room and sat in a corner of one of the big chairs. Ghote went and sat next to her. Gregory Strongbow tactfully went over to a chair on the far side of the circle.

" It was you who took the telephone call for Professor Strongbow?" Ghote asked.

" Yes, it was me," Shakuntala Brown said.

She spoke guardedly, with a hint of being anxious to say only the minimum necessary.

" How did that happen? That you took the call? Was it for you? Did the caller know Professor Strongbow had you as guide?"

" No, I was in here and the professor was out. I think he was down in the permit room."

" I see. And what exactly was said?"

" Just that if Professor Strongbow wanted to know who killed his brother he should wait down by the Brabourne Stadium, on the Marine Drive side."

" That only?"

" Yes. That was all."

Ghote pounced.

" I thought there were instructions the professor should be alone? If that was not said, why did you leave him? You would have been useful. Perhaps his informant would not speak English."

" They did say something about him having to be alone," Shakuntala Brown answered in a sulky voice.

" Then why did you not tell? I asked carefully for exact particulars. Why did you say nothing of this?"

" I happened to forget that," she said with rising sharpness.

" Miss Brown," Ghote said, " what exactly is your position in this business? Who sent you to work for Professor Strongbow?"

" I am employed by the State Tourist Department."

" But you are not Indian national?"

Her back straightened as if on a spring.

" How dare you say that? How do you know? Do you want to see my passport?"

Ghote blinked.

" All right," Shakuntala Brown said, " I admit my father was born English. But he was an Indian citizen for five years before he died. And when he became one I became one."

" I am sorry," Ghote said.

He felt apologies had been called for. But he still had questions to put.

" Now," he said, " would you kindly tell me if anything more was said by that telephone caller?"

Shakuntala Brown's eyes ceased to flash. The wary look Ghote thought he had seen in them before returned.

" I have told you everything," she replied.

" You said that once before. I proved that was wrong. Was there anything more?"

" Hey."

It was Gregory Strongbow.

" Hey, listen, Inspector," he said, " you're questioning Shakuntala as if she was some sort of criminal. All she did was take the call."

Inwardly Ghote could not refrain from cursing him. He wanted to do all he could for him, but if there were going to be protective, chivalrous interruptions of this sort the stock of goodwill he had for him would rapidly run out.

He turned to him now.

" Kindly understand," he said, " that it is most necessary to establish full particulars. I was doing that only."

He went back to Shakuntala Brown. But the interruption had given her time to reconsider.

"Inspector," she said, leaning earnestly forward in the big chair, "believe me, I only want to help too. I genuinely forgot the bit about letting Professor Strongbow go to the appointment alone."

"Very well," Ghote said. "But please to remember it is important to tell everything."

He decided to seize a chance and swung round to Gregory Strongbow again.

"Is that not so, Professor?" he said. "Is it not important to tell everything?"

He gave him a long look. From the momentary hardening of the blue eyes in the handsome face he knew his meaning had been taken. Shakuntala Brown had not been the only one to withhold information.

He waited with anxiety.

"Certainly," Gregory Strongbow said coolly, "certainly it's important to keep nothing back. Unless it happens to be a matter which has no concern with police inquiries."

CHAPTER VI

EARLY NEXT MORNING Inspector Ghote hurried straight to the Queen's Imperial Grand Hotel. The weather had improved with its usual abruptness. But he did not let himself linger to enjoy the freshness of the light breeze coming in from the sea and the sparkle of the first sun. He knew that, had anything gone wrong at the hotel during the night, he ought to have been informed. And he had posted men enough round about both outside and in. But nevertheless he realised he would not feel happy till he had seen Gregory Strongbow with his own eyes.

He felt a strong, quite irrational attachment to the tall American with the unacademically tough set to his jaw and the eyes with the tell-tale wrinkles of concern puckering the tanned skin. This man was in a way his only point of contact with reality in the different world he had so suddenly found himself in. Colonel Mehta was no use : he was too much from another world himself. And every other contact seemed barred by the terms of his orders.

On the shallow marble steps of the ornate pile of the hotel Ghote did allow himself to pause for an instant.

He needed just one second to overcome the ugly thought that it would be his duty for the next sixteen hours or more to watch Gregory Strongbow and wait for the one moment at which he might say what it was that he had learnt from his brother. And in exchange he would be feeding out half-truths about an investigation he was only pretending to control.

He ran into the hotel and made his way to the dining-room.

And there was the American, sitting equably opposite Shakuntala Brown at a big table spread with a heavy white cloth and covered with complicated silver cutlery. He looked utterly at ease. The very sight of him seemed to send Ghote's anxieties sliding away off his back.

He went over.

" Good morning, Inspector," Gregory Strongbow said, smiling. " It's a better day. Have you had breakfast? Will you join us?"

He gestured at the laden table. In front of him two small greasy-looking eggs lay in the middle of a huge white plate surrounded by small and dark slivers of hard bacon. A large coffee cup stood to the right. Towards the centre of the table there was a toast rack containing sixteen small pieces of toast somehow suspiciously limp. Three pots for various sorts of marmalade lay beyond and to the left-hand side was an enormous silver cruet.

" I don't exactly recommend the porridge," Gregory Strongbow said. " There seemed to be lumps in it here and there."

He smiled up at Ghote.

"In fact," he said, "I don't altogether recommend the breakfast at all. I have a feeling it's a British legacy I ought to avoid."

"Thank you," Ghote said, smiling too now, "luckily perhaps I have already eaten—fried vegetables, pickle, crisp wheat cakes, tea."

The professor looked thoughtful.

"I guess there must be a middle way," he said. "Even if I have to make it just a cup of coffee like Shakuntala here."

He looked across at Shakuntala Brown with a grin.

"Mind you," he added, "I'm improving the situation bit by bit. The first morning they tried to bring me something called bed tea. I don't like tea much any time, but to have to cope with it before I'd really woken up. Wow."

But suddenly the smile left his face.

"What is it?" Shakuntala asked quickly.

Gregory Strongbow shook his head slowly from side to side.

"It's nothing really. Just that I remembered joking over bed tea with Hector the morning he went off to Trombay. He told me he'd tipped his on to the floor."

He sighed.

"It was somehow because of that, because of my attitude to that, we decided to go our different ways a bit," he said.

"But you mustn't let that worry you," said Shakuntala. "You shouldn't reproach yourself over what would have only been a tiny disagreement if your brother had lived. That's attaching too much importance to just a few words. Really it is."

She leant forward so earnestly that the American smiled.

"I guess you're right at that," he said. "It's not that I should be worrying about. It's squaring it with Hector for getting him into that trap at all."

He swung round to Ghote.

"Inspector, what is happening? What kind of progress are you making?"

Ghote felt as if he had been slapped.

" We are doing everything possible," he said sulkily. " But it is not just question of arresting a gangster with a tommy-gun. If it was that only, we would do it in no time whatsoever."

Curiously, this hardly-concealed jibe at the America of films about Chicago seemed to mollify Gregory Strongbow. He leant back and took an immense swig of coffee. Ghote felt more than ever obliged to persist in his justifications.

" You must remember," he said, " the man whose name we know in Poona and his associates would have fled their domiciles. This we now have confirmed. And it is bound to take time to track them down. We may have to wait for the advent of an informant. But be assured we are waiting and watching."

The American began tackling some toast. It resisted his knife with rubbery stubbornness.

" I can appreciate all this," he said. " But it doesn't make it any easier for me. I have a duty to Hector. And I don't feel I'm doing it by just sitting around all day."

Shakuntala Brown, up till now sitting quietly sipping at her coffee, leant forward over the massed array of china.

" But there is no need for you to sit," she said. " We can arrange some activity for you that will take your mind off this business."

" I'm sorry," Gregory Strongbow said, " but I don't want my mind taken off this business."

Shakuntala's eagerness was unabated.

" But listen," she said, " what could you do yourself to find out who killed your brother?"

The American shifted uneasily in his chair.

" I know, I know," he said. " But all the same I must do something. I could go around with the inspector here. Keep my eyes open."

" No," said Ghote.

They looked at him.

" I regret, no," he repeated. " Professor Strongbow has been seriously assaulted. It is most likely another attempt will be made. I cannot undertake his safety if he goes here and there about the country, even if he is with me."

Shakuntala answered this with direct indignation.

"But you can't keep him shut up in the hotel here. You can't make him a prisoner like that."

"That's certainly so," Gregory Strongbow agreed.

He gave Shakuntala a glance of appreciation, which emboldened her to go on.

"Listen," she said, "if we were to make an expedition somewhere, say over to Elephanta Island, if we did it without warning, no one would know where the professor was. He would be quite safe then."

"But I don't want to make any expeditions," the American objected.

"You must," said Shakuntala with decision.

She looked at him straight in the eye with all the directness of a schoolgirl discovering the things that need to be put right in the world.

"You must get out and see the beauties of our country," she declared. "You owe that much to yourself. It's what you came here to do. You ought to go on with it."

And the simple vigour of her attack won him over.

"Okay," Gregory Strongbow said. "You could be right, I guess. I'll take this one trip anyhow. Where did you say we'd go?"

"To Elephant Island. It's out in the harbour. It takes an hour and a half or so by boat."

"Sounds okay. When do we start?"

"You do not start," said Ghote abruptly.

He was annoyed with himself for not having squashed this idea more quickly. But he had not counted on Shakuntala being able to sway a man as quietly determined as Professor Strongbow.

"You do not start," he repeated, "because if you go running here and there all over the place I cannot guarantee your safety."

"But Inspector," Shakuntala said quickly, "he will not

be running about all over the place. He will be simply making one expedition. I would be very careless in my duty if I had suggested anything else."

"In any case," Gregory Strongbow said with decision, "I am going. Shakuntala, what time will we get back? We'll give Inspector Ghote a detailed itinerary and he can make all the checks he wants."

Shakuntala looked at the delicate gold watch on her wrist.

"It is now eight o'clock," she said. "We could go down to Apollo Bunder almost at once and hire a boat. I will arrange for a lunch basket and we could spend all day on the island and get back by, say, six this evening. Is that all right?"

She looked at Ghote with an air of challenge.

"I think in any case," he said obstinately, "you are forgetting the weather. It may look calm now, but only yesterday the sea was most high."

"But that was unusual," Shakuntala said.

She turned to Gregory Strongbow.

"Professor," she said, "I have heard the forecast for to-day. I promise you there is no chance of a storm. And I think Inspector Ghote knows that as well as I do."

She turned her intense gaze on Ghote. And, since in deference to the truth he had to admit another big storm was unlikely, his glance fell.

"I guess I'll go then," Gregory Strongbow said.

"In that case I must insist on accompanying," Ghote snapped out in a sudden squall of bad temper.

"Glad to have you," Gregory Strongbow replied placidly.

    : :   : :

Ghote's feeling of resentment lasted until they were well out into the harbour on their way to Elephanta in a battered old whaler, discarded no doubt in years long past by the Royal Indian Navy. It had been the best craft Shakuntala had been able to hire at this late monsoon period when no regular outings took place, but its short-comings only added to Ghote's inner anger.

There were also the doubts that had arisen over their departure from the hotel. Ghote had gone to considerable pains to arrange for the professor to slip out without fuss. But at the last moment he had caught sight of Mira Jehangir behind her brass and teak reception desk taking a close interest in their activities. He had told himself that she obviously took a close interest in everybody who set foot in the big foyer and that it was doubtful in the extreme that she could have worked out that the professor was leaving for a whole day away. But an uneasiness remained.

It had been doubled at least by an incident that took place on the Apollo Bunder just as their decrepit craft had been leaving.

Ghote had been the last to climb down the iron ladder from the low wall at the quay edge down to the waiting boat. As he had begun his descent a rattly old car had drawn up on the far side of the Bunder. He had taken one look at it as he felt down with his foot for the rung below. And just as his head had ducked beneath the low wall at the quay edge a tall, gangling figure in a flapping European-style suit had stepped out on to the rough grey stones of the pavement.

He had been almost sure it was V. V. Dharmadhikar, the journalist. He cursed himself now for not having obeyed his instinct and climbed two rungs back up to make sure. But the others had been waiting and he had felt he ought not to detain them.

And, after all, he told himself, even if it had been V.V., what of it? He had a right to stop his car wherever he wanted. The Apollo Bunder was a reasonable place for a gossip writer to park his car. A liner might be docking at Ballard Pier soon with some celebrity or other on board. In any case it was more than likely V.V. had not seen their party at all.

But he had got into the old whaler feeling unreasonably put out. And matters had not been improved by Gregory Strongbow.

No sooner had Ghote settled himself on one of the sea-smoothed thwarts of the boat than the American had begun expressing doubts about the craft's engine. Certainly there was something pretty pathetic about this piece of machinery. It was an outboard motor from some much smaller vessel and it dangled over the whaler's stern with its little propeller only just below the surface of the water. But Ghote felt that the professor was in some sense a guest and should not have made disparaging remarks about the arrangements. He felt glad that their boatman, a ribby-chested, inward-looking old fellow, apparently understood only Marathi.

" Please do not feel concerned," he had said sharply in reply. " That engine may perhaps stop but if it does it will not be a disaster. No doubt this chap would get it going again in absolutely no time at all. In India we have a great ability for improvisation in the most unlikely circumstances."

For some reason this had seemed to disconcert the American. He had suddenly looked extremely thoughtful. Ghote even wondered whether he could have heard about the village mechanic who had repaired the car of an American family on the Poona road at the time of Hector Strongbow's death. But the report had only come in late the night before. The family had read about the killing and had told the police in Poona that they had unsuccessfully asked a red-bearded American to help them out. Had Hector Strongbow stopped, Ghote reflected, the men who had lit the signal fire might have been chased away by the local villagers before the young American had come through.

In the meanwhile the old whaler's pathetic little engine spluttered on. With every cough it gave, Ghote was convinced that it was going to stop altogether and this anxiety did nothing to improve his resentment of the whole expedition.

But Shakuntala obviously was delighted with the venture. She kept up a continuous, enthusiastic commentary on everything that came in sight.

"Look. Look at that boat there. They have been using dug-outs like that for thousands of years in these waters."

Gregory Strongbow laughed. He pointed away from the long log being laboriously paddled inch by inch through the heavy, pea-soup water over to a distant speedboat cutting its way purposefully along with a wide white wake spuming out behind it.

"That may not be so romantic," he said, "but it takes a lot less out of you."

"All right," Shakuntala replied cheerfully, "if you want modernness, how about those? Indian Navy frigates."

Her pride was naïvely evident.

Ghote looked at the two grey warships moored in the distance with their ominous guns pointing forwards. He found that he too was feeling a similar pride. But he made up his mind that not a hint of it would get out.

"I know America has a much bigger fleet," Shakuntala went eagerly on, "but I bet all those aircraft carriers and things are not one bit more efficient than our frigates."

"I wouldn't be surprised if the frigates weren't a whole lot smarter," Gregory Strongbow conceded gravely.

Ghote felt uneasy. The talk reminded him of Colonel Mehta and his assertions about the efficiency of the Indian Army.

"That's Cross Island over there," Shakuntala chattered on. "And behind it you can see freighters waiting to get into the docks."

Ghote found he could not resist introducing a note of sourness, although it would hardly enhance the tourist attractions of India.

"I hear there is a new strike of dockers," he said. "That is why the freighters are waiting still."

"You should try New York's dockland for strikes," Gregory Strongbow said. "We can certainly beat India there."

But a short silence fell. It was not long however before Shakuntala had perked up again.

"You can see Elephanta quite clearly now," she said.

"To the right of Butcher Island where that big tanker is just coming to its moorings. The oil is for the refineries at Trombay, over there, where you can see the sun on that marvellous white dome. That's the Atomic Energy . . ."

Her voice trailed away.

"I guess that's another field where the U.S. is ahead of India," Gregory Strongbow declared.

There was a much longer silence.

"There is that speedboat again," Ghote said, for want of anything else to break the awkwardness with.

"She's certainly making a hell of a racket," said Gregory Strongbow.

And it was true that the engine of the launch, a big but battered-looking craft, was as noisy as it was possible to be without actually blasting itself to a seizure.

Shakuntala bounced back into the conversation with a display of real interest.

"Oh, I would love to go out in a boat like that," she said. "I never have, you know. All I've ever done is to chug out to Elephanta on the old launches. It must be marvellous to go cutting through the waves in a real speedboat."

They watched the launch's frenzied plume of white wake.

"I dare say you have often been in boats like that," Shakuntala said to the American.

"Why no. Such little sea-going as I've done has been in fishing boats not so much different from those over there."

He pointed to half a dozen high-prowed, lateen-sailed craft winging along on the freshening wind.

"Those are called eagles," Ghote contributed dutifully.

"It's an appropriate name all right. They look light as birds."

"Oh, watch there," exclaimed Shakuntala. "The speed-boat's coming right towards us. I do hope it holds its course. I'd love to see it close to."

The old launch had turned towards them and was noisily approaching now in a straight line so that its long frothed-up white wake was no longer visible. They watched it without talking for a little. A large blotch of rust could be clearly seen near the bows. Ghote felt abruptly depressed that what had once been plainly a beautiful boat should have been so neglected. Beauty deserved care.

And suddenly an unaccountable notion entered his head.

He looked quickly round them. They were almost half-way to their destination and there was not another vessel of any sort nearer than a mile away. He glanced back at the speedboat. It was still heading straight towards them. He shaded his eyes and peered hard at the battered craft. He thought he could make out that the man standing beside the helmsman was holding a pair of binoculars to his eyes and looking dead ahead.

He decided he had to speak.

" I regret," he said, " I do not like the look of that boat. I do not like it one little bit."

Gregory Strongbow whipped round and stared at him. It was plain that he had understood. He turned back and concentrated his gaze on the speedboat still heading towards them in a dead straight line, its engine racketing hard.

" What do you mean?" Shakuntala asked.

" I mean that I think this is another attempt on Professor Strongbow's life," Ghote said. " And I think this time it would not fail."

He looked round again at the empty sea, with the wind breaking its mud-brown surface into small choppy waves.

" But that isn't possible," Shakuntala said, with curious definiteness. " It's quite impossible. I tell you it's just not so. It's totally impossible."

Gregory Strongbow turned towards her.

" How well can you swim?" he asked.

" I can swim quite well, but——"

" I think it will be no use however well we swim," Ghote said. " If they are going to run us down, they will not leave it to chance whether we drown."

Gregory Strongbow's face set hard.

" I guess you're right," he said quietly.

He looked round at the chill, dirty, vacant and unfriendly

sea. Then he looked up and down the length of their small boat from the pathetic little engine choking and spluttering as if every cough would be its last to the worn bow-post pushing its way through the water as it had done for years and years past. There was no help there.

There could be no doubt any more about the intentions of the oncoming speedboat. The three men on board could be clearly seen, the helmsman standing concentratedly over the small wheel, the man beside him who had now let his binoculars fall on the strap round his neck, and nearer the stern a squat figure wearing a singlet crouched anxiously over the engine-well with beside him a long formidable boat-hook.

Gregory Strongbow leant towards Ghote and held his elbow. He jerked a nod towards their boatman sitting contentedly beside his little engine.

"Can you talk to that guy?" he said. "Can't he get some more speed out of that engine?"

Ghote turned and shouted in Marathi.

"Can we go faster?"

The boatman looked across at him as if he thought he must be mad and then dropped his chin on to his chest and resumed his reverie.

Turning away, Ghote saw that the American and Shakuntala were staring as if transfixed at the thundering craft not twenty-five yards away. And their faces were appalled.

CHAPTER VII

THE ROARING ENGINE of the battered old speedboat choked once only. And then it died. The man near the stern in the white singlet dropped his boathook. The clatter as it hit the deck sounded oddly clear in the hush that had come with the cessation of the engine's strident note.

The speedboat continued to slide forward in silence through the muddy brown water towards the little whaler.

But it was steadily losing speed. A few moments later it was obvious that it was going to drift past the stern of the steadily chugging whaler eight or ten feet too far away. The man in the singlet was already working frantically at the engine. In the whaler they heard him curse quite clearly as he put his hand on some part of it that was still hot.

His two companions stood by the wheel looking blackly at the whaler ploughing through the oily water away from them. The man with the dangling binoculars had a heavy, oval-shaped head with slightly greying hair, close-cropped. His chest was like a barrel under his dirt-smeared khaki shirt. The muscles of his arms stretched the short sleeves tight. The steersman was younger, not much over twenty. He wore a bright red check shirt and his stained white trousers were kept up by a length of lighting flex. His dark, thin face was marked by a long scar running from above the level of his eyes right down his left cheek to the chin in a broad gash noticeably lighter in colour than the rest of his face.

" When we get back," Ghote said to Gregory Strongbow, " I would go to the records department and see what we know about those three."

" Should we turn around and make for the city right now?" the American asked.

" I think we had better keep straight on to the island," Ghote said. " It is nearer. And if they get their engine to start again . . ."

They continued to watch the speedboat. It had ceased to have any way on it at all now and was drifting broadside on. The boatman too turned to look.

" Sahib," he said to Ghote in Marathi, " shall I turn and take them in tow?"

With a feeling of total unreality, Ghote realised that the man had all along been completely unaware of what had been going to happen. He must have thought the speedboat, though coming carelessly near, intended to pass just astern of them. No doubt he was used to such unthinking behaviour from the owners of fast craft and had endured feeling his old boat dip and plunge often enough in the heavy wash of vessels higher up the social scale.

"Leave them," Ghote said to him. "They will be all right."

The man shrugged his bony shoulders as much as to say that with mad foreigners on board anything could be demanded. He sunk into his habitual dreamy state, contenting himself with one muttered comment. Ghote only just caught it.

"But to leave a craft at the mercy of the sea : that brings bad luck always."

        : :   : :

Bad luck, if bad luck there was to be, did not appear to have followed them to Elephanta. Everything there seemed to go well from the moment they negotiated the slippery separate concrete blocks of the little pier where the sea swirled and lapped between each one in a mildly dangerous way that Ghote felt he could easily cope with. Surrounded by a noisy band of begging children they routed out an old custodian from his bungalow and set off with him to see the famous caves.

The weather was much more bearable out here, with a little breeze to temper some of the mugginess. They wandered slowly up the spaced steps of the stiffish climb to the open-sided caves. Round a jagged crag of rock, and there they were : an unenclosed forecourt, a flight of smaller steps and the first massive columns rising from the living rock.

The custodian began delivering his set-piece description in a meanderingly quavering voice. His performance filled Gregory Strongbow with continuous amusement. Ghote had expected that Shakuntala would be shocked at this. He had thought she would insist that the looming, impressive beauty of many of the honey-coloured sculptures came first. But evidently the American had more influence on her than might have seemed likely. She abandoned herself completely to the innocent joyfulness of his mood. And before long Ghote too felt himself being infected.

He knew that he ought to be preoccupied with the professor's safety. In whatever way India First had learnt that they were out in the exposed stretches of the harbour in an open, defenceless boat they had certainly been quick to take advantage of the situation. The sudden presence of that powerful speedboat certainly underlined the efficiency of their underground opponents. But somehow in the light-heartedness of the atmosphere on the island it was difficult to remember that any menace lurked for them anywhere.

The guide's vintage electric torch sent its goldeny yellow beam feebly out towards a new group of sculpture.

"This relief represents Siva and Parvati, his consort, seated together, with groups of male and female inferior divinities showering down flowers from above. Behind is a female figure carrying a child on her hip. This makes it clear that the scene represents the birth of Skanda, the war-god. Other authorities state that what is represented is Parvati, the consort of Siva, in a temper."

Gregory Strongbow laughed out loud.

The guide abruptly extinguished his ancient torch, perhaps by way of rebuke. In the suddenly darker gloom Ghote darted quick, nervous glances to left and right. But the big, open rocky cave would have echoed and re-echoed the slightest noise from any intruder and he relaxed once more.

"I guess it's nice not to have to decide between the two theories on that scene," Gregory Strongbow said. "Any technique for holding two contrary beliefs simultaneously gets my vote all right."

The guide laboriously switched his torch on again, having been apparently more economical than offended. At the same instant he picked up his unvarying discourse with a minute description of the next group of statuary "unfortunately mutilated by the Portuguese soldiery about the year 1582."

The professor leant towards Shakuntala and spoke in a voice a little more subdued than before.

"Those soldiery. No wonder India invaded Goa."

Ghote thought he saw the girl straighten a little in the dim light. For a moment he wondered whether she was going to deliver the defence of India's action which had flashed through his own mind. But she simply laughed a little and they moved on.

Before long Ghote felt obliged to inject into the holiday atmosphere one note of warning. He insisted that the tour of the caves should finish as soon as it reasonably could and that immediately afterwards they should eat the lunch Shakuntala had provided and be ready to set out again for the city. His plan, evolved even before they reached the landing-stage, was to wait till some large vessel was passing down the harbour and to make their way back within sight of it. In this way, he thought, they ought to be reasonably safe from a second attack.

They ate their meal on the top of one of the twin linked hills of the island, looking out across the water, which appeared from this height deceptively easy to cross, at the huge, dark sprawl of Bombay city. Ghote methodically scanned the whole expanse of the harbour from the distant spire of the Afghan Church near the tip of Colaba Point to the white dome and chimney of the not-to-be-mentioned Atomic Establishment at Trombay. But he did not see the least sign of the drifting speedboat. He decided that its crew must have got the engine started again and made for the sanctuary of the crowded city.

He peeled another of the little Nagpur oranges that topped their hamper and put aside his troubles.

When they had finished the meal they decided to indulge themselves with a final stroll by going back to the pier along the coast of the little island. It was still tolerably pleasant with the light wind coming off the sea tangy with salt and they spun out the last minutes of freedom from care as long as they could. Every now and again they halted to look down from the top of the little cliff along which the path ran at the sea breaking in small plumes of spray on the rim of black rocks below.

Behind them a tangled mass of trees, creepers and bushes

made a green background alive with the flitting movement of white-faced monkeys, brilliantly coloured birds and darting, gem-like insects.

"The tide's certainly ripping past those rocks," Gregory Strongbow said. "I suppose we'll get away from that pier okay?"

"Oh, yes," Ghote answered. "What concerns me more is to make sure we set out at a time when some suitable vessel is coming into sight."

The professor smiled with some shyness.

"Hell," he said, "I feel like a fool having to be protected like a consignment of bullion or something."

"You don't think they'll try again really?" Shakuntala asked. "I was never so frightened in my life when they were coming down at us like that."

"We'll be all right," Gregory Strongbow said quickly.

He stopped and picked up a short piece of stick from the path at his feet.

"Look," he said, "we can see how strong the tide is."

He strolled over to the edge of the short drop down to the rocks and with a dexterity Ghote envied tossed the stick neatly into the gap between the cliff-edge and the spine of sharp rocks. The water, boiling and bubbling along the narrow channel, seized the fragment of stick and swept it bouncing and twirling out of sight.

Shakuntala clapped her hands.

"Wait," she said, "we must have a race."

"Okay," said Gregory Strongbow, "it's a bet."

They searched the path for a few moments and each returned with the stick of their choice.

"Now, are you ready?" the American called out, standing waiting to lance his craft into the boiling torrent.

And, as if in answer, three figures shot from the thick vegetation behind them as though fired from giant springs.

Ghote had hardly time to register that they were the three men from the speedboat before the scar-ripped young steersman had knocked him to the ground. Struggling to get his hands free to grip the youth, he saw that the squat engineer had swept Shakuntala aside and was crouching in front of the American. Evidently Gregory Strongbow had not been taken quite as much by surprise as the attackers had intended. The barrel-chested, bullet-headed man who had had the binoculars was already on the retreat with a trickle of blood showing under his nose.

But the odds were too great. Just as Ghote succeeded in freeing his hands and getting a grip on the young steersman's long hair, the two others simultaneously hurled themselves back at the American. Ghote twisted his fingers fiercely round the oiled strands of hair and jerked. But suddenly a voice called out sharply.

"Finish. He finished."

Ghote saw the tense mouth beside the long scar just above his own face open wide. Then he felt sharp teeth biting his nose. He gasped with pain. And in an instant the youth was clear, his oiled hair whipping through Ghote's loosened fingers, and his knee coming pounding down into his stomach.

For a moment he was unable to move. Then his senses flowed back and he staggered to his feet. He drew a deep breath to fight off the nausea that almost overwhelmed him and looked round.

Gregory Strongbow was nowhere in sight. And only the sound of rending branches deep in the tangled, luminously green vegetation on the far side of the path indicated that not a minute earlier three violent men had been at work.

Shakuntala Brown, lying where she had fallen on the stony surface of the path, suddenly began to sob.

Ghote forced himself to go to the cliff-edge. At its foot he saw at once the inert shape of the American. He was lying face downwards across a jagged peak of rock with the boiling sea tugging at his feet. Already spray had soaked his light, well-cut suit from head to foot. In the still sunlight it glittered dazzlingly.

Shakuntala came and stood at the cliff-edge.

"We must bring him up," she said.

Ghote looked down at the broken figure.

"Yes," he said, "something must be done. I suppose his relatives will want to have him buried like a Christian. One of us ought to watch here while the other goes and gets a boat round."

"But the tide," Shakuntala said. "It will sweep him away."

Ghote looked down again.

"Yes, it may certainly rise high enough," he said. "But fetching a boat is the only way. To try and climb down would be simply ridiculous. Look at the steepness of the cliff and the spray is constantly wetting it rendering it doubly dangerous."

"But——"

Shakuntala left it at that. Looking down at the broken shape on the rock below, it was only too plain that there was nothing more to be said.

And at that moment Gregory Strongbow distinctly moved. For one instant he raised his head, only to let it fall again as inertly as ever back on to the hard, black, gleaming wet surface of the rock. But the single movement had been perfectly plain. Ghote did not doubt that it had happened for all the apparent lifelessness of the body both before and afterwards.

Shakuntala said nothing but dropped down to her knees and peered over the edge of the cliff with passionate intensity.

I shall have to climb down, Ghote thought.

The speed at which the tide was rising was plain to see. Already the brown suède shoe, which had been only half submerged when he had first looked over the cliff, was permanently below the surface of the racing water. At any moment Gregory Strongbow might have another fleeting return of consciousness. He would need only to raise his head a little higher and he would slip on the treacherous wet surface of the black rock and slide down into the vicious sea. And then he would have no chance at all.

But getting down the cliff would be almost suicidally dangerous. The drop, though of only some twenty feet, was practically sheer. Hardly a single handhold, it seemed, jutted out of the iron face of the rock. And the whole lower third of its surface glittered and gleamed with the spray tossed up from the waves breaking on the spine of rocks below.

Suddenly into his head came the thought of his wife and son in the neat security of their little Government Quarters home across the harbour in the comfortable, crowded city. Surely this was where his duty lay? He had married Protima, entered into a contract with her. They had brought little Ved into the world. Could he go back on claims as strong as these? A running glimpse of Protima's life as a widow shot erratically before him : hanging on in the house of whichever relative tolerated her, without possessions, without position, without anything in her future but a long succession of featureless days.

And all that lay between her and such a life was one tiny slip on these twenty feet of sheerly falling rock which separated him from the huddled body of an American stranger.

He looked downwards once again. Gregory Strongbow's body lay just as it had when he had first seen it.

Only there was a difference.

He knew now that inside that case of flesh a heart was beating, however irregularly. Down there, not ten yards away in a straight line, a man lay in danger of being swept to certain death. He could see him : he would have to go.

He knelt down and slowly took off his shoes. He felt a desolate sadness sweeping over him. Neatly and carefully he placed his shoes side by side on the path.

" Please run down to the boatman," he said to Shakuntala, " and get him to bring the boat round here as quickly as possible."

" You are going down?"

" I must."

" Then I will stay."

" No," Ghote said, " you can do nothing by standing here watching. Kindly go immediately."

Although it was true enough that she could not give him

any practical assistance, it was not mere arguments of commonsense that made him wish passionately that she would leave. He felt acutely that if he was to risk himself in this way he must do so completely on his own. The girl's presence, her fears for him as she followed his progress, would be an added burden. He felt he was entitled to thrust it away as rudely as he liked.

"Please hurry," he said, biting off the words in case they exploded into rage. "Please hurry, time is important."

And to his immense relief she turned and began half-running, half-stumbling away along the stony path. He turned back to the cliff.

By the time he had lowered himself over the edge, he calculated, there would be little more than twelve feet of rock to negotiate. At the bottom, given a certain amount of luck, he ought to be able to get astride the same black jagged spur as Gregory Strongbow. He ought to be able to hold him there till help came. But it would be on the twelve feet of sheer, slippery cliff-face that the end could all too easily come. One slip, one mistake and nothing could stop him tumbling helplessly down into the boiling cataract fanged with black rocks below. He could not escape injury, and dazed and disabled he would be swept within seconds far beyond his limited range as a swimmer. And he did not see how he was to avoid making that one slip.

He lay on his face beside the edge and heaved himself over. Soon his wriggling toes encountered two almost imperceptible projections. Pushing against them with all his force, he lowered himself slowly clear of the top edge of the cliff. He pressed clingingly to the hard surface of the rock and groped about with outstretched fingers. First his left hand then his right found holds of a sort at about the level of his chest. They were mere tiny protuberances, but he set his fingers round them like claws and felt he might trust his weight on them for a little. He took a breath and moved his right leg from its perch. He slithered it downwards searchingly.

Down it went and down on the smooth surface of the

rock. But at last just as it was extended as far as it would go his toes encountered a minute ridge. He explored it carefully. It proved to be about six inches long and at its widest point a little more than half an inch deep. He twisted his leg till all five toes were resting squarely on the tiny flat surface. Then he swung his weight over and took his left leg off its first hold.

The moment he did so he felt the little ridge under his toes begin to move. He knew the whole thing must be slowly coming away in a single big flake. Sweat sprang up all down his front. He felt it salty on his tongue as he licked his upper lip. He felt it where his chest was pressing hard into the rock, and he felt it all the way along the length of his thighs as he fought to stop them trembling.

Forcing himself not to hurry, he brought his free left foot back on to its former hold. Then equally slowly he withdrew his right foot from the flaking ridge and brought it back up again. When at last he had got it securely on the protuberance where it had rested at first, the sense of relief that invaded him was so relaxing that he almost let go of everything.

Then he realised that all he had achieved so far was to get back to exactly the position he had started from.

Why not give up? The thought presented itself to him insidiously. After all, he had tried. Shakuntala Brown was witness to that. He had set off to climb down there, and he had simply found that it was impossible. Surely this was a moment for other claims to be heard? There was a certain value to his life, when all was said and done. He was a trained police officer. He had accumulated a fund of experience over the years that could bring many a wrong-doer to justice, if he were there to do it. At some time in the future it was more than possible that his skill and knowledge, and his alone, would save someone from murder. He owed something to the future too.

But the line of his thoughts carried him on.

If he were to creep back over the top of the cliff now and

lie face downwards in the hot sun not looking at what he had left behind, then he would be letting those three men who had leapt so suddenly out of the trees get away with their crime. He would be cashing in the measure of luck he had been handed when the engine of their launch had stopped at that critical moment. He would be letting India First attain its objective without a fight.

He came to a decision. He must force himself to push away from the comforting face of the rock so that he could see what he was doing on the climb down. Feeling his way blindly was plainly not going to get him to Gregory Strongbow's side.

He counted to three and he forced himself away from the cliff-face.

To his surprise he found that he felt a great deal safer. His sense of balance had begun to assert itself. He was able to look downwards without having to fight back waves of pure terror.

And almost at once he spotted something that looked as if it might solve half his problem. Invisible from the top of the cliff because of the way the shadows fell, there was a long, thin crack running vertically down the face a little way to his right. It occurred to him that if he could jam his toes and the ball of his foot into this, it would give him a hold infinitely more efficient than a crumbly little ridge.

He swung his right leg far out, still keeping himself as clear of the rock as he dared. He just reached the crack. Cautiously he wriggled his toes into it and then his instep. In a moment the foot jammed fast. It was uncomfortable but it seemed to be totally reliable.

He looked down for a moment at his objective, the boiling line of broken foam interspersed with jagged black teeth of rock. And quite suddenly the waves of pure fear came back. He forced his head up till he was confronting the rock an arm's length away and took three deep breaths.

It was enough.

He swung his other foot off its hold and over towards the

crack. He found he was able to observe the wriggling toes below him with clinical detachment as he manœuvred them into the crack in their turn.

It struck him that if the fissure made as good a hold as this for his feet, it might serve equally well for his hands. He would have to put his fingers in as far as they would go and then press them hard outwards against the sides of the crack with his elbows stuck out. He reached across.

Half a minute later he had discovered that he was right. He was crouching in front of the narrow crack feeling almost as safe as if he was standing on the familiar pavements of the city. He began lowering himself neatly down. If he was able to make this much speed, he was almost certain to get to Gregory Strongbow before the tide reached high enough to drag him off his perch and even, with luck, before another bout of returning consciousness made him lift his head again, shift his weight and slide into the angry sea.

After a while he found that, not without unexpected minor complications, he had reached the end of the crack. The cliff on either side was already wet from spray and cold to touch. There were perhaps six feet to go. He began to search around for other holds.

And there was nothing.

This time the cliff really was sheer. A blank surface polished, it seemed, by the constant beating of the waves, glistening and unyielding. He searched it again. And again. But there could be no doubt. There was not the faintest possibility of climbing down any farther from this point. Could he risk jumping? He could not conceivably see what might await him in the bubbling mass of foam at the water's edge. It would be launching himself into the unknown.

There was only one thing to do : to go up again.

Grimly he set out. But going up proved a good deal harder than coming down had been. Not only did he have to tug his weight up, but each danger that he had overcome had to be overcome again, every carefully negotiated passage had to be carefully negotiated once more.

And when he had done it, he reflected, he would be back at the beginning for the second time.

Was this the moment he could abandon it all? Was he being given a second chance to take the sensible way out? Because now he had really tried. He had risked his life in no uncertain way for this stranger. What about those near and dear to him? It was their turn now.

A seagull came screaming up to the cliff near his head. He closed his eyes in a sudden new access of fear. The sound of the bird's harsh, taunting voice dinned in his ears and then seemed to fade. He found he preferred knowing what was happening to the comfort of darkness and opened his eyes again.

He looked round. The bird had flown over the top of the cliff. Below him he saw the shining white patch on the black rock that was the American's inert body.

He began looking for another route downwards.

It was not long before he found it. His eye travelled from a single tuft of tussocky grass to a knob of stone which looked as if he could get a couple of fingers round it, and on to another crack, shorter than the first but useful now that he had learnt the trick. Then there was a whole series of tiny protuberances leading well into the spray zone and finally something that looked like a ridge big enough to plant a whole foot on.

He swung himself off. And almost at once his right foot slid sharply on a tiny area of bird-droppings. His leg shot off the hold altogether. The weight of his whole body tugged at his hands gripping two little rough patches on the rock-face. Inexorably his right hand was pulled away. He tried to gain some support by twisting his left leg round and thrusting upwards. The force of the manœuvre suddenly sent a piece of stone shooting away beneath him and his leg dropped sharply down.

He hung on hard with his left hand, the fingers biting into the hard surface of the cliff-face. Desperately he clutched out for some support with his other hand. But millimeter by millimeter he felt his sweaty fingers sliding from their hold. He registered the moment when the index finger slipped away.

And then came the fall.

CHAPTER VIII

AN AGONISING JAB of pain shot up Inspector Ghote's right leg as his foot hit a submerged rock in the boiling torrent at the foot of the cliff. For a moment he remained upright. Then the force of the water swept him stumbling forward. A sharp edge of black rock seemed to come chopping up towards his face. It struck him on the left shoulder, flinging him sideways.

And suddenly the tug of the racing water ceased to pull at him. His face was clear of the surface, though drenched by successive lashing bursts of spray. He was mercifully jammed hard between two rocks. And safe.

He tried to heave himself up a little and found that he could manage it. Slowly he worked his way round till he was facing in the direction of Gregory Strongbow.

The American was still spreadeagled across the black spine of rock. The distance between them was about three yards. But those three yards were one ominous mass of boiling, bubbling, frothing sea. Each of them could be on separate tiny islands with a deep torrent cutting them off from each other. Or it might be that Gregory Strongbow was only half a dozen paces away.

Ghote began to push himself upright. His right knee darted spasms of pain all the way up his leg. But it seemed to support his weight. Gritting his teeth he tried a step forward. His foot slipped on the awkward angle of the rock underneath it but the rock was there. If all went well, he had only to go forward step by step now and he would reach the American at last. A second pace brought his painful right leg up to his left. Then another advance. Once more forward with the right foot, enduring the dart of pain that this meant. Then another advance with the left foot.

And in an instant he was down.

The water was over his head, beating at him, blotting everything to black confusion. He flung out his arms and felt the peak of rock he had been jammed against before. He scrabbled wildly and his head came out of the water. His brain cleared. He fought his way upright again.

It took him minutes to push against the swirl of the torrent enough to regain his former position. But at last he managed it. He paused to consider, holding his left thumb in his right hand, a superstitious trick that had always brought him luck as a schoolboy.

There was, after all, a deep gap between himself and Gregory Strongbow. He had found out that much. Was it going to prevent him getting to the American? Was he going to be this near and be baulked at the last minute?

Cautiously he set out towards the spine of black rock with the inert, white-suited body flung against it. He calculated that he could take two paces with each foot before he reached the edge of the deep channel between them. One with the left, one with the right. A pause to let the pain ebb away a little. Then one more with the left and another with the right. A longer pause and at last the fiery agony was bearable. He took a deep breath.

And flung himself full length down into the sea. He reckoned that it was the only way. If the deep channel went right up as far as the American's rock, then he would be swept away. If it was a little less wide, he might find something to hold on to on the far side.

He felt his outflung arms slowly going down through the bubbling water. And then there was something solid. He clutched desperately. His fingers made contact. His grip held. He hauled himself forward.

He had made it.

: :   : :

He had had to lie across the unconscious body of Gregory Strongbow on the spine of black rock for nearly an hour. The tide had reached as high as the American's knees and had then slowly subsided. Rescue, when it came, had been comparatively easy. It seemed that deep water went quite close to the foot of the cliff and the boatman was able to bring the old whaler to within a few feet of them. He had been extremely phlegmatic about the whole operation, tossing a rope over to Ghote as if such things happened every time he took a party across to Elephanta.

Between them they had hauled the heavy body of the American into the boat and Ghote had wearily dragged himself on board after. Then he had let go. He had felt that his share was over. He was vaguely aware that Shakuntala was busy with Gregory but what exactly she was doing seemed to be of little concern to him.

Even when she had called out triumphantly that he was beginning to regain consciousness he had hardly stirred. But a short rest at the landing stage and tea provided by the custodian of the caves, who had seemed almost bereft of speech without his monologue to recite, had restored him enough to think what had to be done. He had come to the conclusion that the American was fit enough to get back to the city and see a doctor there, and they had made the journey across the harbour easily enough.

Then it had been merely a matter of getting the boatman to take them to a less conspicuous landing point than Apollo Bunder and bundling into a taxi back to the Queen's Imperial Grand Hotel.

He told the taxi driver to go round to the back of the hotel when they arrived. From his inspection of the building the evening before when he had placed a discreet watch over the American, he knew that there was a back entrance with a short flight of service stairs to the first floor where Gregory Strongbow's suite was.

Leaving Shakuntala to settle the bill, he took the American by the elbow and piloted him in. Less than two minutes later the door of his bedroom was safely closed behind them. And Mira Jehangir, sharp-eyed at the reception desk, would have no idea that he was back and in reasonably good shape. Nor would V.V., if he should happen to be sitting waiting somewhere in the big foyer, be any better informed. If either of them was feeding India First with information, at least a short respite had been gained.

He helped Gregory Strongbow over to the high bed with its heavily flounced counterpane and high mounded pillows.

" Lie here for a little," he said. " Then when you are feeling better we will think where we should hide you."

" I am feeling better," the American declared in rather too loud a voice.

Nevertheless he flopped down on to the big bed and lay quietly.

" Now what's all this about hiding me?" he said. " I don't get it."

" It is quite simple," Ghote explained, fighting against a feeling of weariness. " The India First people do not know their attack failed. If we can hide you safely away somewhere and get you proper medical attention, they will never learn."

The American thrust himself up off the soft bedding.

" And I'm nice and tidily kept a prisoner?" he said.

" No, no. Not in any sense a prisoner. But it would be best for your own safety."

" I'm not doing it."

The American still kept himself up on his elbows and glared at Ghote.

" I'm not doing it, I tell you. I might as well go scuttling back to the States. But I'm not going to do that either. I'm going to stay here and stay a free agent. No one's going to order me around and keep me cooped up. That's for sure."

Ghote sighed.

" You are a free agent," he said. " You can do what you want."

" Then I stay right where I am."

Gregory Strongbow flopped back on to the pillows and closed his eyes.

" But one thing I insist," Ghote said.

" What's that?"

" That you see a doctor without further delay."

There was a short silence.

" Okay," Gregory Strongbow said at last. " I guess I do feel a little beat."

This admission alarmed Ghote after the American's toughness of a moment before. He felt a new flood of energy and hurried into the suite sitting-room to the telephone. He found that the hotel regularly used a Dr. Udeshi who lived only a few minutes away.

When he got back to the bedroom Gregory Strongbow seemed to be asleep. He sat down on a little cane-seated chair by the foot of the huge bed and waited. After about five minutes the American spoke.

" I don't feel so bad after all," he said cheerfully. " You know, all I need is a drink. Let's take a stroll down to that Bulbul Permit Room and see what a little whisky can do for us."

" No," said Ghote.

" Hell, why not?"

" To begin with you are plainly not really well. And in the second place, though the India First people are bound to find out you are back here before very long, I wish to keep it secret while I can."

" Very sound reasoning," the American replied.

Ghote registered that the oddly forced tone he spoke in must mean that he was by no means well. There was more than a hint of delirium in it.

" I tell you what though," Gregory Strongbow continued in the same hectic tone. " I tell you what. We can have a drink up here. It's legal. It says so on that little notice by the door. Drinking's allowed by permit-holders of the following classes, one, visiting Sovereigns, two, foreign visitors. And I'm a foreigner in these parts."

He began heaving himself up from the downy plumpness

of the bed and groping round for the bell push. Ghote
wondered if he ought to restrain him by force.

Mercifully a loud knock came on the outer door. Ghote
hurried away to answer it. It was Dr. Udeshi. Ghote led
him in without stopping for formalities.

And Dr. Udeshi, portly, solemn, with an immense,
stubbly, grave jaw, would not hear of any alcohol being
taken in any circumstances.

" My dear sir," he boomed after examining the American, " one week in bed, one week, nothing less. I cannot
undertake to avoid complications unless strict rest is enforced for at least that period. I cannot undertake it."

And the relentless pressure of such a personality was too
much for the American. He lay back on the huge plateau
of the bed and looked up at the high ceiling, where no
fewer than seven long-bladed fans twirled rhythmically.

" If that's what you say, Doctor," he murmured.

" I absolutely insist. Absolutely. Already you are showing decided symptoms of fatigue. Decided symptoms."

" I guess I do feel tired."

Dr. Udeshi rose from his little chair beside the bed and
administered an injection.

" I will leave you now," he said. " I advise a short,
refreshing sleep and afterwards a light meal. There is
nothing you need particularly avoid. Choose whatever will
stimulate the appetite."

His head inclined in a grave, permissive bow. He replaced his hypodermic in its appointed place in his black
leather Gladstone bag.

" I will return to-morrow morning at approximately ten
a.m.," he said. " But if you should need me before that
time, do not hesitate to telephone. I am always available."

Wafting a dense aroma of reassurance in every direction,
he made his way out.

Ghote turned to Gregory Strongbow.

" I too will leave when I have seen Miss Brown," he
said. " But before I go I want you to promise me one
thing."

The American turned his head and looked at him. He seemed less feverish after Dr. Udeshi's ministrations.

"What is it?" he asked quietly.

"Not to leave this room under any circumstances without telling me," Ghote said.

The American's eyes were wide open.

"All right," he said. "It's a promise."

His eyes closed. He was asleep.

:   :   :   :

Ghote encountered Shakuntala in the broad corridor outside Gregory Strongbow's suite. Three bearers squatting together a little farther along looked at them curiously.

He told her briefly what Dr. Udeshi's findings had been. She looked serious but relieved.

"He has ordered a week's complete rest," Ghote said. "Kindly make certain Professor Strongbow obeys those orders. I must be sure he does not leave his rooms."

Shakuntala nodded solemnly.

"You can trust me for that," she said.

Ghote gave her one sharp, critical look.

"Can I?" he asked.

She looked back at him earnestly.

"I give you my word."

:   :   :   :

Ghote decided not to report to Colonel Mehta till the next day.

When he did so, toiling once more up the interminable flights of neglected stairs to the little office in the topmost cranny of the big building in the Fort area, he felt much better able to cope with whatever the colonel might have to say. A night's long sleep had restored him, and only an occasional twinge of pain in his right knee remained as a tangible sign of his buffeting in the torrent at the foot of the Elephanta cliff.

Colonel Mehta, sitting upright at the totally bare little table in the bare office, heard in silence his account of the two further attempts the India First thugs had made on

Gregory Strongbow. When Ghote had finished he looked up at him under his bushy eyebrows.

"And the professor," he said, "did he express his gratitude for you saving his life?"

Ghote thought for an instant.

"He was very tired last night, sir," he said. "Almost in a state of delirium until the doctor saw him."

"Hm. Have you seen him to-day?"

"No, sir. I came straight here. But I telephoned the hotel. He is well."

"Then you'd better get round there and receive his thanks, hadn't you?"

"I do not expect to be thanked," Ghote said stiffly.

"On the contrary, Inspector. You will put yourself in the way of being bloody well thanked."

"But——"

"And in the aftermath of that gratitude, Inspector, you will take the opportunity of asking your man just what it was his brother said to him when they met after that appalling visit to Trombay."

Ghote considered this in silence for a few seconds. Was he going to take advantage of the American's natural feelings in this way? Was this the sort of order he was bound to obey?

"Well, man?"

"I will do what I can, Colonel."

"I should bloody well hope so, Inspector."

"Colonel."

The colonel's hard eyes looked up at Ghote standing in front of him. There was an expression of incredulity in them at the prospect of an order about to be questioned. But Ghote had no intention of doing that.

"Colonel," he said, "may I ask what progress you yourself are making?"

Colonel Mehta's mouth snapped to under the line of his bristling moustache.

"I will remind you, Inspector," he said, "that the activities of the Special Investigations Agency are top security matters."

" Sir, it had occurred to me only that it might be possible to get at the controller of the India First through whoever is spying on Professor Strongbow. I was wondering only if such a step was still necessary."

Colonel Mehta permitted himself a token smile.

" Such a step is still necessary, Inspector. India First is not the sort of organisation that can be broken in a couple of days. But don't deceive yourself into thinking you're going to get at their Number One in that way. There is such a thing as the chain-of-command system, man."

" Yes, sir. But it is the only way I can do anything. And unless something is done the murder of Hector Strongbow will go unsolved."

The colonel looked up at Ghote speculatively.

" There's still plenty of the policeman about you, isn't there, Inspector?"

" I hope there is always, Colonel."

The colonel shrugged.

" Carry on if you want then," he said. " But don't think you'll advance matters one little bit."

" Thank you, sir."

: :   : :

So before Ghote went to call on Gregory Strongbow he permitted himself the luxury of setting in train a few police inquiries. The familiar routine lapped briefly and comfortingly round him.

He sent to Records for anything they had on the three thugs from the launch. He got in touch with the inspector in charge of harbour crime about the launch itself.

He telephoned Poona and checked on Shakuntala Brown.

Yes, she was the daughter of a British forest officer who had eventually taken Indian nationality. And, yes, she was employed by the State Tourist Department.

He made a few inquiries among his headquarters colleagues and unearthed the history of Mira Jehangir, receptionist at the Queen's Imperial Grand Hotel. She was, it appeared, the sort of person about whom his colleagues were likely to have a good deal of information, even though she had never come under their professional notice. Her father had been a jewel merchant, who from over-ambitiousness had run himself into bankruptcy and then had promptly died. His penniless sixteen-year-old daughter had become the mistress of a whole series of businessmen, but had reached the end of each association no better off than at the beginning. Until at last she had thrown in her lot with Mr. Wadia, the widower manager of the Queen's Imperial Grand. If the gossip was true, she was doing her best to induce him to marry her. But once again she seemed to be getting the worst of it. Instead of being the exigent adored one, she had become a more than usually hard-worked employee, without pay.

About V.V. he had little need to make inquiries. He was known to everyone as a journalist, always poking into anything that looked at all unsavoury. He could be expected to be sniffing around the Hector Strongbow case, but what his motives were only he himself could say.

Happier for this short interlude back in his proper harness, he went to see Gregory Strongbow. Almost at once he found that, like it or not, he was carrying out Colonel Mehta's plan for him.

Gregory Strongbow lifted himself up from the heaped mound of his pillows the moment he came in.

" Inspector," he said, " I've been hearing from Shakuntala more about what you did for me. You saved my life."

An instinct to thrust this aside overwhelmed Ghote. He smiled down at the tall American.

" Well," he said, " please to take care of that life then. Do not let me hear of you getting out of bed one moment before Dr. Udeshi gives permission."

Gregory Strongbow grunted.

" That guy," he said. " He was in here already. He's not going to let me out of his clutches if he can help."

"That is an excellent thing. After concussion it is necessary to take great care. Doctor's orders should be scrupulously obeyed."

"I'll do that. But in any case I gave you my word not to go gadding out, remember. That'll keep me in here more effectively than any doctor."

Ghote relaxed. The danger seemed to be averted. And it looked as if he was not going to be able to obey Colonel Mehta's instructions. If it was not in him, it was not in him.

"But you are looking much better," he said cheerfully to the professor.

"Yes, I'm feeling much better. I guess last night I was pretty well delirious. But I'm in my right mind now all right. In one way that's why I'm glad I didn't do anything about thanking you then. I'd rather you didn't think it was just delirious ravings."

"But—but there was no need."

"Yes, there is a need. You saved my life. You did more. You climbed down that cliff when anyone could see it was beyond the line of duty. And I'm going to say straight out that I'm never going to forget that. Never."

A warm rush of emotion swelled up in Ghote's heart. He darted up to the big, high bed and seized the American's broad hand where it lay on the deep fold of the white sheet.

The American shifted about a little.

"Hell," he said, "I can't go on calling you Inspector all the time. I want to call you by your first name from now on."

He grinned a little.

"I only hope it's something I can pronounce," he said.

Ghote smiled.

"It is Ganesh. Ganesh. Quite easy."

"Ganesh. Thank you, Ganesh, for saving my life."

Into the rosy flow of feeling in Ghote's head a tiny hard thought surfaced like a blue-black spike of rock in a wide river.

This is the moment, he found himself thinking. This is

the moment that I have got to ask him, to ask Gregory, what it was that his brother said to him as he waited to catch the Poona train.

"Gregory," he said, "if your life has been saved, it is true also that your brother's was lost. I would prefer not to mention, but this is not the time to be ruled by fear of hurting another person's feelings."

The American reached across to the tall, polished teak bedside table. From it he picked up a small black and white object, his brother's C.N.D. badge.

"I got Shakuntala to fetch me this first thing to-day," he said. "I'm not forgetting what happened to Hector."

"No," said Ghote, "I see that you are not. That badge shows me. Does it mean that you are going to take up where Hector could not go on? Gregory, what did he tell you in that talk outside V.T. Station?"

Gregory continued to look at the thin disc in his hand.

"We had a talk," he said. "I don't think any purpose would be served by going into it all."

"Please, Gregory, I need to know what your brother said."

The American glanced up at him briefly. Ghote caught one glimpse of cautious, appraising blue eyes.

"Do you really need to know, Ganesh?"

"Yes, Gregory, I need to."

He put all the conviction he could contrive into the words.

"I don't think so, Ganesh. Ganesh, I'm going to ask you a favour, friend to friend. Just don't ask me that any more. All right?"

Ghote looked down at him. His head had flopped back on the immense mound of bluey-white pillows at the top of the bed. He was staring expressionlessly up at one of the seven long-bladed fans swinging whiningly round from the ceiling.

"I regret," he said, "it may be necessary at some stage of my inquiries to ask you that question again. I am a police officer."

He felt a sudden burning fury at having used just those words at this moment. He was a police officer. But if ever there was work a police officer should not have to do this was it.

"All right," Gregory said slowly. "If you have to, you have to."

The big fan swung round and round above him at the end of its long shaft.

: :   : :

Ghote left the American as soon as he felt he decently could. Outside the suite he checked and double-checked his security arrangements. A major hotel in a fashionable part of Bombay ought not to be a place where a murder can be committed. The organised forces of society had a right to expect something. But he was going to take no chances.

He had personally selected the constable stationed by the internal telephone at the end of the corridor outside the suite. He was a moon-faced fellow, not over intelligent but trustworthy as a trained dog. He looked up at Ghote now, his eyes wide with determination to absorb every minutest particular of his orders.

"Now," Ghote said, "your duty here is very simple. You are guarding Professor Strongbow, the big American. You know him?"

"Yes, yes, Inspector sahib, I know well. He is American. He is tall. He has the face of a lion and kind eyes."

"And if anyone except his room bearer goes to the door of his suite, what do you do?" he asked.

"Ring, ring, ring on this telephone, Inspector sahib. Double quick time."

"Good man."

Ghote went outside and looked up at the windows of the professor's suite and the long wooden balcony with the dark area of greenish monsoon mould below it. He studied the whole surroundings hard, but simply confirmed his earlier finding that the balcony was accessible only to the half dozen grey crows that perched along its hand-rail.

Finally he decided that he could go back to his office and

safely pursue his inquiries into the three possible India First spies.

Shakuntala was his main object. The promptness with which she had arrived at the professor's side after his brother's death was a fact that had itched obscurely just under the surface of his mind ever since he had realised why Hector Strongbow had been killed. So far his inquiries on the telephone to Poona had produced only the answers that might have been expected. But there was a lot more that could be asked, given time to ask it.

He pulled his chair into his little scored and scratched desk, picked up the telephone and got through to Poona. He felt comfortable. This was his work. Patiently unearthing facts, comparing them, checking for the inconsistencies. The sheets of scrap paper piled in front of him began to be covered page by page with scrawled notes. He shuffled through them, marked words here and there, thought for a little, put in yet another call.

He forgot about getting anything to eat.

Some time in the afternoon he rang the Poona police again. It was only to check one tiny point. But to do so he had to explain at length who he was and what case it was that he was investigating.

No wonder the crime rate is so bad, he thought. When everything takes so much time.

" Inspector Ghote?"

A new voice at the end of the crackling, buzzing, appallingly bad line.

" Inspector Ghote speaking."

" Good afternoon, Inspector. It is Inspector Phadke speaking. I think I have something to interest you."

" Yes? Yes, what is it?"

His thoughts raced round the subject of Shakuntala Brown, the too-Indian English girl.

" I am holding a certain Kartar Singh, Inspector. He is a cousin of Harjeet Singh."

He had almost asked who Harjeet Singh was. But he stopped himself in time. Harjeet Singh, the man Poona had provisionally identified as the Sikh leader of the ambush party. Not to have known about him would have been to give this Inspector Phadke a very low opinion of Bombay efficiency. He owed more than that to his colleagues here.

"A cousin of Harjeet Singh," he said thoughtfully into the telephone. "And is he talking?"

Inspector Phadke laughed cosily.

"Soon he will be talking, Inspector."

"Then I will have a report when you have something to state," Ghote said.

He had not liked the sound of Inspector Phadke's laugh. No doubt often a policeman owed it to the forces of law and order to extract information from a suspect. But he owed it to himself not to enjoy that sort of thing.

"Goodbye, Inspector," he said, putting down the receiver.

He stopped and thought. Kartar Singh was something Gregory should be told about. Pulling him in represented a real advance in the hunt for the actual killers of Hector Strongbow. It would be a pleasure to have something to tell Gregory that reflected nothing but credit on Indian police-work.

Carefully he gathered up his notes, Shakuntala Brown, Mira Jehangir, V. V. Dharmadhikar. He clipped them in three separate bundles and put them in the top drawer of his desk, the one he could lock.

: :   : :

There was no answer when he knocked on the tall, dark door of Gregory Strongbow's suite.

He frowned sharply. Even if Gregory was dozing, Shakuntala Brown ought to be there.

He knocked again. A noisy tattoo.

And still no answer. He tried the door. It was unlocked. A sudden fury swept into his head. Surely they could at least have taken the simple precaution of keeping the door locked? Was it up to him to think of everything?

And all the time the possibility that the suite might prove empty had to be thrust down. It could not be empty.

Gregory had promised. Shakuntala Brown had declared he could trust her for that.

He shouted.

He ran through the deserted sitting-room into the bed-room. On the big, high, flounced bed the huge mound of bluey-white pillows was deeply dented where Gregory had been lying. But of Gregory himself there was not the least sign.

Ghote tore over to the door of the bathroom, his last hope. He flung it wide. The huge, slightly rust-stained bath stood solidly in the middle of the bare, white-tiled, narrow room under the high ceiling. There seemed to be dozens of mirrors, large and small, mostly a little blotched. He saw himself reflected and re-reflected. But nothing else.

No one.

CHAPTER IX

INSPECTOR GHOTE ran out of Gregory Strongbow's empty suite. The thought which he had thrust away so hard was simple reality now: Gregory had gone. He really had broken the promise he had made not to leave without giving warning. And Shakuntala Brown had done nothing to stop him. Surely this meant she was working for India First? And if this was so, then Gregory was heading for danger once again.

At the end of the long tan-carpeted corridor he saw his carefully selected constable, sitting almost to attention on a small gilt-painted chair.

"What happened? What happened, man?" he called out.

The constable jumped to his feet.

"Is all right, Inspector sahib," he said. "Professor Strongbow is outside as of now."

"Outside? Outside?"

" Yes, Inspector. The party left thirty-five minutes ago, accompanied by other party."

" Other party? You mean Miss Brown?"

The man's expression of patent anxiety to please wilted.

" I am not knowing her name, Inspector. Please, I am very sorry."

" Never mind her name. An English-looking girl, but wearing a sari."

The woebegone moon-face brightened.

" Yes, Inspector. That is quite right. A green sari. It was dark green."

" But why did you let them go?"

The constable's face was solemn again.

" Inspector, I had orders."

" Yes, orders to protect Professor Strongbow at all costs. He cannot be protected if we do not know where he is."

"No, Inspector. Not those orders. Orders to telephone pretty damn' quick if anyone tried to get into professor's room."

Ghote sighed.

His sense of justice compelled him to recognise that the man had indeed obeyed orders. Only too faithfully.

He swung away and hurried down to the public rooms. But as he expected there was no sign of Gregory or Sha-kuntala in any of them. In the foyer at the reception desk he saw the familiar, watchful form of Mira Jehangir.

He went quickly over.

" Professor Strongbow?" he snapped out. " Did you see him leave?"

But as he might have expected he did not get a straight answer.

" Professor Strongbow leave?" Mira Jehangir said, look-ing down at the long, painted nails of her elegant, jewel-covered hands.

" I know Professor Strongbow has left," he said. " What I am asking is when he went, and whether he told where he was going."

" You want to see the professor then?"

"I asked if you knew where he has gone."

Mira Jehangir's flickering eyes at last came to rest looking at him.

"Perhaps he just went to buy something," she said. "There is the American Express in Dadabhai Naoroji Road also."

"Did he say that was where he was going?"

Ghote tried to induce her to continue looking at him but in vain.

"Inspector, he tells me nothing," Mira Jehangir said with a hint of bitterness. "He hides in his room and I do not know whether he is dead or alive."

For a moment Ghote was tempted to pursue this answer. But he foresaw the great quagmire of evasiveness that any such questioning would produce.

"But you saw him go out," he said. "Did you see which way he went?"

"Through the swing doors it is not possible," Mira Jehangir replied regretfully.

Ghote glanced across at the tall doors. It was certainly true that their tinted glass blurred all figures outside them.

"How long ago was it that he left then?" he asked.

"Professor Strongbow?"

"Look," Ghote shouted. "Already you have told that he left. I am asking how long. How long?"

Mira Jehangir shrugged her elegantly thin shoulders.

"Ten minutes perhaps," she suggested.

"As little as that?"

"No. No, perhaps it was a little more. Perhaps it was nearer half an hour, or an hour. It was probably about an hour ago."

Ghote found his hand was gripping the little brass rail of the faintly nautical counter with such force that the fragile tube was in danger of breaking. He took a deep breath and turned away.

After a moment's thought he hurried back up to Gregory's suite again. Perhaps he could tell from what clothes the American had taken where he was likely to be heading for. He worked his way through the rooms systematically. But as far as he could tell nothing had gone. A lot of clothes still hung in the two tall wardrobes. There was a faint mouldy smell when he opened them, but that was almost certainly just the time of year. The sitting-room was exactly as he had last seen it with the heavy chairs grouped round the small central wicker table. There was no sign of a note.

It was just as he was leaving the bathroom that he saw it. He had dealt with the bathroom in a few seconds. There was little to see. The rust smears on the bath and the blotches on the mirrors could tell him nothing. Except that on the small mirror fastened to the back of the door there was a message. Just five words scrawled in lipstick.

Gone to Sewri—Launch there.

He understood immediately. The launch. That must be the launch that had come bearing hard down on them in the harbour. Somehow Gregory must have learnt that it was up at Sewri. There were plenty of berths along the waterfront there where a boat such as the launch could be tucked away out of public notice. So the stupid idiot had rushed off at once to see if the three men who had gone for him on Elephanta were waiting there.

But the message in lipstick must surely have been left by Shakuntala? What could that mean?

There was no time to think.

He bounded down the wide sweep of the main staircase two steps at a time. What a piece of luck that he had come over in the truck.

He skated across the chequered desert of the foyer, barged through the heavy, tinted swing doors and shot across the wide, startlingly hot pavement towards the truck. The driver, the same nutty-faced fanatic perpetually in love with his internal combustion engine, was standing by the open bonnet, tinkering as usual.

Thank goodness for some loyalty to something.

" Quick," he shouted to him. " Up to Sewri. Somewhere there we must find a launch. A big one, painted white."

The man turned to him, his eyes shining at the prospect of putting his truck over a fast obstacle course through the buffeting traffic from the crowded southern tip of the city all the way to the Sewri dockland on the north-east shore. For an instant he turned back to the opened engine, unable to resist the temptation of a last, lingering wipe with his bundle of cotton waste. Then he slammed the bonnet back home, nipped like a monkey into his seat and a moment later they were jockeying out into the traffic stream.

And at that second a contrary thought jumped into Ghote's head. For all his eagerness to be pushing on, something that he had half-noticed in the foyer of the Queen's Imperial Grand sirened obscurely for his attention.

The truck jerked to a sharp halt as a flock of pedestrians waiting to make the broad crossing coming up to Flora Fountain suddenly decided it was now or never.

The abruptness of the stop seemed to shake the realisation of what he had seen in the foyer to the forefront of his brain. It had been the tall, gangling figure of V.V. Or had it?

Ghote found that he could not be sure. He had gone through the lobby at such a speed. He had the clear impression of the tall, dark-suited form of the journalist in his mind's eye now. But was it simply the result of an overworked imagination? Or had he really been there? Spying once again at a critical point, with that uncanny knowingness that seemed to be the hallmark of India First?

They were edging their way round Flora Fountain itself now, the impassive portly nymph looking down on them from a swirl of frozen draperies as cars, bicycles, lorries and buses bullied and banged in a fume-heavy tangle of shouted obscenities, racing engines and squealing brakes. Ghote decided he would never know the answer to his questions for sure. He tried to sit back and conserve his energies.

But progress was maddeningly slow. For all his driver's pouncing concentration and the smooth reliability of the vehicle, they were still only in Dadabhai Naoroji Road. Drifting slowly past on the right was the mass of the

Municipal Offices, its domed tower loftily clear of everyday preoccupations against the metallic sky. He remembered the capricious fact that the statue in front was of Sir Pherozeshah Mehta.

The name presented him with the image of Colonel Mehta. He would be sitting at this instant in that bare, pared-down office, waiting to receive the information he had ordered so confidently. Ghote moved his shoulders uneasily. Would he ever match that military standard of efficiency?

Another Parsee honoured in statuary by a grateful city, Sir Dinshaw Petit, surrounded by his little oasis of greenery, slipped behind them. But the enormous, red-brick bulk of V.T. Station seemed to be taking hours to float by. Ghote looked out at the pavement. It had been somewhere here that Gregory had had that short conversation with his brother which he was so unwilling to talk about. Could it really be that they had simply discussed some deeply private family matter? It was possible. There were things that one owed it to all the history of one's childhood days not to chaffer in the public eye. But would he ever manage to find out whether it was something like this now? A few minutes before he and Gregory had been sworn friends. Gregory had acknowledged the saving of his life in the most solemn way. But now he had wantonly broken an equally solemn promise not to go anywhere without giving full information. So what chance was there of learning his inner feelings now?

Ghote glared at a dirty, bright blue truck ahead of them. It was loaded high with roped crates coming away from the Government Dockyard and it was progressing, with all the deliberateness it owed to such an important load, to some distant destination beyond the city. At the back was a small notice saying " Horn Please." And using the horn was forbidden.

" Get a move on, damn you," he shouted suddenly at the square rear of the vehicle.

" I will cut past before we get to Crawford Market," his

driver said philosophically. " Paltan Road would be best."

Ghote sat back. It was terribly sticky and close.

Sure enough, just as they passed the *Times of India* office on the left they slipped round the outer side of the truck and slid neatly into the stream of traffic intending to fork right into Paltan Road. But the sight of the newspaper office plunged Ghote back into depressing thoughts about V.V. once more and he got no pleasure from the success of the manœuvre.

If V.V. was an India First spy and had been there in the foyer, then already they would know he was heading this way. They would make sure Gregory had been dealt with before he stood a chance of getting anywhere near. It had been the merest luck they had been defeated up to now. It could not go on.

And progress through the traffic was still infuriatingly slow. Away on the left as they crept jerkingly along the narrower width of Paltan Road the clock tower of the Crawford Market stayed in sight far longer than seemed possible. At the complex junction where Carnac Road crossed their path it took hours to cut their way inch by inch round to the right. And even when they reached the point, just before the bridge over the railway, when they were able to head directly north again into Dongri Road there were still miles to go.

Ghote groaned out loud.

Gregory and Shakuntala knew where they were heading for. It might be the India First thugs' launch or it might be simply another false rendezvous but they knew where to go. While he himself had to search the whole waterfront at Sewri when he did get up there.

He cursed the note on the mirror for being so short. The lipstick surely meant Shakuntala had written it, but why had she said so little? Perhaps it had been because Gregory had insisted that they should go without leaving him any message, and this had been all she dared say out of a sense of loyalty. Always provided that she was not India First's spy, planted on Gregory with businesslike calm before he even knew his brother's death was anything more than an accident.

They were making quite reasonable progress now along-side the noisy railway lines of Dongri Road. But he re-mained wrapped in gloom.

They passed Masjid Station. Perhaps Gregory and Shakuntala had not used a taxi. Perhaps they had simply caught a suburban train to Cotton Green? It might be a quicker way to get to Sewri, if you were lucky. But a taxi seemed more likely. If Shakuntala were really wanting to help him follow, she would probably have insisted on a taxi. It would give her more chances of getting another message back to him. Only was she on his side?

He cursed.

She was out there in front of him somewhere. She and Gregory hurrying to some point on the waterfront. The answer to the whole enigma was there. But maddening stretches of road, infuriating conglomerations of traffic lay ahead.

At the big crossroads where Sardar Patel Road cut at right angles across their route they were held up for a clear five minutes. They broke through at last and shot away at a good speed but still not fast enough to obliterate the sheer space cutting him off from all he wanted to know.

Sandhurst High Level Station flitted past. They swung left and turned sharply into Mazagon Road with barely a glimpse of the massive outline of the J.J. Hospital a quarter of a mile away to the west.

And, for all that he knew it was ridiculous, Ghote could not stop himself sitting forward in his seat and peering at each car ahead. Something might have delayed them, and making progress like this, they might catch them up.

He spotted the yellow and black of a taxi.

"Do you see it?"

"What do I see, Inspector?"

"The taxi, you fool. The taxi. Can you go any faster than this?"

" Going as fast as possible, Inspector," the driver replied, with a touch of sulkiness.

Ghote forced himself to say nothing more.

At the crossroads with Nesbit Road a heavy stream of lorries was rolling across their route from the left going in the direction of the P. and O. dockyard. The taxi ahead was forced to stop and they drew up alongside. Ghote whipped round and peered into its dark interior.

A fat lady in a very pale pink sari sat in deep communion with a large sticky sweetmeat, holding it in front of her between a finger and thumb and nibbling reverently.

Ghote flopped back against the hard, hot seat.

At this very instant, he thought, Gregory may be teetering on the very edge of the trap.

The truck jerked sharply forward as his driver tried to cut ahead of the other vehicles lined up waiting to move on. Ghote noted that he was trying to get over to the centre of the road so as not to be held up by cars forking off down Love Lane a hundred yards or so ahead.

I should have had a man waiting outside the hotel day and night, he thought. I should have had someone there to follow Gregory the moment he showed his nose outside those tinted swing-doors. That was what a really efficient police officer would have done. He would have trusted no one. He would have put his whole reliance on the system, and nothing else. The simple facts dictated that if a police guard was being kept on someone then that person must never be allowed to get out of police surveillance. It was as simple as that.

And he had failed : he had let himself be ruled by his feelings about Gregory. He had simply trusted him to keep his word. It was ridiculous. And in an hour's time, or at the end of a search lasting till far into the night, he was going to find Gregory's body with a knife in it, or half a dozen bullets, in some out-of-the-way corner of the waterfront.

He looked up. His surroundings were now as depressed-looking as he felt himself. Big, grimy-walled mills arrogantly squatted wherever they pleased, leaving only narrow, black passages between for the tumbledown shacks of little human ants. Solid, tall chimneys exuded serpents of thick smoke. Behind the high, dirty blank walls the clank and roar of remorseless machinery could be heard even above the noise of the truck engine.

The driver began to swing to the right.

" What the hell are you doing?" Ghote snapped. " Straight ahead. Straight ahead."

" Quicker to cut down into Reay Road, Inspector," the man said placidly.

Ghote drew breath to shout him down.

But it would be quicker, he realised. Once into the straight run of Reay Road, in these more outlying parts of the city they would really be able to shift.

" All right then," he said.

But the truck had made the turn well before he had given his agreement.

At Reay Road Station they did indeed begin to move. Ghote sat forward again, intent on the chase. In no time they were snaking into Sewri New Road and ahead of them were the grounds of the European Cemetery.

" Turn right, Inspector?"

" Yes. And fast as you can till we get to the docks. Then as soon as we do, dead slow and keep your eyes open."

The truck hummed and whined as they took the clear road along beside the cemetery at top speed. In less than a minute they were at the docks.

Now, thought Ghote, just one bit of luck and we will find them.

" Go left or right, Inspector?"

Ghote took a long look to the right, towards the great area of the Grain Depot. The launch could be there. But equally it might not. One thing was certain : there was no black and yellow of a taxi.

" Go left. And take it dead———"

He stopped.

From the far side of the junction a figure had come suddenly running from the narrow passage between two towering godowns. A figure in police uniform, a sergeant. And it was plain that something was wrong.

The sergeant, a tough-looking veteran with a bar of grey moustache across his upper lip, came to a halt on Ghote's side of the truck breathing heavily, his face streaked with runnels of sweat.

He saluted.

"Inspector," he said, "seeing the blue of your Dodge was like a miracle. I have got Pal Bedekar trapped in there."

He looked over towards the black slit of the passage between the two huge godowns. Obviously he expected Ghote to know who Pal Bedekar was.

"Good man," Ghote said, trying to sound as enthusiastic as he could.

It was clear that this was an event of importance for the sergeant, who probably had spent twenty years in this particular, crime-ridden section of dockland. But the thought of Gregory Strongbow somewhere ahead of them, perhaps not fifty yards and in mortal danger was hammering incessantly at Ghote's brain and he could give his attention to nothing else.

"Only one thing, Inspector," the sergeant went on gravely.

"Yes? Yes?"

"He is carrying knife, Inspector. On my own I cannot be sure to get him out. And if I am waiting too long he can climb out."

The claim was blatantly staked.

A red fury seized Ghote. Why should this idiot stand there so seriously doling out the history of some petty dock-side thief? Of all the times to have chosen to make his great capture, why had he picked on this, the moment that Gregory Strongbow was there, so near, waiting for help?

He forced himself to speak casually.

"Sorry, Sergeant. You are out of luck. I have an important . . ."

He saw the look of sheer incredulity spreading up from the grey bar of the man's moustache.

Damn him, he thought, I cannot do this to him. The climax of a long career. To throw away all those patient years.

"Well, I can give you five minutes. You want me to come after him with you?"

"Three minutes only, Inspector sahib. With someone to help, I can deal with Pal Bedekar in three minutes only."

He turned at once and made for the narrow passage between the two tall, windowless godowns. Without hesitating for a moment he marched in.

There was not room for Ghote to walk beside him. He followed a pace behind, peering hard into the deep shadow ahead. When they had gone about fifteen yards down the passage he saw the sergeant's Pal Bedekar. He certainly looked as if he would take some dealing with. He was a heavily-built man of perhaps forty, naked all but for a cloth round his middle, crouching at the end of the passage, his hands held in front of him ready for action. And he had only one eye.

Ghote felt a snicker of apprehension go through him in spite of himself. A one-eyed man : the traditional figure of ill-omen.

"All right, Bedekar," the sergeant shouted. "You are coming out now."

The heavy, crouching figure at the end of the passage grunted contemptuously. Ghote saw the glint of a knife as his right hand moved a little.

"Do you want me to take him, Sergeant?" he asked.

"Oh, no, please, Inspector. For this I have waited a long time. Just as long as you are there in case I make mistake."

He advanced steadily towards the heavy, crouching figure. Ghote followed two paces behind, ready to jump the moment he saw how their opponent had reacted.

Suddenly the sergeant dived. The smack of two bodies coming into collision was like a thunderclap in the narrow passage. There was a swift manœuvring of arms and legs in the gloom. Ghote saw the glint of the knife as it moved jabbingly twice. For an instant he lost it. Then he saw it again.

He darted in. With a jet of animal pleasure he felt his fingers digging hard into a muscular forearm. He heaved his full weight to one side and twisted for all he was worth. The knife fell to the flagged ground with a clatter. It was all over.

A minute later the sergeant was marching a glowering, defeated criminal out into the harsh light of the road. Ghote, who had stopped to retrieve the knife, came after. He noticed a patch of dark blood spreading over the sergeant's shirt.

" Are you all right?" he said to him.

" Is nothing, Inspector. A dog like this could do nothing to me."

The sergeant gave a savage jerk to the arm he had doubled up behind his captive's back.

"We can handcuff him to some building for a few minutes," Ghote said. " I have a missing American visitor to go after."

" An American?" the sergeant said.

He turned round to address Ghote directly.

" An American got out of a taxi here just before I spotted Bedekar," he said. " Would he have a girl with him? American too perhaps, but wearing a sari?"

" That is him," Ghote said. " Almost certainly. How long ago was this?"

" Only twenty minutes, Inspector. They hurried down that way."

He pointed to a gap between two godowns a little further along the road. Ghote did not wait to hear any more. He ran full tilt into the dense shadow.

For a moment the comparative darkness forced him to check his pace. But without waiting to accustom his eyes to the gloom again he plunged on. A discarded piece of mango peel or something equally slippery suddenly sent his right foot skating along under him. He thought he was bound to fall. His flailing arms encountered the walls of the go-downs on either side of the narrow passage. He spread his hands wide and saved himself. And then he was out in the light again.

The passage had led on to the quayside itself. Almost directly in front of him a small steamer was being loaded with cotton. A pair of derricks swung the big, bursting, white bales from a great square stack up through the air and down into the ship's holds. There was a knot of dockers round the stack, absorbed in their task, moving with unhurried skill, occasionally calling out some comfortable intimate joke.

Little use asking them if they had seen an American with a white girl wearing a sari.

He looked along the quay the other way.

And at once he saw the old launch with the rust-blotch near the bows. It was tied up at the foot of a flight of slimy, broken-down steps. None of the India First thugs was to be seen.

Moving fast but with caution, he made his way along under the shade of a row of godowns towards the top of the steps. No one was working up at this end of the quay and everything was curiously silent. He took care not to bring the heels of his heavy shoes down hard on the stone surface for fear that any purposeful sound would give a warning to whoever might be down in the launch cabin. The donkey engine working the two derricks behind him chugged muffledly away and occasionally the dockers could be heard making one of their loud, almost meaningless, jokes. But as he approached the tumbledown flight of slimed-over stone steps there was not the least noise and nothing seemed even to be moving.

A single brooding kite was perched totally motionless on the top corner of a high blank square of wall just at the point where the steps began.

As Ghote reached the pair of dark-rusted bollards marking the head of the steps he took one last cautious look behind him and to either side. Nothing. Nobody.

And suddenly at his feet the launch engine broke into violent life.

CHAPTER X

THE NOISE of the launch's heavy engine shattering the silence of the deserted quay went through Inspector Ghote numbingly. Gregory, he thought. If Gregory Strongbow is in that boat, I have got here just in time to see him disappear.

He took one despairing look round. Away from the wall of the quay the dirty brown water stretched into the far distance with nothing breaking its surface. A craft like the launch could roar out into the wide reaches of the harbour and head away straight down south into the limitless stretches of the Arabian Sea.

The powerful engine settled down from its first crashing roar into a deep throb of contained power. It was ready to send the boat surging through the water at the flick of a lever. All that was needed was for someone to come out of the cabin, unwind the rope at the stern and toss it away. Then nothing could detain them.

Ghote took four steps along the quay and hurled himself outwards.

He landed by pure luck on a part of the launch's deck near the stern where there was nothing to injure him as he sprawled forward. Under him the boat canted sharply over and swayed heavily back. He began pushing himself up.

With a crack like a pistol shot the door of the cabin immediately in front of him banged back. The barrel-chested man who had hurled Gregory Strongbow over the cliff on Elephanta stood there.

Ghote, swaying slightly from side to side with the rocking of the boat, looked at him blankly.

What shall I do, he thought. I have made things no better charging blindly out here like this. Why did I set myself up all alone against people like India First? This man will be too much for me by himself. And the other two are probably there behind him.

All I can do is to make it hard for them.

In the open doorway the barrel-chested thug let his jaw drop wide. Ghote registered the fang-like yellow teeth.

Then suddenly the man shouted.

" Police. The police. Quick."

He bounded forward. Ghote could not prevent himself glancing into the darkness behind him. The other two thugs were there. And that instant of missed concentration was all the barrel-chested man needed. He hurled himself at Ghote like a battering-ram.

Ghote felt himself go down with a thud that knocked the breath out of his whole body.

This is the finish, he thought. I have let the whole police force down for ever.

It was a moment of overwhelming despair.

And then he realised that nothing more had happened. The big thug had not flung himself down with hands searching for his throat. The others had not rushed to help.

He jerked up his head.

The three of them were already at the top of the slimy stone steps. They were making off as fast as they could. He guessed then what must have happened. They could not have believed he was on his own. They were trying to get away before the rest of his men were on to them, the forces of justice always at his command.

He scrambled to his feet.

In the black space of the cabin doorway Gregory Strongbow appeared. His face looked very white under the locks of curly brown hair. He stared up at Ghote.

" How did you find us?" he said. " How did you? You were just in time."

The sound of his voice unlocked a torrent of emotion in Ghote's mind.

"It is not question of how I found you," he shouted. "It is question of how you came out to here."

He took an impulsive pace forward so that the boat swung and swayed again.

"Yes," he said, "that is what you have to answer: why, when you gave your word to me you would not leave the hotel without telling, did you go all the same? What is the good of giving trust when straight away it is broken? What is the good at all?"

Gregory blinked at him.

"Hell," he said, "I have to sit down somewhere."

He looked round him with the hasty selfishness of someone taken unexpectedly ill. By the craft's low rail there was a coil of rope deep enough to sit in. He took a couple of swaying paces towards it and sank down.

"You are well?" Ghote asked with sudden concern. "They have not done something to you? And Miss Shakuntala Brown? Where is she?"

The American smiled wanly.

"She's okay," he said. "Come out, Shakuntala."

Shakuntala appeared at the cabin doorway. She too looked pale, but seemed otherwise all right.

"No," Gregory said, "all those guys had done so far was sneak up on us and keep us in there. What they were fixing to do was scheduled for later, I guess. When we were well out to sea."

"You are all right, Gregory?" Shakuntala said, looking down at him anxiously.

"I'm okay, more or less. It's just that I should never have got out of bed. Your Doctor Udeshi was quite right."

"And why did you get out of bed?" Ghote asked. "Why did you come out here? That is what I want to know. That is what I think I have a right to know."

For some time Gregory did not answer. Then he looked slowly over towards Ghote.

"Yes," he said, "you have a right. I feel bad about this. A fine time to feel bad too, I suppose, when I've got myself into a hell of a jam and you've got me out of it."

He grinned, and then immediately looked totally serious again.

"I want you to believe this," he said. "I felt badly about all this before ever those guys sneaked up on us. I really did. Before we even saw the launch I wanted to call you and tell you what was happening. But, damn it, you never see a call-box in this city."

"You have to go into a shop and make request," Ghote said.

"You do? I'll know next time. But that doesn't make it any better, me taking off like that in the first place."

Again he looked at Ghote with honest, serious eyes. Ghote looked coldly back.

"Well, damn it," the American said, "I was lying there in that fantastic fluffed-up bed with nothing to do but think. And I reckoned you didn't seem to be interested in anything except what I had happened to say to Hector. So I thought I should try and do something for myself. I owed it to Hector, didn't I? Didn't I?"

But Ghote was prickling.

"I am not interested in anything?" he said. "But a great deal was being done."

"It was?" Gregory answered with abruptly rising sarcasm. "I didn't see too much of it."

Suddenly he rubbed his hand across his face.

"No," he said, "I didn't mean that. I'll tell you the truth. I did think it. Cooped up there, I thought Indians couldn't run a police force in Paradise. But that was only a kind of patriotic nightmare. Honestly it was."

"A full-scale hunt was taking place for this very launch," Ghote replied stiffly. "Men were proceeding northwards, both along the beaches on the east side and along the docks this side. Here they had already reached the P. and O. dockyard at Mazagon."

"Where's that?" Gregory asked.

Shakuntala answered.

"It's about a mile south of us. They would have

reached this place quite soon. Our Mr. Batliwala sounds a bit unnecessary now."

She smiled at Gregory with a hint of conspiracy.

" Mr. Batliwala?" Ghote said sharply.

" A terrible private eye I hired," Gregory explained. " I used the telephone and went on asking till I got hold of a detective agency that specialised in docks security. That was Mr. Batliwala."

" And you told him everything?"

Ghote did nothing to keep the outrage from his tones. Although Gregory knew nothing of Colonel Mehta and the Special Investigations Agency, the thought that he had chosen to tell some nasty little private detective all about India First and the real reason for Hector Strongbow's death made him feel black with betrayed despair.

" I told Mr. Batliwala one whole heap of fantastic nonsense," Gregory said. " I owe Hector at least that. I can still be trusted for something, you know."

" And so can the Bombay Police be trusted," Ghote answered quickly. " Do you think we had done nothing? Not only had we nearly found this boat, but we knew the names of those thugs. They had records. They were willing to do any dirty work round the harbour for a hundred rupees among them. And if we had been left in peace we would have had them behind bars."

Gregory shut his eyes.

" You can't make it any hotter for me than I'm making it for myself," he said. " And you got me out of it all too. You still haven't told me how you got here just in time."

" I can explain that," Shakuntala said.

" I left a message for the inspector," she said. " I scrawled it in lipstick on a mirror in the bathroom just as we left. I am sorry. You believed I'd stick by you."

Gregory shook his head.

" You weren't under any obligation to me," he said. " And I'm the one who ought to be doing the apologising. Apologising all round."

He pushed himself to his feet and came across to Ghote holding out his hand. Ghote took it.

" No more helping me without telling ?" he said.

Gregory grinned.

" No more," he said. " Not ever."

He pumped Ghote's hand again.

" And how about you ?" he went on. " No more bothering over what Hector did or did not say, eh ?"

Ghote dropped his hand.

" I regret," he said, " I must keep freedom of action in all cases."

The American looked as if he had been suddenly jabbed viciously in the ribs. After a moment he shrugged.

" As you like," he said.

: :   : :

That night Ghote looked in on Gregory just before he made his final security arrangements at the Queen's Imperial Grand. He found him alone in pyjamas and a thin, red silk dressing-gown drinking a final whisky-and-soda in his sitting-room.

" I wanted only to tell you that I am making full arrangements for your protection to-night," Ghote said.

He began backing out into the suite's little vestibule still occupied solely by the heavy, antiquated ironing-board.

" No, no," Gregory said hurriedly. " Listen, Ganesh, come in a minute, will you. There's something I want to say."

Ghote closed the heavy teak door behind him with reluctance and stepped into the sitting-room. He felt that relations between himself and Gregory had fallen back into a state of chill neutrality. And, since he was pledged to discover something Gregory plainly did not wish to make known, he preferred on the whole that this state of affairs should continue. And now with this invitation to " Ganesh " it looked as if Gregory had other ideas.

" Sit down, sit down," the American said. " Look, what about a drink ?"

" No thank you," Ghote said.

But he placed himself compliantly on the chair next to Gregory's.

The American sat in silence. He picked up his glass, looked at it, leant forward and replaced it on the little central wicker table.

Ghote felt obliged to say something.

"You wish to hear more about the activities of the police in clearing up the matter of your brother's death?"

Gregory shook his head wearily.

"No, I trust you for——"

He broke off and swung round in his heavy chair to look directly at Ghote.

"It's Shakuntala," he said.

"Shakuntala?"

"Yes, don't you see? When we went out to Sewri she was the only one who knew where I was going. And no sooner had we got there than those thugs of yours blew in."

"But you are forgetting she left message for me," Ghote said.

Gregory's revelation of what was worrying him had taken him by surprise. He was not concerned to pretend that Shakuntala could not be an India First agent. It was something he had even wanted to talk over at length with Gregory. But finding the American suddenly so keen to make out a case against her, he felt constrained to come to her defence. He felt he was obliged to say what he guessed Gregory really wanted to hear.

But a look of obstinacy settled on the American's openly handsome face.

"No," he said, "I'm not forgetting that message. But that could have been to draw suspicion away from her. I've been weighing this thing up."

His hands were twisting nervously together on his lap as if they were fighting one another.

"Look," he burst out, "I like that girl. It so happens I liked her the moment I saw her. She's darned sympathetic."

He looked over at Ghote as if he was relying on him to understand more than he had been willing to say.

Ghote felt the responsibility, and resented it a little Gregory was too distant from him to have a right to expect such a degree of understanding. He was a foreigner. If he wanted to tell him something, then he ought to say it straight out and in plain terms.

Yet he felt that he ought to take up the challenge since it had been made. If there could ever be real sympathy between people of such different backgrounds, then this was the test.

He coughed a little primly.

" There is something I have to ask," he said.

" Yes?" Gregory said hopefully.

" At home, are you a married man, Gregory?"

The American smiled slowly.

" I guess you took my point," he said. " Well, the thing is I was married. Until about a year back. My wife—— Oh, hell, she went off with this man. In the end we had a divorce. But the point is now that I care for Shakuntala. I really care for her. And yet she could be working for the outfit that had my brother killed."

He flung his twisting hands apart in a gesture of hopelessness.

" But she is not the only possibility," Ghote said earnestly. " I agree that a group as well-organised as India First almost certainly has an agent watching your every move. But it does not have to be Shakuntala."

" Well, who else could it be? Look at the way it all ties up. She came along at just the right moment to have been planted on me. She took that call for me to go to meet the guy at Brabourne Stadium. She was the one who wanted to go out to Elephanta. Of course I think she's sympathetic : it's her duty to be."

" But on the other hand," Ghote said persuasively, " it was perfectly reasonable for her to answer the telephone for you. And after all she was in the boat with us when it looked as if we were certain to be drowned. And there are others who are equally suspicious."

" What others, for heaven's sake?"

" To begin with there is Miss Mira Jehangir, the receptionist at the hotel here."

The American frowned in thought. Then his face cleared with almost comic suddenness.

" It could be," he said. " It certainly could be. That woman's the most darned curious female I ever met. There could be good reason for that. Do you think she was planted here to spy on me?"

" No, she was not planted," Ghote said. " But it is still possible that India First may have bought her. We know they do not hesitate to purchase just what they require, whether it is dacoits on the Poona road or the use of a fast launch in the harbour."

Gregory shifted a little in his chair.

" All the same," he said, " you're not just producing the possibility of this Miss Jehangir—is it Jehangir?—just to confirm for me that it really is Shakuntala all along?"

" No, no," said Ghote. " There is even another possibility. You are knowing V. V. Dharmadhikar, the journalist?"

Again Gregory's eyes lit up.

" The guy who interviewed me," he said. " That certainly fits in. What do you know about him?"

" He is a journalist," Ghote replied. " It is his duty to interview people like you. Certainly, he seems to hang round the hotel a great deal, but that too might be through excessive loyalty to his paper. No, we must keep all three in mind."

" All three?"

" All three."

Gregory put his chin in his cupped hands.

" So where do we go from here?" he asked.

"There is one thing that could be done," Ghote answered. " I was going to tell you that the Poona police have arrested·on suspicion a certain Kartar Singh. He is cousin of the leader of the dacoits, an impudent fellow who thought it would be safe to come back to his home already. I was wondering whether to go to Poona to question him myself. I think now I should go, and you should come with me."

"Fine, if we're going to get on to the India First top brass that way."

"Good. Now who shall we tell that we are going?"

For a moment there was a look of perplexity in the American's eyes, then he understood.

"If we make sure only one of the three knows," he said. "That makes sense all right, even if it does mean I have to act as a decoy duck."

He thought for a moment.

"Can the one we tell be Shakuntala, please?" he said.

Ghote looked at him intently.

"You are sure you want?"

"Certain."

On the way out Ghote was careful to give clear instructions to the best man in the guard party to stand by to follow Gregory Strongbow if he as much as set foot out of his suite.

: :   : :

Ghote, making his way through the jostling mass of people in Dadabhai Naoroji Road with Shakuntala Brown next to him and the tall form of Gregory Strongbow on her other side, looked back for the twentieth time. The high red brick arches of Victoria Terminus lay just ahead. But this might be the moment India First would choose to strike.

In the turbulent crowd, a dazzling confusion of white-shirted, dark-headed figures with here and there a turban or a Gandhi cap or the vivid splash of a sari, how could he hope to pick out one individual manœuvring closer for the kill?

Of course there ought not to be anyone. It was not that he had not taken precautions. His men outside the Queen's Imperial Grand had been alerted in good time. If anybody lingering there had suddenly left just after they had set out themselves, he would not have been allowed to get far. Yet it was India First that he was up against. And somehow India First always seemed one jump ahead.

He turned back and glanced over at Gregory. It was almost time he fulfilled his part of their agreement. Would he bring it off? He forced the query down. It was not a particularly difficult thing to do : he must trust him.

And at that moment Gregory looked up at the ornate mass of the huge station just ahead and turned to Shakuntala with all the innocence in the world.

"You know," he said eagerly, "you could catch a train from there in just a few minutes' times and be in Poona in under four hours. Up in the cool, pretty good."

He is doing it perfectly, Ghote thought. I ought to have known he would. After all, we worked it out carefully enough together.

Suddenly Gregory stopped dead just where he was.

For a moment Ghote believed the attack had begun, something he could not make out. Then he realised that it was part of the American's performance. A tiny doubt sprang up in his mind. Was it quite right that he should be able to act out something invented as well as this? But there was no time for speculation. He listened carefully. At any second he might have a part to play himself.

"It's a great idea," Gregory was saying. "We take off right now. We give ourselves a really good break."

Shakuntala was looking very doubtful. Now was the moment.

"An excellent suggestion," he said forcefully. "It would not be a break only, it would be a very good protection for you, Gregory. To set off without a single moment of notice."

"But—— But we can't just go off to Poona like that," Shakuntala said.

She seemed very much put out.

"I mean we wouldn't get there till it would be much too late to get back to-day."

"We'll go to a hotel," Gregory said cheerfully. "That Wellesley place was okay. We could stay maybe a couple of nights. Why not?"

"But we have no clothes. Nothing. By all means let's

go to Poona if you want to. It's certainly much too hot and sticky to be in Bombay unless we must. But let's go to-morrow, after we've packed a case each."

"No, no," said Gregory. "It'll spoil it to make out a great schedule and everything. That train goes in a few minutes, the Madras Express. We'll just climb into it and buy some pyjamas and a toothbrush in Poona."

"That would be perfectly possible," Ghote slipped in. "Certainly for one night. I would ring my headquarters when we get there."

Shakuntala looked all round her.

"All right," she said, "if you both insist. But we could still get back to the hotel and pack. The train's almost bound to be a bit late leaving. If we take a taxi both ways we'll do it."

She began searching the noisy, jerking stream of traffic for the black and yellow of a taxi.

A spasm of anxiety went through Ghote. She was almost certainly right. They had not judged the moment quite perfectly. There probably would be long enough to get to the Queen's Imperial Grand and back. And once back there, so many opportunities would arise for someone to see that they were off somewhere, that the whole plan would be riddled with holes in five minutes. If their eliminating device was to work, no one must know except Shakuntala. If she was really working for India First, she could tell them where Gregory was easily enough in Poona.

But Gregory seemed equal to the occasion.

"We'll miss the train for sure if we start trying to do that," he said, with what appeared to be genuine feverish-ness. "You can't be certain it'll leave late. When it says on the schedule that a certain train leaves at a certain time, you just have to be there if you want to get on it."

Ghote wondered whether these were his real sentiments. They were what Americans were supposed to feel. It was possible that Gregory had succeeded in persuading himself that the situation they had contrived between them was real.

He decided that in any case he must help.

"Look at the traffic," he said. "A taxi might get caught up in the most deplorable jam."

"Quite right, quite right," Gregory said. "Just come on."

And by sheer force he swept them into the great station concourse, past, round, and even over the hundreds of people standing, sitting and lying there, and on to the ticket office. There at last he suffered a check as they found the end of the right queue and stood waiting while it gradually approached a tremulous and white-bearded clerk at the ticket-window.

All the while Gregory kept shooting looks at the station clock as its long minute-hand twitched judderingly towards their departure time. And when at last they reached the old clerk and he fumbled and dithered interminably over issuing three air-conditioned class tickets to Poona the American's impatient fury was a sight to see.

Shakuntala turned away from the ticket-window.

"Really," she said, "you haven't any need to worry. The train is certain to leave late."

"Then it darn well shouldn't," Gregory snapped.

He glared like a gorgon over Shakuntala's shoulder at the white-bearded old clerk. And the old clerk simply stopped his palsied hunt for the correct tickets and blinked interestedly back.

Ghote reflected that Gregory's unshakable attachment to the highest ideals of punctuality was certainly making this stratagem look life-like. A feeling of impatience was beginning to disturb even his own equilibrium. What if someone spotted them before they were safely out of sight aboard the train?

At last Shakuntala stepped back from the window holding the correct tickets, all in their correct form and order. Gregory heaved a gigantic sigh of relief and began striding out towards the platform where the Madras Express was waiting.

Ghote found himself almost equally relieved. In less than

a couple of minutes they would be safe in the train. And then they would be out of Bombay. They would be dodging for a little the constant, ominous watchfulness of India First. Up to now, he felt, India First might have attacked Gregory in any one of a hundred ways at any moment they chose. In Poona events would be much more under his own control. Either India First would lose the scent altogether, or they would pick it up only after a warning from Shakuntala, if she was their agent. So their attack would be limited by the need to act quickly and by having to be carried out in a new area. The pressure would be off. It seemed almost too good to be true.

And this sudden move would take him out of the orbit of Colonel Mehta for a little, he reflected. No doubt the colonel would be furious at losing contact even for twenty-four hours. He was that sort of man, always wanting to be in control. But it would be worth a dose of his anger to feel free for a while now.

He would be free, too, to do some real police work. That was in a way the biggest gain of all. After these days of floating in the void without contacts of any sort, to have to deal with a simple, ordinary criminal like the man the Poona police had caught would be to eat real food again after a diet of air. He would be working on his regular routine of questioning instead of trying to decide what people completely detached from all the realities might take it into their heads to do next. It would be like coming back to life.

He marched along with brisk, short steps behind the enormously striding American.

" Professor Strongbow. Professor."

The voice calling from behind them was unmistakably loud and clear.

CHAPTER XI

INSPECTOR GHOTE swung round. Caught. Caught within yards of the Madras Express waiting with steam up to whisk them from under the noses of India First. Caught within minutes of getting clean away out of Bombay and the network of dangers all round them.

As he had thought from the sound of the voice that had called after them so insistently, V.V. was standing there peering from his considerable height over the heads of the crowd. When he saw they had stopped he came over to them in his usual series of long, erratic strides. And as usual he began talking while still a good distance away.

"Hallo there. So nice to bump into you."

"You followed us," Ghote shouted. "You tracked us down."

V.V.'s eyelids dropped over his unnaturally bright eyes.

"I like to know what is going on," he said.

Ghote glared up at him.

"Why did you follow?" he said. "I want explanation. Now. Or I would know what to do."

"Inspector," V.V. said, in a tone of exasperating reasonableness, "I have a most simple explanation: Professor Strongbow is here. Professor Strongbow is a most distinguished man. What he does, where he goes, is news, Inspector."

"Where he goes?" Ghote snapped. "What is it to you where Professor Strongbow goes?"

"Inspector, it is item of public interest. If Professor Strongbow revisits Poona where he was staying when his brother was killed that is a matter which my readers would like to know."

"Poona? Poona? Who said we were going to Poona?"

"Perhaps you are not, Inspector," he said. "But it is

strange that one of your party is carrying tickets, air-conditioned class, just for Poona itself."

But by now Ghote had recovered from his surprise and chagrin at being caught out like this.

"Yes," he said, "it is true we are going to Poona. I tell you that frankly. But of course off the record. Naturally the professor does not want at this time to be the subject of public curiosity."

V.V.'s eyelids drooped once more over his prominent eyes.

"But all the same may I ask the purpose of your Poona visit, Professor?" he said.

Gregory was caught on the hop.

"Well, why shouldn't I go to Poona?" he blustered. "It's very hot and sticky here in Bombay. Isn't that reason enough?"

V.V. smiled.

"But is it your reason, Professor?"

Gregory looked anywhere but at V.V. His eye caught the juddering minute-hand of the big station clock.

"Darn it, I won't get to Poona at all if I don't make that train this moment," he said.

V.V. put a bony hand on his forearm. "You are showing touching faith in the Indian railway system, sir," he said.

But Gregory snatched his arm away, swung round and headed like a maniac for the snorting, belching Madras Express. A porter with three cardboardy-looking suitcases balanced on his head wandered into his path. Gregory brushed past at such speed that the topmost case slipped and crashed to the ground. Its tinny lock sprang open and the contents of the case disgorged themselves over the platform.

Ghote wondered whether he owed it to the unfortunate owner to apologise for the American's rudeness. He knew that he did, but decided he had better run on, or Gregory would possibly leave for Poona without him.

And as it turned out no sooner had they found three vacant seats in one of the Madras Express's air-conditioned apartments, than with a hellish shriek of steam from its whistle the train pulled out dead on time.

Shakuntala laughed.

" Well, Gregory," she said, " your faith in the Indian State Railways was totally justified. V.V. will be most upset."

" V.V.? Why should he be upset?" Ghote asked.

" Didn't you hear?" said Shakuntala. " He followed us all the way to the platform explaining the train couldn't possibly leave on time."

" He followed us? He must be very keen to find out why we were going to Poona."

Shakuntala settled herself in her seat.

" Well, it was a good thing anyway," she said. " It gave me a chance to send a message back to the receptionist at the Queen's Imperial Grand."

Ghote stared at her.

" To the receptionist? To Miss Mira Jehangir?"

" Yes, of course. She is the one who would need to know we are only going away for a day or two. It was kind of V.V. to say he would tell her."

Ghote sank back in his seat. So now all three of his suspects would know Gregory was going to Poona. And, worse, even if Mira Jehangir was not working for India First, she was certainly capable of retailing this bit of information to anyone who persisted in asking her about Professor Strongbow. She would expect to get some morsel of gossip in return, and that would be that.

If only they had made the trip by car. It would have been much more convenient. But the thought of driving Gregory past the very place where his brother died had been too much.

With a long dying sigh of steam the Madras Express came to a halt. Ghote looked out of the window. They had hardly left the station.

Shakuntala giggled.

For a long time nothing seemed to happen. The huge

locomotive up in front was totally silent. The Goanese waiters hurried along the corridors with their trays of tea, toast and jam, trying to get as much of their task done as possible before the train started swaying and rattling over the criss-cross of lines leaving the city. The group of young people taking up most of their compartment began talking in loud voices about the break they were going to have sight-seeing in the mountains round Lonavla.

Suddenly there came a sharp, but deferential tapping on the carriage window. All eyes turned. The silk-suited businessman occupying the corner seat heaved himself up. He lowered the window. Balancing on the footboard out-side was a shirt-tail flapping clerk. As soon as the window was down he thrust a bundle of letters into the business-man's outstretched podgy hand. Shaking his head wearily at the rigours of his life, the latter thumped back into his seat, placed the letters carefully on the flap-table in front of him and began signing away for dear life. Opposite him his wife, looking on plump and cross-legged, allowed herself just the faintest twinkle of amusement behind her gold-rimmed pince-nez.

: :   : :

The bulbous American Ford taxi which had brought Ghote and Gregory Strongbow from the Wellesley Hotel across the Fitzgerald Bridge and up to the massive walls of Poona Gaol came to an impressive halt. The voluminously bearded Moslem driver pressed hard on the horn button in front of the huge closed main gate.

"This was one of the gaols where Gandhiji was im-prisoned," Ghote said.

The American looked at the implacable stone walls.

"Gandhi, eh?" he said dutifully. "All that seems a long while ago."

He turned round to look the other way. In the distance dotted here and there on the smooth turf of the golf-course parties of players, probably Army officers, could be seen moving slowly from green to green.

"Yes," Gregory said, "I guess Gandhi is pretty well all history now."

"History, yes," Ghote said. "But it is history we should not forget."

A warder came out through the big gate. Ghote lowered the taxi window and explained what they had come for. There was a slight delay while the man checked by telephone.

Ghote found he could not help contrasting his present situation with the days of the struggle for Independence. The task of discovering whether an American visitor did or did not know the secrets of India's atomic energy establishment was far, far away from the simplicities of the mass struggle against the British. No doubt there had been dilemmas of loyalty enough then, but surely not this terrible empty world of severed links and no trust by anyone for anyone.

The warder came back out to them.

"It is Inspector Phadke who will be seeing you, Inspector," he said with a smart salute.

The taxi rolled forward into the central courtyard of the gaol. Gregory looked round at the lowering, grim building.

"So this was where they held Gandhi," he said. "The very place."

A man in the uniform of a police inspector came down a flight of stone steps to greet them. It was clear that he was far from adhering to the austere precepts of the Mahatma. His tautly plump flesh stretched the cloth of his uniform tight. Above the strained collar his face was full and rounded with prominent lips, a thick nose and luxuriant eyebrows.

In spite of his bulk, however, he ran easily down the steps and crossed over to their taxi on the balls of his feet.

"Inspector Ghote? I am Phadke. Please to come in. I take it you will want to see the prisoner right away. I will take you down myself."

He spoke with a briskness that contrasted sharply with

the softly rounded curve of his chin. Ghote thanked him and, as he got out of the taxi, explained that he had brought Gregory with him because he had been the victim of a series of unexplained attacks since his brother's death.

Inspector Phadke looked a little put out by this unexpected addition to the party. But with a slight shrug of his well-padded shoulders he led them in. They followed him along a number of high, stone corridors echoing loudly to their steps. They went through several iron-barred gates and at last down a deep and narrow stone staircase. At the bottom there ran a corridor between two ranks of cells, their outer walls consisting solely of close-set, dark-rusted iron bars running from floor to ceiling. Apathetic prisoners scarcely lifted their heads as they passed. The air was sharp-smelling.

At the end of the two ranks of cells there was another barred gate. Past it, they descended a short flight of chill stone steps and came into a little square, stone-walled room lit by a single dim electric bulb. At the far side there was a small barred door. Inspector Phadke tugged a heavy key from his pocket and with a grating squeak turned it in the lock. He stepped back and hauled the door open. In a tiny cupboard of a cell there half-stood, half-crouched an almost naked man.

"Here you are, Inspector," Phadke said. "Kartar Singh, or what is left of him."

It was impossible to see more than the dull gleam of naked flesh at the back of the tiny cell.

"Out," Phadke shouted, taking a lunge forward towards the open door.

The dimly seen figure did not budge.

"Out. Or do you want me to come and get you?"

Again the figure kept utterly still.

"All right," Phadke said slowly, "we will have to see what we can do to make you move."

He took a lounging step forward towards the cell, a faint smile beginning to show itself on his full lips.

And suddenly the man in the darkness leapt forward. Phadke jumped sharply back.

Kartar Singh stood just outside his tiny cell and laughed shakily.

" You tell me to come out," he said to Phadke.

They could see now that he was a tall man, though he still stooped as if it would be a long while before he could stand upright again. In the little cell he must have had to have bent almost double.

He looked round slowly. The eyes gleamed in the gaunt face under the heavy crop of uncut Sikh hair. The jutting gush of his beard was matted and foul. But it was his naked body that attracted attention now that they could see it under the dim light of the single bulb. It was criss-crossed by dozens of heavy welts leaving hardly an inch of skin unbruised. Many were still crusted with dried blood, others had already begun to fester.

" Well, there you are, Inspector," Phadke said. " As nasty a dog as you could find."

He stepped forward and thrust his heavily jowled face into the Sikh's.

" However, we are beginning to show him that insolence does not pay," he said. " Isn't it? Isn't it?"

Just for an instant the stooping, broad-framed, battered Sikh appeared to quail. Then he drew himself up painfully until he could look down on Phadke.

" Little inspector," he said, " it would take more than you to make me tell anything of my friends, more than you and all your men."

Inspector Phadke brought the edge of his open right hand swinging up into the Sikh's face. The thud of the blow sounded like an explosion in the little, square, stone-walled room. Kartar Singh swayed from the impact. But not by the slightest sound or change of expression did he acknowledge that anything had happened.

Phadke turned away.

" Well, Inspector," he said, " do you think now we could be doing more?"

Ghote looked from the plump, firm figure of the Poona inspector to the gaunt, glaring-eyed Sikh.

"No, Inspector," he said, " I am certain you are doing your utmost."

"Then shall we go?" Phadke said.

"Yes, by all means. I do not think there is anything I can do here."

Ghote detected a rustle of protest from Gregory at his side. The American had been increasingly restive ever since they had seen the crouching form of Kartar Singh at the back of his cupboard of a cell with its inescapable stink and back-breaking lowness.

"Come along, Gregory," he said quickly. " I am sorry I had to bring you here."

Gregory said nothing more as they followed Inspector Phadke back past the ranged cells of the other prisoners and up into the politer regions of the administrative offices. Every now and again Phadke tossed them a cheerful remark over his shoulder.

"It is better when they are a bit tough," he said, as he opened the door of his own office. " There is more to getting them to talk then than just one hour's work."

"And so far you have got nothing at all from Kartar Singh?" Ghote said.

Phadke laughed sharply.

"So far nothing," he replied. "But do not worry yourself, my good Inspector. It will not be long now before he betrays all his friends. And in the meantime I am quite happy."

"Inspector," Ghote said, " all the same I would like a word with him."

"With Kartar Singh?"

Inspector Phadke sounded genuinely startled.

"Yes, with Kartar Singh."

"But you have just seen."

"I know. And now I have had time to think about him, and I would like to see again."

"As you wish," Phadke said with a gusty sigh.

He began to close the office door.

" No," said Ghote. " Up here."

" Up here? In my office?"

" If you object, perhaps in some other room."

Phadke looked round his office. It was a spacious and airy room, looking out on to a wide balcony where one of the prisoners squatted, naked except for a loincloth, heaving interminably at the rope of an antiquated punkah wafting in sluggish gusts of air. His services were retained apparently in spite of two large-bladed fans with their wires running, bare and unpainted, across the ceiling and down to a switch near the door. In the centre stood a large, glossy desk with a telephone and three heavy glass ashtrays on it. The chair behind was sturdy and comfortable-looking with arms curving embracingly round. To one side there was a large, leather armchair with a low table placed conveniently near it and another ashtray, on a stand. Two big carpets added even more to the air of luxury. And even the harshness of the bare stone walls was softened by a pair of bright calendars hanging on either side of the big clock in places where the mortar was friable enough to take a nail.

Ghote noted that the calendars were from past years and each rivalled the other in the scantiness of the clothes its girly wore.

" Well, if you insist, Inspector," Phadke said. " We can have him in here as well as anywhere else."

" But I am wishing to see him alone," Ghote said flatly.

" Alone? You do not——"

Inspector Phadke pulled himself up.

He laughed, tersely.

" Very well, Inspector. If that is what Bombay wants. I will have him brought up."

He walked out through the still open door. In the corridor he stopped and turned back.

" But please, Inspector," he said, " do not treat him like a baby."

" I do not think Kartar Singh is a baby," Ghote said.

Inspector Phadke evidently decided to take this as the

nearest he was likely to get to a promise. He turned and marched off down the echoing stone corridor.

Gregory Strongbow hardly waited till Ghote had pushed the door closed.

" Ganesh," he burst out, " this can't be allowed to go on. Why, you've only got to take one look at that Kartar Singh to see he's worth a dozen of your Inspector Phadke."

" Yes," Ghote answered, " Kartar Singh is a man whose determination in not giving away his friends is most admirable."

" But can't you do something?" Gregory said passionately. " That Phadke, he'll kill him before long. I swear he will."

" You are probably correct. Kartar Singh would let himself be killed rather than betray his companions."

Gregory's eyes shone.

" Then you will do something? You can order him to be taken out of here?"

" No," said Ghote.

A look of incredulity appeared on the American's open face.

" But—— But, look here——"

Ghote interrupted sharply.

" Those men Kartar Singh is protecting so loyally killed your brother," he said.

The words at least had the effect of making Gregory think. He stood in front of Ghote almost visibly preventing himself saying anything more. After a little he swung away and went to stare out of the broad window in front of the wide balcony where the punkah-wallah still swung at his rope like an automaton.

" All the same," he said, " that man . . . Well, he is a man. Hell, I don't know."

The sound of steps in the corridor outside stopped him saying anything more. The door opened and Inspector Phadke came in followed by Kartar Singh, held on either side by a hefty warder twisting an arm behind his back.

" Here you are then, Inspector," Phadke said. " Would

you like these two to stay? They are most skilful at holding a man down while he is questioned."

"That will not be necessary," Ghote replied.

Inspector Phadke smiled.

"Very well," he said. "But do not think you will get anywhere by using fair words to this raper of his own sister. I know him better than that."

He jerked a nod at the two warders. With a single concerted movement they hurled the battered, blood-stained Sikh to the ground at Ghote's feet. Then they turned and left the room. Inspector Phadke followed, still smiling.

Ghote waited in silence till the door was shut and the sound of steps on the far side had faded away. Then he looked down at Kartar Singh, who had remained where he had been flung on the floor with his head just resting on the edge of one of the big carpets.

"You can get up now," Ghote said.

Kartar Singh moved his head a little and looked upwards suspiciously. Then in one swift movement, which still showed how lithe he must have been not long ago, he was on his feet. He stood in front of Ghote, arms folded across his chest, looking down with an expression of disdain.

"I see Inspector Phadke has been treating you roughly," Ghote observed.

"That son of a dog could do nothing to me."

"I think he could," Ghote said.

"Then you are a fool."

The Sikh infused the words with insult.

"This is what I will do," Ghote said. "You tell me where your cousin and the two others are hiding, and I will have you taken to Bombay out of the hands of Inspector Phadke."

"Inspector Phadke."

Kartar Singh spat on to the floor, missing Ghote's right shoe by little more than an inch.

Ghote, who was watching the Sikh's gaunt and battered face, heard Gregory Strongbow draw in a sharp breath. But he did not let his eyes move for an instant.

"Well, Kartar Singh, will you tell?" he said.

"You think I will tell a boy like you? I have not let out a word to that Phadke, for all he has done."

"I think all the same you will tell me."

The Sikh did not even reply.

"Very well," Ghote said, "I will come and ask you again. When shall it be?"

"I do not care when you come or when you go."

The Sikh turned away with elaborate unconcern. He looked across at the big window. Outside the sky was pale blue and half a dozen kites were wheeling lazily across it.

CHAPTER XII

FOR ALMOST a full minute Ghote watched Kartar Singh as he looked out at the sky and the wheeling kites. Then he spoke sharply.

"That is all you have to say? That you do not care when I come again?"

Kartar Singh stiffened slightly but remained silent.

Ghote went over to the door, opened it and called along the corridor to Inspector Phadke's two warders.

"You can take him back now."

The two men hurried in, grabbed at the Sikh with plain delight and thrust him in front of them through the door.

"I will come to-morrow at noon," Ghote said.

He turned to find Phadke stepping in casually from the balcony.

"Well, Inspector Ghote, you did not have much success, I fear."

"No," Ghote replied, "I did no better than you."

Phadke smiled.

"But I am going to win in the end," he said. "And in any case I shall enjoy the struggle."

"I expect so," Ghote said. "But I would like to see him

once more all the same. In this office, if you would not mind. Just at noon to-morrow."

Phadke shrugged a little.

"The requests of Bombay are our command," he said. "I will have him up here at the time you state. But you will not mind if I first remove the carpets?"

With the toe of his gleamingly polished brown shoe he obliterated the mark of Kartar Singh's spittle.

: :   : :

When Ghote and Gregory got back to the Wellesley Hotel, eager to wash and relax since they had gone up to the gaol as soon as they had reached Poona, someone was waiting for them. Sitting comfortably installed with Shakuntala at a veranda table with glasses of lime juice, looking cool and inviting, was none other than V.V.

Ghote felt a spasm of disproportionate annoyance.

He marched straight up to the gangling dark-suited journalist.

"V.V.," he said, "what are you doing here? How did you get to Poona so soon? We left you in Bombay. You were going back to the Queen's Imperial Grand."

V.V. smiled.

"It is very simple," he said. "I did not take your message to the hotel in person. I telephoned from the station. And when I had finished I found your train still waiting at the end of the platform. So I decided to accompany. Poona is much pleasanter than Bombay just now."

"That may be," Ghote snapped. "But have you no duty to your paper? Will your editor be content to know that you are up here in the cool when he must be down in the damp and heat?"

But V.V. remained undisconcerted.

"I have good reason to be here," he said. "Professor Strongbow is here."

"But that is no reason for you to come," Ghote shouted. "What reason is that? Professor Strongbow is visitor only.

If he comes to Poona when the weather is sticky and unpleasant in Bombay, is that a newspaper story?"

But V.V. only let the eyelids fall across his prominent eyes and said nothing.

"Listen," Ghote said earnestly. "What if I should tell you that it is specially important that Professor Strongbow should be left alone?"

V.V.'s eyes opened wide for a moment.

"It is specially important?" he said.

For a second Ghote calculated.

"Yes," he replied. "I will trust you and be completely frank. A matter of national security is involved."

V.V.'s bony face looked up at Ghote.

"Inspector," he said, "you are telling nothing I do not know already."

Ghote checked his rising temper.

"If you know that," he said as icily as he could, "then it was your patriotic duty not to have come up here, bullying and badgering."

V.V. shook his head in disagreement.

"Inspector Ghote, you have a lot to learn," he said. "You·must not think that you have only to pronounce the magic words 'national security' to be able to do whatever you like without any attention being paid to you. That is very far from the case."

Ghote let the temper rise, and boil over.

"How dare you say such things? When it is national security matter, it is national security matter. The Press and its stories of this and that do not count one bit any more."

V.V. pushed himself out of his small wicker armchair.

"And who is to be judge of when it is really national security?" he asked. "Is it to be the people who have most to cover up? Inspector, you should be glad there are newspapers in this country. Glad to the bottom of your heart."

He stalked away along the veranda, a big, black, untidy crow of a figure. Ghote glared at him.

: :   : :

But for the rest of the day they saw little of V.V. and next morning Ghote, who had made sure that he was up very early, was comforted to find from a bearer he questioned that at least the journalist was still sound asleep.

When Gregory Strongbow came out of his room almost an hour later Ghote was outside waiting for him.

"Good morning," he said to him, "I hope you slept well."

"Once those guys with the scooter-rickshaws had quietened down I did," Gregory answered.

"I am sorry," Ghote answered, "but I had to insist you had a room at the front. At the back someone could have crept in without being once seen."

"So that was why," Gregory said.

"I had to take every precaution. Especially when I had deliberately brought you here to be attacked," Ghote answered.

He would have liked to have gone on to discuss the failure of his elimination plan and what they should do about Shakuntala in consequence. But he found it difficult to broach the subject. All the way to Poona in the train the day before Shakuntala had chattered away about the wild romantic scenery of the mountains as they crept up the Western Ghats. She had been full of the ancient days when the legendary hero Shivaji and his faithful horsemen had defeated the powers of the Mogul armies in daring engagement after daring engagement. And Gregory had watched her with shining eyes.

He had laughed at her and had questioned her more extravagant assertions, like the story of how Shivaji had giant lizards at his command trained to scale perpendicular cliffs with ropes attached to them. But Ghote saw that though Gregory liked to tease her with such doubts, it might be a very different matter should anyone else doubt Shakuntala herself. He decided to wait for a little at least.

Gregory looked round about him cautiously.

"You think they'll try something to-day?" he asked.

"It is very probable," Ghote replied. "We have one

advantage though. They will want to make their attack look like an accident. They would not want to have two American tourists murdered within a few days."

"So we keep our eyes skinned for an accident happening on purpose," Gregory said. "Where do we begin?"

Ghote smiled.

"By having breakfast," he said. "We owe it to our bodies to look after their wants."

In the dining-room, where Gregory managed to evade the sternly British breakfast in favour of papaya, yogurt and jasmine tea, Shakuntala soon joined them.

"Oh, I do hope we can stay here for a bit," she said. "There is so much more to show you, Gregory."

The American grinned.

"Sure," he said, "I've heard such a lot about Poona, you know. All those old British colonels and the pukka sahibs. What was it I read on that War Memorial yesterday? Something about going forth to fight for the Empire? That's the stuff."

"But no," Shakuntala exclaimed passionately.

And then she realised that she had been kidded and gave Gregory a look of mock exasperation.

"For that," she said, "you'll spend all morning going over the ruins of the old Saturday Palace built at the height of Poona's real greatness. The gates have spikes on them to halt elephant charges, and not far away there's the street where the really big traitors had the privilege of being trampled to death." The waiter, at that moment placing in front of her half a yellow papaya sprinkled with lime juice with its cluster of black seeds gleaming in the middle, suddenly gave a loud chuckle.

"You are lucky if you go there to-day," he said. "Most likely you would see an actual trampling by two elephants."

Gregory leant back and looked up at him.

"Oh, come now," he said, "I may be only a hick American tourist but you can't expect me to believe that."

The waiter grinned till every tooth in his head was showing.

" Oh, yes, sahib," he said, " is perfectly true, I am assuring you."

He adjusted the table-napkin on his arm.

" Is a film unit present there to-day, sahib," he said.

Gregory suddenly grinned back at him.

" You mean that? A film unit down at—where is it?"

" In the Shanwar Peth, sahib. This very morning, a.m. There will be film-unit making a big filming."

: :   : :

But when they arrived in the Shanwar quarter of the city they found they were by no means the only ones to have heard about the filming. The whole district seemed to be filled with one single-minded crowd so that even the wide streets had become impassable.

Ghote was less single-minded.

" We will never get there and back in time in all this," he said. " We should go somewhere else. I am told that Visram Bagh Palace should not be missed. Or in the Empress Gardens it would be nice and cool."

" And miss the elephant trampling?" Gregory said. " Why, that waiter would never forgive us. Come on."

He plunged with determination into the jammed mass of white-backed figures in front of him. Shakuntala adroitly took advantage of the vacuum formed by his wide shoulders. Ghote could only follow at a distance.

But before long the American got himself entangled in one of the numerous bicycles of Poona and Ghote managed to catch up.

" Please, Gregory, listen," he called out. " Remember I must be back at the gaol at noon exactly. I cannot afford to be late."

Gregory lost his expression of idleness.

" Okay," he said. " But there ought to be time for one quick look. It's early yet."

Ghote felt he could not deprive him of his pleasure. After all he was the victim of a tragedy. He was entitled to what passing happiness he could get.

" One look we will risk," he said.

He hoped that as they got nearer the street where the filming was to take place the crowd would get so thick that even Gregory and Shakuntala would decide to back out. But he had reckoned without the colour of Gregory's skin. Suddenly people began to notice that they had a guest among them. The inextricable jam of humanity mysteriously opened and in no time at all they were in the very street that was being kept clear for the filming.

"Up there, up there," Ghote heard people shouting.

"Yes, the balcony. He will see from the balcony."

He looked up. A narrow balcony ran for most of the length of the street. Already it was packed to danger point with onlookers, but within five minutes he found himself up on it with Gregory and Shakuntala somewhere ahead of him.

He looked at his watch. Only nine o'clock. With any luck the filming would be well over before he had to set off to keep his appointment at the gaol. He began to look about him.

He could have wished Gregory had not been hustled up to the balcony ahead of him. Five yards of squeezed together spectators were separating them and even in the security given by the very density of the crowds the tall American was a vulnerable target. But he decided there was nothing he could do for the present. And in fact Gregory was probably more in danger from the frailness of the balcony than from any form of attack from a distance. The delicate structure creaked with ominous sharpness every time a new eddy of movement occurred among the dozens of people crowding its narrow length. And its filigree iron railing was already in a precarious enough state. At one point, he noticed, a whole stretch had been carried away at some already distant date. An old piece of red silken cord, the relic of heaven knew what luxurious palace at the height of the British Raj, stretched across the gap just by the spot where Gregory and Shakuntala were standing to a point about four yards farther on.

It looked as if it would stand almost no strain at all. But probably there would be some warning if it did begin to break. It would fray rather than snap, and there was a decorative iron lamp-bracket or two on the house wall to clutch on to. In any case the drop was not all that great.

Ghote looked along to the far end of the cleared street. Towering above everything else there was a pair of massive elephants, standing patiently while their mahouts arranged their heavily decorated caparisons on the directions of one of the film unit. There was a lot of shouting and argument going on. Other members of the film unit stood talking to each other or sat waiting in upright canvas chairs. Ghote wondered if any of them were stars. Raj Kapoor might be there, even. It would be something to see him act in the flesh. Or would the magic vanish? He thrust the doubt away.

It became very hot, even though the balcony was in the shade. After a while the women in the house behind began passing out refreshments of various sorts, brass tumblers of buttermilk, lengths of sugar cane, smallish mangoes cut in half. He accepted one of these. The flesh turned out to be pithy and so sharp-tasting that it set his teeth on edge. Just as he was about to drop the piece over the balcony railing he realised that one of the women was watching him from inside the house. He put the half-fruit up to his mouth again and pretended to eat.

The woman smiled to herself amusedly and he realised she had known all along that the mangoes were acid.

And still there was no sign of progress from the film unit. He looked at his watch and was startled to find it was already past ten o'clock. He began to calculate how long it would take them to get back to the Wellesley Hotel if they had to leave before the filming was over. At all costs he must not miss seeing Kartar Singh at the gaol at exactly noon.

Could he safely leave Gregory behind? What if Shakuntala was with India First? If she saw him going, would she contrive to arrange an accident herself? Or signal to an accomplice in the crowd? No, Gregory would have to come with him.

He looked at his watch again. Ten past ten.

He started to try and catch the American's eye. But it was not easy. The five yards of balcony separating them were jammed with a score and more of people, and Shakuntala was keeping Gregory busy as she pointed out with great animation various incidents among the crowd opposite. Was this some sort of plot of hers to make Gregory stay where he was?

He shook his head angrily. Fantasy was no help at all.

At last he succeeded in gaining Gregory's attention. He held up his right arm as high as he could and tapped the watch on his wrist with the index finger of his left hand. Gregory obediently looked down at his own watch. Then he twisted round to the packed crowd behind him and shrugged his shoulders helplessly.

Ghote looked along towards the film unit. To his surprise there had been a sudden spurt of progress. The two great elephants had been dressed to someone's satisfaction and were being manœuvred into position looking down the street. A camera on a small trolley had been wheeled forward. A clapper-boy was parading up and down the empty street enjoying the laughing applause of the crowd nearby. The canvas chairs of the director and other important figures were being assiduously repositioned.

From a small, brightly painted van two men brought a floppy dummy dressed in all the glory of eighteenth-century Mahratta costume with four papier-mâché iron balls bouncing and bobbing from wrists and ankles. They laid it carefully in the victim's place. There was a last flurry of shouted orders and counter-orders. The mahouts gave the tails of their animals vigorous twists. As one, the two beasts lifted up their trunks and roared.

"Sound. Cameras. Action."

The triple yell hushed the crowd into instant, respectful silence. One more twist of the elephants' tails, another agonised double roar of protest. And the charge was on.

Shoulder to shoulder in the confined passage of the street, swaying and bumping into each other, trunks extended, enormous feet lifting and stamping, the beasts charged.

For a moment Ghote felt himself back in those more brutal days. For an instant even he shared the desperate, pounding fear that the chained and weighted victim, only days before a proud aspirant to the seat of power, must now be feeling.

And two seconds away from the moment of destruction the elephants halted. The leading beast looked at the sprawled figure. Its eyes glittered with suspicion. Slowly it reached forward with its trunk. It felt at the staring, wide-mouthed, horror-stricken face.

And with a practised jerk it tugged off a convenient morsel, conveyed it to its mouth and happily munched.

At the far end of the street the director fell into a rage which must have been a lesson and inspiration to his actors. Ghote shut his eyes tight and wished he was far, far away.

After a little he began trying to signal to Gregory again. But he and Shakuntala were completely absorbed in watching the tantrums in the distance. He tried to work out if, after all, there was a route from them along the crammed balcony and in at a window. Perhaps they could all three meet inside the house.

And it certainly seemed that beyond them there were fewer people to the square inch. Perhaps the view was less good from that angle. He saw that one man was already moving. He watched with interest. The man was young and wore dark glasses. He was bare-headed, with a rather spoilt-looking, plumpish face. When he raised both arms to work his way past a portly matron in a maroon sari, Ghote saw that he was wearing a deep-blue bush-shirt, very clean and fresh.

He seemed to be making steady progress by means of discreet shoving combined with an occasional desperate wriggle. Ghote thought that he could easily do the same.

He looked over at Gregory wondering how, amid all the jabber of excitement, he could possibly attract his attention. And to his delight he saw that the big rage scene at the far end of the street had mysteriously evaporated. The director was talking earnestly to one of the mahouts while the other urged both elephants back into position for a new charge. An assistant was kneeling beside the victim rapidly moulding his face into respectability again.

Ghote once more consulted his watch.

Eleven o'clock all but two minutes. If the trampling went all right this time, with the crowd pouring away they should be able to get up to the gaol in time still.

Once more the clapper-boy paraded in front of the camera. Once more the director called for sound, camera, action. The mahouts leapt forward and jabbed their charges with short pointed sticks viciously in the rear.

Immediately the beasts let out prodigious roars of pain and disapproval. They shot forward into the empty street. Their ears were spread wide, their tusks flashed, their trunks were raised high. They trumpeted defiance and lumbered unstoppably down on their victim.

And at that moment Ghote saw the young man in the dark-blue shirt.

What distracted his sight from the overpowering spectacle of the careering elephants he never knew. Perhaps it was because the youth's arm in the crisp, blue material was the only thing moving besides the rampaging, terrified, stop-at-nothing beasts. But whatever it was, he saw what was happening up on the balcony with the concentrated clarity of a scene lifted out of a jumbled illustration by a giant magnifying glass.

The young man was hacking away at the red silk rope with a short-bladed knife.

In two seconds it was bound to snap. And the consequence was equally inevitable. The press of spectators leaning forward to see the stampeding elephants would tumble irresistibly down.

The drop was not great. Few of them would even be injured. Until the elephants reached them.

And the timing was perfect. Ghote glanced quickly towards the shrilly trumpeting beasts. They would arrive at the point where the people on the balcony would fall before anybody had even had time to pick themselves up. And Gregory was foremost among them.

"Stop. Stop."

Ghote shouted with all the force his lungs could muster. But he knew it was useless. A mere shout was not going to stop the young, intent, plump figure sawing so concentratedly at the last strands of the red silken rope. And in all the noise from the elephants no one else was going to hear.

The short, glinting blade hacked its way through at last. With one appalling lurch the crowd on the balcony tumbled to destruction.

CHAPTER XIII

GHOTE, safe himself on the part of the balcony with the iron railing, could only watch helplessly as events took their course. For a few seconds even he thought the India First man's plan was going to fail after all. Gregory, the instant he had realised what was happening, had swung round and grabbed for one of the lamp brackets on the wall behind him. He had reached it and it had taken his weight.

But then Ghote, still powerless to intervene, had seen Gregory look back and try to catch hold of Shakuntala. But she had been well beyond his grasp. And he had let go of the bracket.

Ghote even wondered whether he had seen what he thought he had. The whole sequence of events had all taken place so quickly. At one moment the old red silken cord had been intact with the blue-shirted India First agent sawing away at it. Then it had snapped. At once the crowd on the balcony had lurched forward in one slow, solid mass. Gregory had shot out an arm towards the lamp bracket, had turned almost as soon as his fingers had come in contact with it, and then had let go at once when his effort to seize Shakuntala had failed.

But whatever had happened, both of them were down in the tangle of struggling people in the street now. And the charging elephants were hardly ten yards away.

Ghote flung himself suddenly forward as the people around him, their faces shocked with fear, scrabbled wildly away from the gap in the railing.

If Gregory hopes to help down there, he thought incoherently, then I can too. I can at least try to land on my feet and get between them and the elephants.

He found himself poised to jump.

And, in a totally unexpected burst of lucidity, the whole scene seemed caught for ever just as it was at that instant. The elephants were frozen with their great front legs raised in the charge, never to descend. The tangled mass of people in front of them stayed fixed in its inextricable confusion waiting for imminent destruction through an eternity. The young assassin, slipping dexterously away from the scene of his crime, was caught in an attitude of slinking evasiveness as by a lava flow. The red silk cord he had just cut dangled, still swinging slightly, held unmoving as if it were a delicately observed detail in some huge allegorical painting.

The red silk cord.

The frozen instant passed. Ghote knelt swiftly and seized the end of the cord still attached to the railing beside him. Immediately below Gregory was rising to his feet among the chaos of limbs. Ghote shouted. He shouted with every atom of his strength.

" Grab the rope."

At the same instant he flicked the loose end towards the tall American. And Gregory saw it. He shot out his arm and snatched it.

A moment later he had taken a good turn of it round his

wrist. In another moment he had seized Shakuntala from the mêlée. He kicked his feet clear, reached up with his free hand and grabbed the rope again three feet higher up, and heaved.

Ghote, twisting a leg round the railing beside him, leant over as far as he dared, and further. He got his hands behind Gregory's back. He tugged upwards. Gregory, with an enormous grunt of effort, propelled himself towards him and swung Shakuntala, perhaps unconscious, perhaps merely dazed, on to the balcony. A second later he was kneeling beside her. Below the elephants reached the struggling mass of people.

Ghote shut his eyes.

As if by an iron drop-curtain the thought of what must be going on in the street below was shut out from his mind. And in its place came the insistent buzz of his own affairs.

He had a duty to perform. Getting Gregory to safety was only one part of it. Someone else had a claim on him too : Kartar Singh.

Up in the silence of the gaol nothing of the tumult in the Shanwar Peth would penetrate. There a different set of circumstances awaited him. With urgency.

: :   : :

The whole time that it took Ghote to impress on Gregory how urgent the situation was and to get him down through the house and out into the lane at the back was one confused jumble of shouting and expostulation. Sudden, unexpected, pointless questions kept presenting themselves. The American showed a tendency to wander dazedly in any direction but the right one. Could they try to revive Shakuntala, he asked. Was it really safe to leave her behind?

Ghote knew that he was snapping unnecessarily in fighting off these suggestions. Someone confronted with an experience like Gregory's in a foreign land and without friends might be expected to be in a difficult state. To counter it, he himself should have been calm and reassuring. Instead he had shouted, grown excited, been thoroughly unreliable.

Only when at last they both stood in the lane at the back of the house did he succeed in gathering himself together. Then he knew at once and clearly what he had to do. He had to get the pair of them to the gaol as quickly as possible. Nothing else at all mattered, not even setting anybody on the assassin's trail.

He looked at his watch.

It was 11.45.

They certainly could not hope to get to the gaol in fifteen minutes by foot. It was a question of how easily they could get hold of a taxi, tonga or scooter-rickshaw.

"Follow me quickly," he said to Gregory.

The American obediently loped after him as he ran down the length of the lane, past a vermilion-coloured temple bright with profuse pictures of the gods, and out into the broad street beyond. At once Ghote realised that getting transport of any sort was going to be almost impossible. The news of the disaster with the elephants had spread like a leaping flame. People by the hundred were hurrying to the scene. Others were struggling equally furiously to get along in the other direction, either to fetch help or to avoid the unpleasantness. Together they blocked any fast progress.

And now that the crowds were involved in something more than a simple outing Gregory had lost all his foreigner's magic. No one pushed him courteously to the front any more. Instead he was someone more in the way than other people, bigger, different, more irritating.

Ghote wondered whether to abandon him.

Without him he would certainly get along faster. Wriggling and squeezing his way through alone, he might knock minutes off the time it would take him to get to the gaol. But he knew he could not do it. Gregory was in his keeping. And he had already had a sharp enough lesson about the seriousness of his danger. The young man in the blue shirt might already be aware that his plan had failed. If so, he would be doubly keen to strike again. India First were not the sort of people to take reports of failure calmly.

Ghote twisted round and dug his shoulder viciously into the gap between the two people in front of him.

Darting through and tugging the lumbering American after him, he suddenly saw just off the entrance to a nearby lane a cluster of bicycles abandoned by their owners when the filming had begun. He realised at once what they could do. They could take a machine apiece and, pedalling for all they were worth, make a wide detour beyond the crowded city centre, through the wide avenues of the Cantonment area, and round to cross the Fitzgerald Bridge at last and head for the gaol. They would have to go like the wind to do it, but with luck it should be possible.

They would also have to steal the bicycles. The policeman in Ghote rose up in protest.

He turned to Gregory.

" Out this way," he said. " We are going to take two of those bicycles."

The American was quick to grasp the notion.

" Good idea," he said. " And we go round some back way?"

" We will have to steal the bicycles," Ghote said.

" Come on then," said Gregory.

The bicycles were piled up against the steps of a small square tank with a line of washing fluttering above it and a couple of buckets standing on the edge. But no one was bathing or doing the laundry at that moment. There was nothing to stop them going up to the heap of bicycles, selecting the two fastest-looking and wheeling them away. Ghote felt during every second that a uniformed constable of the Poona force ought to materialise from nowhere to stop the crime. But no one anywhere took the slightest notice.

They rode off as fast as they could go.

At the end of the lane they cut across a wide street and plunged into another passage on the far side. Here all along a row of little, open shops men were squatting beating at small brass pots with a cumulatively deafening sound. Two minutes later they emerged into a broad road much less crowded than before. They shot along it at a fine rate, swerving only occasionally to avoid a goat, another cyclist or a speeding scooter-rickshaw.

Past St. Mary's Church, swing left, up through the Indian Infantry Lines, past the Polo Ground, under the railway, and they were shooting across Fitzgerald Bridge.

As they did so, Ghote held his hand as steadily as he could in front of his face and tried to read the time on his watch. Seven minutes to twelve: about a mile to go.

"We will do it," he called back over his shoulder to Gregory.

Then a quick flutter of doubt assailed him. He turned backwards again.

"But hurry."

As they sped along beside the golf course on a mercifully clear road, he wondered whether there would be any difficulty at the gaol gate. After all, they were criminals, bicycle-thieves.

But he was also an inspector of police. The warder on duty recognised him, made no comment on his mode of transport and ushered them both in.

Again Ghote looked at his watch. They had done it easily. Three minutes to go.

At the foot of the staircase leading up to Inspector Phadke's office they met the inspector himself, standing exuding an aura of satisfied calm. Ghote was briefly conscious of how quickly his breath must still be coming after their wild ride and of how sweat-stained he must look.

"Good morning, Inspector," he said, as cheerfully as he could. "Is my man ready for me?"

"Of course, Inspector," Phadke replied, with a little bow from his paunchy waist. "Naturally a request from you would be obeyed to the letter."

"Thank you," Ghote replied. "I am sorry to have troubled you."

He began to make his way towards the stairs.

Phadke put a hand on his arm.

"One moment, Inspector," he said. "I would much appreciate if I could be present at your interview."

Ghote looked back at him.

"I am very sorry, Inspector. I will not keep the man a moment. But I am convinced that if I am to get anything out of him I must do it on my own."

Phadke's hand tightened a little on his forearm.

"Nevertheless, Inspector," he said, "I want to be present."

Ghote dropped his arm sharply and swung round on the lowest step till he was facing Phadke squarely.

"I much regret," he said, "but I cannot agree."

Phadke smartly climbed two steps till he stood a little higher than Ghote.

"The man is under my charge, Inspector," he said.

"And the case is under mine," Ghote said.

"Then we will have to see which is the most important."

"No."

Ghote looked at Phadke intently.

"Inspector," he said, "you know as well as I do that I am officer in charge for the whole business. The fact that you have custody does not affect issue."

Phadke smiled broadly.

"Of course, of course, Inspector. But cannot we discuss in peace? Let us go into that office there and see what we can decide without unpleasantness."

He nodded towards the open door of an office on the other side of the broad passage.

Ghote looked at his watch.

"Inspector," he said, "there is one minute only till noon."

He set off up the stairs, nodded to the two warders outside Inspector Phadke's office and entered. Kartar Singh was standing looking up at the clock on the wall facing the desk.

"It is Inspector Ghote," he said. "You are not late."

"Of course not," Ghote said. "I promised for twelve o'clock."

The battered Sikh contrived to smile.

Then for a moment it looked as if he was going to fall, so suddenly did he sway to one side. Gregory, who had been following Ghote closely as a shadow, put out a hand to save him.

Kartar Singh shook it off.

He turned to Ghote again.

"Well, Inspectorji, since you have been such a good boy you shall have sweetmeat."

Ghote kept utterly still.

"A temple in the Sahyadri Hills," the Sikh said. "You go to Peral village and take the track to Narjat. By a little lake you turn right. It is half a mile along the path."

"You are lying," Ghote said quickly.

Kartar Singh looked at him, stony-faced.

"You can prove. Go there."

"We will go," Ghote said. "And if we find you have told the truth, I will have you transferred to Bombay straight away."

Suddenly the Sikh seemed to choke back a sob.

"I do not care if I stay or go," he said. "I have sold them to you now."

Ghote turned to Gregory.

"There is nothing to keep us here any more," he said.

: :   : :

They took the bicycles to get back into the city again. It seemed the easiest thing to do. They went nearly as fast as when they had been racing to get to the gaol by noon but they rode side by side now and a few shouts of conversation were possible.

"Listen, Ganesh."

Ghote turned his head to indicate that he could hear.

"I want to thank you again."

"But nothing is necessary," Ghote shouted back.

They swished on over the even surface of the road.

"It is necessary," Gregory shouted. "It's very necessary : I thought you were fouling up the Kartar Singh business."

Ghote did not turn his head. There was nothing to turn for.

A moment later more shouted words came past him.

"How did you work out he'd break up like that?"

"By looking," Ghote shouted. "He seemed to be at his end of tether. But he is a proud man : he could not give in at once."

"You certainly timed it right anyway. And now what?"

"To go and see if I was right. We must hire a car. But first I have to call at the police station."

"Why is that?"

"I want a gun. They will be armed. Even for just seeing if they are really there a gun is necessary."

"A gun?"

The shout floated into the air. They pedalled on in silence.

It was only when they were outside the police station that Gregory spoke again.

"What's the procedure for collecting this gun then?" he asked.

Ghote hurried into the building.

"I shall have to get them to telephone Bombay perhaps," he answered. "But it should not take long."

"Listen," Gregory said, catching him urgently by the elbow, "could you fix one up for me too?"

Ghote stopped in his tracks.

"Certainly not," he said.

Gregory looked astonished, and a little hurt.

"I can handle a gun," he said. "I used to captain my college pistol team as a matter of fact."

But if he was hurt, Ghote was furious. The thoughts tumbled through his mind. Irresponsible. Playboy. Gangster. American.

He swung away.

"Absolutely impossible."

Gregory followed him into the big, echoing entrance hall.

" I guess you're right," he said with mildness. " After all, I haven't done any shooting in a long while. It's somehow not considered dignified for a professor to fool around down at the range."

: :   : :

As soon as they got back to the Wellesley Hotel, Ghote with a heavy Service revolver bulging his pocket and banging against his thigh, they saw Shakuntala. By association of ideas Ghote at once looked round for V.V. But for once he was nowhere in sight.

With luck, Ghote thought, we shall get away without him knowing.

In the meantime he registered the way Gregory was greeting Shakuntala. The sight of her apparently safe and sound had obviously overwhelmed him. He was fussing like a mother reunited with her lost child. Ghote left him to it and went over to the reception desk. The clerk was quick and helpful and in a couple of minutes he had arranged for a self-drive car to be brought round to the hotel entrance straight away.

Ghote went over to Gregory and told him. The American looked abruptly sheepish.

" Look, Ganesh," he said, " can I have a quick word with you?"

Ghote frowned slightly.

Gregory took him by the elbow and fairly pushed him across the lobby away from Shakuntala.

" It's like this," he said in a low, urgent voice. " Can we take Shakuntala with us? I know there may be objections, but it means a lot to me."

A new fountain of fury swooshed up in Ghote's head. This American. Always wanting something more. Never for one instant content. If only there was not the responsibility of making sure he was safe, he would tell him to go off with the girl anywhere he liked.

And then he remembered the way the American had accepted the snub over the gun.

" All right," he said, " she may come, if she will do exactly as told."

Gregory looked like a schoolboy given an unexpected half-holiday. He positively frisked across the lobby to tell Shakuntala. Following him, Ghote felt suddenly depressed.

" Hell," Gregory said to him, " you look as if the bottom had fallen out of the world. But we're doing all right, aren't we? We've got a pretty good idea where those guys are hiding out, and we're on our way to check. What's eating you all of a sudden?"

Ghote felt unable to explain.

" Perhaps it is those bicycles," he said, unwilling to seem at a loss. " I do not like to have been responsible for adding two more items to the Poona crime figures."

Gregory and Shakuntala burst into laughter, looking at each other as if they alone could appreciate this to the full. Through the window behind them Ghote saw a little green Hindustan like the one Shakuntala had first driven Gregory in. It was drawing up outside the hotel and a man in a grease-stained shirt and a white turban was getting out.

" I think this would be our car," Ghote said tersely.

: :   : :

Ghote drove. Gregory and Shakuntala had elected to sit together in the back of the little car. Nobody spoke much. Ghote was concentrating on getting along as fast as he could and on one or two private problems that were worrying him. Behind, Shakuntala and Gregory did not seem to feel the need for spoken communication.

One of the things Ghote considered, when the abruptly descending road down the wooded, crevassed slope of the Western Ghats allowed him time to think, was the matter of the assassination spot. They would have to pass it. It was only some ten miles beyond it that they would have to fork off the main road to get to the Sahyadri Hills. What would Gregory's reaction be to passing the exact place his brother had been killed?

And quite suddenly they had completed the descent.

The verdant, after-monsoon woods on either side abruptly gave way to level, caramel-coloured fields. The heat took on a new steaminess. Ghote was able to push the little green Hindustan along the now straight road at a good pace without having to concentrate hard. But the opportunity for good, hard reasoning did not seem to help.

All too soon he spotted in the distance on the left the slightly rounded rise in the level ground with on top of it, standing clearly out, the huge Flame of the Forest tree under which Hector Strongbow's killers had waited so patiently. Somewhere beyond and on the other side the line of smoke from the signal fire must have risen. And now straight ahead, not far away, there were the road works. Little seemed to have been done since the time that Bholu's bullock cart had halted there, neatly blocking the whole road at just the moment Hector Strongbow had driven up so fast.

Why had he been going so fast, Ghote wondered yet again. All the driblets of information he had gathered had mounted up to that. The young, red-bearded American had been going towards Poona as if getting there was almost a matter of life and death. Why had he been in such a hurry?

Ghote looked up at the driving mirror and adjusted his position a little so that he could see Gregory's face. The serious, deep-set eyes were fixed absorbedly on the girl at his side.

Suddenly Ghote made up his mind. He would stop at the place. The vivid reminder might be just what he needed.

And then they were there. The cluster of palm-thatched huts of the little village flicked by, and a moment later the road narrowed to a single lane. Ghote pulled up.

"Hey," Gregory said from behind him. "Why are we . . . ?"

Shakuntala leant forward quickly.

"Do we have to stop?" she said. "Can't we just go past?"

"I think Gregory would like to get out for a little time," he said.

In the mirror on the top edge of the windscreen he noticed the broad-shouldered form of the American shift restlessly.

"Well, yes, Ganesh," he said after a moment, "of course —I mean, Hector was—— But hadn't we better push on? There'll be other times."

"A few minutes only," Ghote said inexorably. "A short rest will be a help to me. Let us get out."

Without waiting for an answer, he opened the car door. Gregory came out a little more slowly. Shakuntala quickly followed him and he turned to her at once.

"Shall we walk to the place his car stopped?" Ghote said.

"All right," said Gregory.

His mouth was set and he was looking straight in front of him at the neat heap of stones of the roadworks.

Ghote led the way. Gregory followed a pace or two behind. He put out his hand and Shakuntala took it. They walked in silence up to the place where Hector Strongbow's hired car had halted and where there had been that sudden volley of shots.

They stood there. Ghote watched Gregory hard out of the corner of his eye. He saw his hand was gripping Shakuntala's tightly.

Quite soon it would be the moment to take Gregory aside and ask him the question that Colonel Mehta so badly wanted the answer to. And perhaps now, in this instant of strain, his mission would be accomplished. He would hear just exactly what it had been that Hector Strongbow had said to Gregory outside V.T. Station. He would realise why Hector had been driving to Poona so fast. And he could feel that that task was over.

He felt a spurt of excitement at the thought that he could then go on, a free man, to hunt down Hector Strongbow's actual killers. He could drop back, released of all untoward responsibilities, into the familiar police routine. It would be a good moment.

Suddenly a car, coming from the direction of Bombay,

pulled up just in front of them with a prolonged squeal of brakes.

Irritated, Ghote looked up. The vehicle, an oldish but still flashy-looking American convertible with its hood up, had slewed half across the road with the violence with which it had been braked. Ghote frowned. Such driving, a disgrace to the Indian motorist.

And his mouth opened in astonishment.

CHAPTER XIV

THE DRIVER'S WINDOW of the flashy convertible, slewed so appallingly across the road, had been rapidly lowered and there looking out at them with an expression of wild hopefulness was Mira Jehangir.

"You," she said. "All of you. Here. It is a sign."

She shot the car door open, tumbled out and came over to them at a run.

"It is a sign," she repeated with jerky emphasis.

They looked at her in silence. None of them seemed able to think of any possible reply. At last Ghote took a step forward.

"Miss Jehangir," he said, "may I know what you are doing here?"

"I have run away."

"Run away? Who from? What for?"

"He is brutal. Brutal. I could not endure one moment longer."

Tears began to pour down her face. For a little she let them run. Then she started to brush them away with the back of her wrist so that a black smear of eye make-up spread all across one cheek.

"Please," Ghote said with some sharpness. "Who has been brutal? What is this? I do not understand."

"Why, him, of course," Mira Jehangir said impatiently. "Mr. Wadia."

"Mr. Wadia," Gregory said. "That's the manager of the Queen's Imperial Grand."

"Very well," Ghote said with calmness, "you are running away from Mr. Wadia. You state that he has been brutal. Does a question of preferring charges arise?"

"Charges? Charges? I want nothing more to do with that pig."

Ghote received this stolidly.

"Now," he went on, "this matter of a sign. That is a further point I do not understand."

Mira Jehangir gave him a look of pure scorn.

"It is a sign meeting you," she said. "A sign meeting Professor Strongbow."

"Me?" said Gregory.

He was so surprised that his voice went almost squeaky.

Mira Jehangir turned her full attention on him.

"But a most wonderful sign," she said. "I was coming to look for you. I knew you must be somewhere in Poona. I risked everything on being able to find you. And now I have met you standing there in the road, it is a sign."

Ghote reflected that the sign was hardly a very wonderful one. If Mira Jehangir had happened to start out a little earlier, the meeting would certainly still have occurred. Only it would have been in the commonplace setting of the Wellesley Hotel.

"And why did you want to find Professor Strongbow?" he asked.

Mira Jehangir ignored him.

"I had to warn you," she said to Gregory. "I had to warn you above everything else."

"To warn me?"

Gregory sounded suddenly wary.

"You are in danger," Mira Jehangir said passionately. "In great danger. I have found out that much."

Ghote marched straight up to her.

"Miss Jehangir," he said, "you will tell me everything you know."

"But it is so obvious, don't you see?" she answered.

" There were those men yesterday. The ones who pretended to be from the car-hire firm. All those questions they asked about where the professor had gone. I realised at once that they were not what they seemed. And as soon as they had gone I proved it. I rang the firm. They had no such employees."

" What questions did they ask?" Ghote demanded.

" About where he had gone. Whether he had taken all his luggage. Everything like that. Of course I told them nothing. I knew I had to put the professor's interests first."

She turned and gave Gregory a glance of burning loyalty.

" You told them nothing? Nothing at all?" Ghote persisted.

She let him have a moment of her attention.

" Nothing," she said. " Not until they forced it from me. And then I knew that I had to warn the professor. Men like that do not want to know where someone is for nothing, and already his brother had been killed."

" So you set out for Poona?" Ghote asked.

" At once. At once."

" And this question of Mr. Wadia's brutality? Where does that fit in?"

" I told you. I told you. He had made life impossible for me. I had to leave him. So I took the pig's car and set out for Poona. I knew that when I had warned the professor, he would be truly grateful to me."

She looked at Gregory, standing there tall and reliable in his clean, well-cut tropical suit.

" I thought too you were all alone in India," she went on. " I thought you would need a friend."

And suddenly her tone changed.

" But I see I am too late," she added.

She looked pointedly downwards. Gregory was still holding Shakuntala's hand in his broad palm. He dropped it as if it was something he had picked up without realising what he was doing. He licked his lips.

" Look, Miss Jehangir," he said, fixing his eyes on a place just beside her. " Look, I feel—well, I'm really more than thankful to you for telling me all this. As it so happens, it came as no surprise, but——"

"Then I have been of no help," Mira Jehangir broke in, in a voice harsh with emotion. "I have been of no help here. My last hope."

"No, look," Gregory said.

He pushed his hand into his inner pocket and brought out his wallet.

"Hell, this is difficult. But you seem to be in a jam. I mean, you may have no job to go to. I don't know what resources—well, look, I'd like you to have this."

He stepped forward and shot out a bundle of notes towards her. Ghote could not see exactly how much was there, but there were certainly some hundred rupee notes.

Mira Jehangir looked downwards.

"No, no, I cannot," she said. "Or, well, it must be just a loan. A temporary loan."

Gregory turned smiling with relief to Ghote.

"I guess we should be taking off again," he said. "We can't lose too much time."

He began to walk back to where Ghote had stopped their car. Mira Jehangir drew back her shoulders.

"I too must go," she said in an unnecessarily loud voice. "Yes, I must go. Even though I have nowhere to go to."

She began stalking back to her own car, or rather to Mr. Wadia's.

"Well then, goodbye," Gregory said. "That is, goodbye for the time being."

Shakuntala took his arm and leaning close to him whispered something energetically.

"Er—no," Gregory said. "I don't think so, not just at the moment."

"But, yes," Shakuntala said more loudly. "You can't let her go just like that."

Gregory looked down at her with a perplexed frown.

"I just don't see what good I could do," he said.

"You can talk to her."

"But, hell, I haven't anything to say."

Gregory was beginning to sound embarrassed.

"She needs you," Shakuntala said determinedly.

"Well, I dare say she does. But you can't go to every-body who happens to think they need you."

Shakuntala looked up at him with eyes starting to spark.

"You must go."

"Look," Gregory said with some heat, "I gave her money, didn't I? A hell of a lot of money, if you want to know. And, damn it, there's nothing else I can do."

"You can't just let her drive away like that," Shakuntala replied.

She was speaking loudly enough now for Mira Jehangir, sitting at the wheel of Mr. Wadia's flashy convertible look-ing straight in front of her, to be able to hear every word.

"You Americans," Shakuntala went on, her indignation blossoming instant by instant. "You Americans think money solves everything. Well, let me tell you it's no sub-stitute for ordinary, decent kindness as between one human being and another."

"Look, I never said money cured anything. I just gave her some because she was broke, or said she was. And I did it out of kindness, pure kindness."

Gregory was speaking quietly, but with considerable emphasis. He swung round now to Ghote.

"Come on," he said, "we've got a job to do."

"You mustn't go," Shakuntala said, as loudly as before. "If you do, I'll stay."

Gregory simply stood where he was, looking at Ghote inquiringly.

"Well," Ghote said, "we have got to hurry, of course. But perhaps a few minutes' delay, if you wanted, Gregory."

"I don't want to stay here one single second more," Gregory said flatly.

"All right then," Shakuntala cut in with sudden iciness. "I will see you later, Gregory. Somewhere or other."

She waited for perhaps two seconds, but Gregory did nothing. Then she turned and walked over to Mira Jehangir's car. She went round the far side and got in beside her.

"For heaven's sake, let's go," Gregory said.

Ghote followed him as he strode with enormous paces back to the hired Hindustan. They got in without a word being spoken. Ghote pulled at the starter.

They drove in steamy silence till they reached the point where they had to leave the Bombay road for the cross-country route leading to the region of the Sahyadri Hills. Here, Ghote had made up his mind, was where he would say what he had to.

So, although the side road was much less good and required constant watchfulness, he spared a moment to turn and look at Gregory. He was sitting looking straight ahead with hunched shoulders and an expression of dark sombreness.

He decided to begin with caution.

"Gregory," he said, "I do not think you should expect too much from this temple."

"I'm not expecting too much," Gregory replied morosely.

"So," Ghote went on circuitously, "in the event of not finding these men, or of them escaping, when we bring in men to capture them, or of them refusing in all circumstances to talk, it will be necessary then to make another approach."

The American did not ask him what approach.

"It will be necessary then," Ghote resumed manfully, "to make an approach by means of Miss Brown."

"Shakuntala?"

At least Gregory had reacted.

"Yes, you see, although it is now possible she was not responsible for the attack on you in Poona, it is still possible that she was. There is still a lot against her. Showdown will be absolutely necessary."

"All right, all right. You're not telling me anything I don't know. Go right ahead."

Ghote reflected dispiritedly that this was only half of

what he had promised himself to say to Gregory. He took a deep breath.

" There is another matter also I would like to get cleared up," he said.

Gregory was staring broodingly at the pot-holed road ahead.

Ghote gave a prim little cough.

" It is the matter of your talk with your late brother outside V.T. Station before you set off for Poona," he said.

Gregory swung round towards him so violently that he gave an involuntary twist to the driving-wheel. The car swung wildly towards the edge of the road before he regained control.

" Look here," Gregory shouted, " I've said once and for all. What Hector told me and what I told him is a personal, family matter and of no concern to you at all. Do you get that?"

" Yes, Gregory," Ghote said.

In even blanker silence they drove on till they reached Peral village. Here Ghote stopped and made inquiries from the small crowd that at once surrounded them. They still did not talk as they set off again along the cart-track to Narjat which had been eagerly pointed out to them.

Fields gave way to jungle as they bounced along the deeply rutted track, and Ghote had plenty to think about merely keeping the floundering little car pointing in the right direction. Eventually their steady climb was interrupted by a short level stretch, and there at the end of it was the little lake Kartar Singh had spoken of. Ghote felt a sense of relief that at least so far the tortured Sikh had not misled them.

He halted the car in the shade of a giant banyan with the white-washed stone of a wayside shrine lurking in the depths of its canopy of multiple dangling roots.

" We would have to foot it from here," he said.

They were the first words either of them had uttered to each other since Gregory's outburst. But they seemed to do nothing to break the ice.

Gregory simply grunted an acknowledgment, and Ghote locked up the little car without another word.

It was true that any question of driving was impossible. The track Kartar Singh had indicated was scarcely a yard wide, a mere trodden earth-line in the rich vegetation that now faced them.

" It would be half a mile only," Ghote said.

He spoke cheerfully, not because he hoped to alter Gregory's mood, but because quite suddenly he had felt the need for reassurance himself. This was unknown territory to him. The close alleys of the Bombay slums where even in the full glare of midday there were patches of black darkness held few terrors any longer. Even the most lawless criminals there were within his scheme of things. He knew the way their minds worked. They were, in a way, friends. But in this jungle ahead of them now there were animals. How did their minds work? In no circumstances could they ever be friends.

" If you are ready," he said to Gregory, " we will go."

" Okay."

They set off down the soft winding path. In less than two minutes it was impossible to get the slightest glimpse of the car or the huge banyan by the lake. The jungle surrounded them.

High elephant grass towered over their heads. Great trees turned the sunlight into a shimmering, darting mystery. Long creepers plunged downwards immobile and sinister. On all sides there was noise, chattering, twittering, suddenly breaking out into wild screaming. And everywhere there was sharp movement, insect-jabbing, unexplained writhings, flowers and butterflies bright, beautiful and somehow wrong.

The thought of pythons, of cobras, of deadly kraits entered into Ghote's mind and would not go. Abrupt clumps of thorn bamboo caused the path to twist and circle till all sense of direction was utterly confused. It was oppressively hot with a thick steaminess which wetted the whole body from head to foot.

Gregory, who had been forced by the narrowness of the path to drop behind, suddenly spoke loudly.

" Hey," he said, " when Kartar Singh told us it was half a mile, did he mean half a mile along the path or half a mile as the crow flies?"

" I do not know," Ghote said.

A sharp-edged blade of grass swept across his forehead. The sudden contact hurt and he put his hand up to rub the place. He saw it was streaked with blood.

Blood, he thought.

An unreasoning fear began palpitating somewhere inside him. He was smelling of blood. He was bait.

" Say, would there be tigers in jungle like this?" Gregory asked.

" No," Ghote snapped.

He had no idea. But he could at least will that there should be no tigers.

He plunged forward. The path seemed to get even narrower till leaves were constantly brushing him on either side. And from behind after a long period of grunts and heavy breathing Gregory suddenly spoke again.

" Gee," he said, " I don't mind admitting it : I'm scared."

Ghote stopped where he was and let the feeling of relief pour through him. He turned round. Gregory certainly looked very apprehensive with his face sweat-streaked, his cream-coloured suit green-smeared and dusted with layers of pollen and with a short, triangular tear on one sleeve.

" I am somewhat scared also," Ghote said.

He smiled a little.

Gregory grinned back.

" Come on, let's push on," he said. " It can't be so far now."

Ghote turned happily.

" No, I am sure you are right," he said. " We will see."

He strode forward. The path took a turn round the bole of an immense sal tree. And there was the temple.

The jungle cleared ahead of them and in the middle of the small open patch the temple stood. It was not a large building and it was in a state of some neglect. But beyond doubt it was the place Kartar Singh had described.

Ghote wondered how it had got there at all. Perhaps at some time in the distant past a meteorite had fallen at this remote spot. Such an event would bring worshippers quickly enough. But with the passing of time fewer and fewer would make the long journey with the inhospitable jungle waiting at the end. You could not expect people to be faithful for ever.

And now the deserted building had been picked on as a hiding-place by Hector Strongbow's killers.

Ghote felt in his pocket for the heavy, dangling revolver. Beside him Gregory parted a clump of tall elephant grass to get a better view.

" If they're there, they're inside somewhere," he said in a low voice.

" We must creep right up," Ghote replied. " They cannot see us. There are no windows."

Gregory gave him a quick smile.

" Should be easy up to there anyway," he said.

Ghote took the gun out of his pocket. For a moment he struggled with the safety catch.

" Listen, Ganesh," Gregory said, " you're sure you wouldn't like me to handle that thing?"

" No thank you," Ghote answered, with a new touch of stiffness. " I have not served in Chicago. But during my training I passed in range practice. Sixty per cent."

" Go ahead, go ahead. I shouldn't have spoken."

Ghote forgave him.

" We shall go then?"

" Right away."

They crept forward. On the soft, moist earth their shoes made no sound. They reached the beginning of the clearing. Ghote looked at the American. He looked back at the temple. All was silent there. He advanced across the short grass. No challenge came. Out of the close jungle it seemed strangely quiet without the constant buzz and hum of the insects and the calling and twittering of the birds.

They reached the cover of the outer wall of the temple and stood with their backs to it trying to regain some calm. Some three yards away was the entrance, a square archway six feet wide and five high.

After a moment Ghote nudged Gregory. Then he dropped to all fours and crawled along the wall till he had reached the corner of the arch. Very slowly he put his head round the jamb at ground level where a watcher inside would be less likely to realise what was happening.

When he had got his head sufficiently far round the square stone pillar of the jamb he lay still and waited till his eyes were accustomed to the gloom inside. Bit by bit he began to make out the main features of the temple interior.

There was little to discover. The building consisted apparently of one low-ceilinged hall unsupported by columns. At the far end, black against the light brownish stone of the back wall, there rose up from a low stone platform the short, round-topped, pillar-like form of a lingam, carved for worship perhaps from the original meteorite which had fallen on this spot.

And this was all. Nothing else to see. No one.

He got to his feet. Gregory sidled quickly up to him, an expression of inquiry on his face.

" We had better go in," Ghote said.

He stepped sharply through the archway. And, as he had expected, nothing happened. The temple was bare and echoing. He felt a welling sense of despondency. Having found that the temple did in fact exist, somehow he had never expected that Kartar Singh was still going to turn out to have cheated them.

" No, look," Gregory shouted suddenly.

Seizing Ghote's arm, he dragged him helter-skelter over to one of the walls. Then he pointed.

In the darkness behind the jutting lingam Ghote saw what it was Gregory had spotted. There was a second chamber to the temple. A much smaller archway, directly behind the lingam, led into it. It was possible still that India First's hired thugs were waiting there.

Ghote pointed the revolver in the direction of the dark oblong of the archway and advanced. He waved Gregory to silence and crept forward on tip-toe, straining every muscle to catch the slightest sound from the darkness of the inner chamber. Step by step he approached and not the faintest noise of any sort disturbed the ancient calm around him.

Then at last he was within a pace of the squat doorway.

One sharp jump forward.

And he laughed shortly.

"Empty," he said. "It is hardly big enough to take all three of them."

Gregory came up and peered in his turn into the little dark chamber.

"Well," he said, "I guess that Phadke was right after all. Your Kartar Singh has led us on a pretty fine wild goose chase."

CHAPTER XV

INSPECTOR GHOTE stared mournfully into the darkness of the little cupboard-like room behind the temple lingam. Even with prolonged peering, it was still so far from the light that it was possible to make out little more than the fact that the hiding-place was bare.

He slowly straightened up. He was unable to restrain a long, deeply disconsolate sigh. And then he jerked back to the short doorway.

"Wait," he said.

He darted forward and knelt down. A moment later he got up again.

"Look at these," he said to Gregory.

The American looked intently down at what he was holding in the palm of his hand.

"Cigarette butts," he said. "And a bit from a packet."

"The sort of people who might come to worship here, if anyone does come, do not smoke factory-made cigarettes," Ghote said. "And touch them, Gregory."

Obediently Gregory put out a finger.

"They're warm," he said. "Still warm."

Ghote took them across towards the light coming in from the main entrance.

"Cavander's," he said. "They are very common, of course. But on the other hand the packets found under the Flame of the Forest where the dacoits waited were Cavander's also."

"Heck, Ganesh, I'm sorry," Gregory said. "I was too quick with that wild goose stuff. Listen, those guys must have heard us coming. We weren't too quiet in all that high grass. They must have——"

"Sssh."

He stopped like a jammed machine at the sight of Ghote's tense, listening face.

After more than a minute he whispered very quietly into the inspector's ear.

"You're dead right. They're coming back."

For a little they both waited, standing tautly by the temple entrance, craning to hear more. And bit by bit they did hear. The sound of the tall, dry-topped elephant grass rattling as it was parted, the noise of a body lunging through a tangle of vegetation, grunting and muttered speech.

Ghote pulled the revolver from his pocket again.

"Quickly," he said, "one either side of the archway."

Gregory understood at once. He held out his hand briefly as if asking whether after all he should not have the gun. But the instant Ghote shook his head he moved quickly into position and stood poised in ambush beside the bright rectangle of vibrating sunlight that the archway presented.

The sounds of the approaching enemy grew louder and louder.

Then a distinct voice called out.

"Inspector Ghote. Inspector Ghote. You are there?"

Ghote and Gregory looked at each other.

"They cannot know it is me here," Ghote said, quite loudly. "Those men would not know my name even."

"Help. Help. Oh, please, help."

The cry was agonised and pathetic.

Still pointing the gun, Ghote stepped out into the bright sunlight.

He had been ready to find himself the victim of a trap, but had not really seriously expected it. And nothing in fact occurred.

The shouts began again. He ran towards the jungle where they seemed to originate. Behind him he heard the thump of Gregory's feet. At the edge of the jungle an old peacock from the top of a dead, leafless tree let out a strident warning cry.

Ghote stopped.

"Please help."

The cry came again. Ghote plunged down the path. And less than ten yards into the jungle he had his answer.

Of all people, V.V. was standing there, looking wildly in every direction, the tail of his ridiculously sombre dark jacket caught firmly in a small clump of thorn bamboo.

"What the hell are you doing here?" Ghote exclaimed.

V.V.'s wild cries ceased.

"Inspector, Inspector, it is you."

"Of course it is me. But what are you doing here?"

"Is the temple near? Did you find? You did not get lost? You were not attacked by some animal?"

The questions shot out, and the gangling journalist's huge Adam's apple jerked and bobbed with them.

Ghote took him firmly by the arm, disengaged the back of his jacket with a sharp tug and piloted him back to the path.

"The temple is just here," he said. "And I think you would be better out of the sun inside it."

And, surely enough, almost as soon as he had entered the cool darkness of the deserted building, V.V. began to recover. He launched into an insistent tirade of gratitude.

Ghote cut him short.

"What are you doing here?" he barked. "Still you have not told."

V.V. blinked his prominent eyes.

"But, Inspector, I was about to say. It is perfectly simple. I followed you. At the Wellesley they told me you had left just that moment, by hired car. So I also hired and I took the risk of choosing the Bombay road. Perhaps I would have missed you. But luckily I encountered Miss Shakuntala Brown, and——"

Gregory Strongbow's broad hand slapped suddenly and swiftly down across the journalist's mouth and was held there hard. Ghote looked at him in astonishment. But the expression on the American's face instantly explained everything.

Someone else was approaching the temple.

Ghote listened. And this time there was a difference in the sounds which reached them in the temple interior. They were more definite, more controlled. From time to time a voice called softly and received an equally confident and quiet answer. It was plain beyond doubt that now several men were moving towards the temple, coolly ready to deal with any opposition.

And suddenly the calls took on a changed note. They ceased to be quiet instructions going from one of the oncomers to another: they became sharp shouts directed at the temple itself.

"Come out. Come out. You in there, come out. Both of you. With hands up."

Ghote thought quickly. Then he put his mouth close to V.V.'s left ear as Gregory held him.

"You hear those men calling?" he said quietly.

He saw the whites of the journalist's eyes flick towards him.

"Those men are dacoits," he went on, "the dacoits who shot Hector Strongbow. And now they are coming for us. On the orders of India First."

As he spoke he watched V.V.'s face with every atom of concentration he was capable of. And the look of understanding that came into his prominent eyes at the mention of India First was unmistakable.

Ghote decided to take a risk.

"Let him go," he said to Gregory.

After an instant's hesitation, the American obeyed. V.V. shook his head as Gregory's grip loosened. For a moment Ghote thought he was going to call out to the advancing thugs that he too was an India First man.

But he shut his mouth again and looked at Ghote with eyes wide with curiosity.

"You know about India First then?" Ghote said.

"It was the story I was after," V.V. replied. "It would be the story of a lifetime."

"You will not have any lifetime if you are not careful," Ghote replied brusquely. "Just listen to me."

A new look of fear came on to V.V.'s face.

"Listen," Ghote went on rapidly, "those men called out just now 'Both of you.' They said 'Come out, both of you'."

He glanced up at Gregory.

"You see what this means? They think that you and I are in here only."

Gregory's eyes gleamed.

"You could be right," he said.

"We must risk that I am. Now, V.V., flatten yourself by the wall just there, next to the archway. And wait. Gregory and I will run back to a little room behind the lingam there. We will make as much noise as we can doing it. If we are lucky, the three of them out there will rush in after us. And then you will slip out. Do you understand?"

V.V. was looking sick with fear. But he nodded agreement.

"Very well," Ghote said. "If you get out without being seen, then get up that path as fast as you can. Get in your car and drive like hell along the Bombay road to Panvel. There are plenty of men in the police post there. Get them back here just as quickly as you can."

"But will there be enough time?" V.V. said.

"It will not be easy to get us behind the lingam," Ghote said. "We have a gun. But hurry only."

V.V. nodded again and licked his lips.

He tiptoed over to the wall beside the archway and stood waiting. Ghote looked at Gregory.

"Are you ready?"

"Okay."

"Then, now."

They turned together and ran towards the darkness behind the lingam on its low platform. Ghote brought his heavy shoes banging down hard on the stone floor and the sound of the double set of footsteps rang out and echoed in the temple hall.

"Back. Back," Ghote shouted. "Get right to the back."

Then, just as he swung round one side of the lingam and Gregory swung round the other, the light coming in from the archway entrance was suddenly blotted out. He dived for the black doorway of the little chamber an instant after Gregory.

As he scrambled round he saw three figures rushing across the hall on the far side of the lingam platform. He jabbed the gun in their direction and pulled at the trigger.

The noise of the shot in the low-ceilinged temple was like an explosion. It halted the onrush of the thugs as if they were figures from a stopped film.

And as the echoes at last died away there was a long silence.

Gregory came and knelt close to Ghote under the low arch of the chamber entrance.

"Do you think V.V. did get away?" he whispered.

" I could not see," Ghote answered. " But if he stayed where he was we will know quite soon. They cannot miss seeing."

They waited and waited. And then at last the thugs began talking to each other in low voices.

" I cannot make out what they are saying," Ghote whispered. " But it must mean V.V. got out. They are all three talking."

" Pity you didn't manage to get one of them when you used the gun," Gregory replied. " We can't have all that much to shoot with."

" Six rounds," Ghote whispered back.

He felt suddenly acutely depressed. If only he had fired with less panic. If he had succeeded in putting one of the dacoits out of action, they would have been a great deal better off.

" Never mind," Gregory said. " At least your friend V.V. got away, and that's what's going to mean most in the end."

" My friend? Why do you say he is my friend?"

Gregory grunted a laugh.

" You certainly trusted him if he wasn't your friend," he said.

" I thought it was the only thing to do to take the risk," Ghote answered.

The thought that he had taken the risk, and that it seemed to be paying off, comforted him.

" What made you think he might be safe after all?" Gregory asked.

" What he told himself : that he thought he had story of a lifetime. I thought that it might be that what had made him follow us through the jungle and everywhere was just getting story for his paper. I think it comes above everything with him."

" You could be right," Gregory said. " I always felt there was something a little over-zealous about that guy. Dedicated to getting the truth in the news, eh? Well, we have 'em that way back home."

" Let us hope we are right," Ghote said. " Because unless

he sticks to his story now, we are going to be left here until it is too late."

"Yes," Gregory agreed. "I don't think we can hold out in this little cubby-hole for ever. I could do with some light for one thing."

Ghote did not reply. There was nothing to say.

In the darkness they crouched together listening and peering out. Occasionally they heard the dacoits exchanging muttered comments. Ghote suspected that they were evolving some plan. They were certainly taking good care that nothing they said could be heard.

And then, without the least warning, the second attack came.

A shot banged out. Ghote heard the bullet smack into the wall just above the archway. It sent down a scatter of stone splinters.

Then he glimpsed a figure darting across the hall. He brought the gun up quickly and, as he did so, another bullet hit the wall over his head. It seemed to be nearer this time and the noise was deafening. The figure in the gloom was still running. He fired.

But there was only a redoubling of the booming echoes in the low hall in front of him.

"Heck," said Gregory, "the guy's got to the back wall here. Kind of puts us in a cross-fire if we put our heads out from the doorway."

With a sinking heart, Ghote realised that what Gregory had said was only too true. Only by coming well out from the doorway was there a hope of getting at the man on the back wall, and coming out that far would present the other two thugs with a sitting target. The situation had turned sharply against them.

He nudged Gregory.

"Please," he said, "take."

He held out the gun to him, butt foremost.

"Hell, no," Gregory said. "That was a pretty tricky shot you had there. Anyone might have missed it."

"No," Ghote said. "There was time to have hit. I would like you to have the gun."

"Well, I'll take it for a time anyway," Gregory said. "You need a rest, I guess."

He took the revolver and waited, kneeling on one knee, as far forward into the low archway as he dared to risk going.

But it seemed the dacoits were in no hurry to exploit the advantage they had achieved. Once again they began calling out to each other. This time they had to speak more loudly because of being separated, and Ghote was able to make out what they were saying. He translated for Gregory's benefit.

"They are complaining there is not enough light."

"They are? What about us? Still, I guess they're right. We must be pretty hard to see in the gloom here."

"They are saying something about torch."

"A torch? Do they have one? If they do, it could be pretty bad."

"They are going to fetch. One of the two by the main entrance has gone."

"Do you think he'll be long? Maybe this is the time we ought to try a bit of action ourselves."

"No," Ghote said. "It is definite we must stay here. It would be quite easy for the two of them, the moment we show our heads."

Gregory laughed sharply.

"Guess it would be shooting a couple of sitting ducks all right," he said. "And those characters aren't going to stick to any sporting rules they got from the British."

"No," Ghote replied soberly. "They believe in shooting to kill. That is certain."

Once more they waited.

It was a long time till the torch arrived. But eventually it came, as Ghote had known it must. The man bringing it called out cheerfully that he was back. There was a brief discussion. And then—click—the light came on.

It was obviously ideal for the dacoits' purpose, a good,

strong light sending a hard white glare right into their little hiding-place.

And at almost the instant the light shone out the third attack began. Shots banged out in quick succession both from the pair near the temple entrance and from the third man on the back wall. And this time the bullets were not all smacking harmlessly into the wall above them. Some were getting right into the little chamber itself in spite of the screen which the lingam and its platform gave.

And a few moments later Ghote was hit. It seemed to be a bullet that ricocheted off the wall behind him. He felt it as a sudden, totally unexpected, searing pain in his right arm. And with the shock he simply yelled out loud.

There was a shout of triumph from the dacoits. Ghote felt his head swim. Then nearer to him he heard Gregory fire.

And a few seconds later the torch went out and a long silence followed.

" You all right?" Gregory said quietly.

" I think I am," Ghote said. " I think it was my arm only."

He felt at the place where the pain was with his left hand. There was a lot of blood, but the bone seemed hard and firm still.

" I think it was flesh-wound only," he reported.

He felt braver for having used the words, and found himself able to make a confession.

" I screamed out," he said. " I regret. But I am not used to being wounded."

Gregory laughed.

" It was a darn good thing you did yell," he said. " Those guys thought they'd finished us. They came out with a rush and I'm pretty certain I got the guy along at the back here."

" I should have given you a gun in Poona," Ghote said.

Gregory chuckled.

" Well, I'm in better practice than I ever thought I'd be," he admitted.

He glanced back at Ghote.

"Look, you should try to get that shirt off," he said. "You're losing a hell of a lot of blood."

"All right," Ghote said.

He gritted his teeth and began easing his shirt past the wound. New blinding waves of pain came with every movement but he forced himself to go on.

Suddenly the two dacoits near the entrance switched the torch on again. Gregory leant forward tensely and Ghote stopped his work on the shirt. But no attack came.

"Must be making sure we don't try creeping out," Gregory said. "Gives me a good light to get a bandage on you anyhow."

Ghote went back to getting the shirt off while Gregory turned to his sentry position again. After what seemed an interminable time Ghote was able to tell Gregory that he was ready.

"You watch and I'll work," the American said.

Ghote, whose head was beginning to swim in earnest now, managed to crawl to the chamber entrance and look out into the dim hall beyond the lingam. He heard Gregory rip the shirt into strips and then felt him deftly winding them round the wound.

"Good thing I did do this," the American said after a little. "You're blood from here down, boy. If you'd gone on like that, you'd have been out cold before long."

"I am feeling better already," Ghote replied.

"That's great. Now just make a knot here, and you're okay for a bit anyhow."

Gregory tied his knot. Then suddenly he spoke in a voice so loud that it seemed almost indecent.

"Hey, wow. Do you see that?" he said.

"What? What is it?" Ghote exclaimed.

"Gee, sorry, did I startle you? To tell you the truth I was a little startled myself. I just saw the walls of this little hidey-hole."

Ghote looked. The walls of the little chamber were now steadily illuminated by the strong beam of the distant torch.

And what neither of them had had any time to see since the torch had come on was for the first time starkly apparent: every inch of the walls' surface was covered with an exuberant foam of miniature carvings, and every one of the figures represented was in direct and unequivocal celebration of the art of love.

"Yes," Ghote said, "they are called mithunas. They are well-known. Though these are the first I have seen, except in books when I was younger. But I had not heard of any in these parts."

"I've read about mithunas, all right," Gregory said. "Most people have."

He looked along the lines of little, sensual figures running along the wall beside him, moving determinedly from one voluptuous group to another. From time to time he stopped to take a quick, sharp glance out into the temple hall where the two dacoits waited in silence.

"Yes," he said, "I'd read about them. The books talk about 'playful sculptures.' Playful. Playful, heck."

He went back to the archway entrance and made a long, slow survey of the hall beyond. After a little the two dacoits began talking again, but kept their voices too low for it to be possible to make out what they were saying. The light from the torch fell so steadily that Ghote decided they must have found somewhere to prop it.

Still looking outwards, Gregory spoke again.

"What do you make of them, Ganesh?" he said.

Ghote knew that it was not the dacoits that he was talking about.

"Well," he said carefully, "they are carvings of things we know exist only."

"Yes. Yes, I guess so," Gregory said thoughtfully.

He fell silent again. Ghote's head was throbbing angrily now and he was grateful for the peace. He decided he would close his eyes for a little.

"Yes, that sort of thing exists all right," Gregory said suddenly, after what seemed to have been a long time.

Ghote kept his eyes closed.

"Yes," Gregory went on, " it exists. I mean, that was the trouble with Irene. My wife. My ex-wife I ought to call her."

Again he lapsed into silence.

After a little Ghote, overcome by a sudden anxiety, opened his eyes wide. Gregory was still kneeling on one knee at the chamber entrance, looking out watchfully. To his side the torch still shone steadily on the rows of riotous little figures in their entwined, inward-looking, self-absorbed groups.

Ghote closed his eyes again.

"You wouldn't have thought she was a frigid woman," Gregory said. " Hell, no one in the States is allowed to look like a frigid woman. But, well, she——"

He broke off. Ghote opened his eyes again and forced himself up into a position of alertness. But there seemed to be no change in the situation.

"No," Gregory said, with sudden firmness, " I don't want to go around crabbing at American society. I despise people who do that."

Ghote found he could summon up little interest. His head was throbbing with a numbing ache. His arm seemed a lot more painful. He explored the bandage with his good hand. As he expected, there was a sticky patch of blood on the outside.

He would have liked to have let himself slide away. But he knew that he must not. Gregory would need him. After all, they had only the one gun and three rounds of ammunition while the dacoits seemed to have plenty of ammunition and were alert and dangerous. Gregory would want all the help he could get.

But perhaps he could afford just two minutes' rest.

"Hey," said Gregory.

Ghote struggled to his feet.

His head gave a screech of pain that seemed to shoot through all his body. He swayed.

"They're moving the flashlight," Gregory said. " What are they getting at?"

He peered forward. Behind him Ghote seemed to see the locked couples in the stonework move with the moving of the shadows.

"They're saying something out there," Gregory went on. "See if you can pick it up. I get the feeling they're planning something fresh."

Ghote moved forward leadenly till he was nearer the entrance arch. Out in the temple hall the two dacoits were certainly talking, and they were moving from side to side with the torch. Just by Ghote's head now one of the little pairs of stone figures, one more ordinary than the others, seemed to start a stately little dance together.

He suddenly wished with all his heart that he could be somewhere else. Somewhere wrapped up. Safe. Cocooned. He wanted to be at home in the quiet of the night.

"What's it they're saying? For heaven's sake?"

Gregory's voice grated harshly on his ear.

He must listen. He might manage to hear something that would save Gregory. And simultaneously the other thought burgeoned in his mind. Dark. Comfort.

The torchlight wavered to and fro.

With an almost physical jerk Ghote forced himself to concentrate on the two distant voices at the far end of the hall.

"It is all right," he said after a moment. "They are trying to see further in only. And they have just decided that they cannot succeed."

A merciful blackness welled up in him. He was vaguely aware that he was slumping down against the wall.

A moment later he felt Gregory gently hauling him up.

"Hey, feller, don't conk out on me."

"I am okay," Ghote managed to say. "Thank you for your kind attention."

"Now, I'll prop you up here. Then you can keep a bit of a watch-out and get some rest too."

Gregory was handling him with great care and deftness. He gave the carnal figures on the wall opposite one last look and closed his eyes once more.

He lost count of how long he stayed where he had been propped, in a dreamy state of half-wakefulness. But suddenly he was alert again.

Someone was calling him.

"Mr. Policeman. Mr. Policeman."

He started to scrabble up.

"It's okay, Ganesh," Gregory said. "It's just those guys. They seem to want a parley or something. Can you handle it?"

"Yes. Yes, I can," Ghote said.

He looked at Gregory. The American was crouching in the archway, the gun in his right hand pointing steadily forward.

Ghote pushed himself cautiously off the supporting wall. He was conscious that the convenient handle he was using to haul himself up was the miniature carved representation of a graceful, full-figured girl curved voluptuously round her partner. It did not seem to matter.

"What do you want?" he called to the dacoits outside.

"Come out," one of them shouted back.

"Throw your guns down and we will come," Ghote answered.

The men laughed coarsely.

"Throw away our guns, Policemanji? When we are winning? You are wounded. We have seen that. It will not be long. But if you like, we are ready to make bargain."

"What bargain is this?" Ghote called back.

He could not understand what possible offer the dacoits could have to make, and the effort of dealing with them seemed to be taking an unfair amount of his remaining strength.

"It is a very easy bargain, Policemanji. Tell the American to come out with you and when you come we will make sure no harm comes to yourself."

"No."

The dacoits did not seem put out by the refusal. The one doing the talking went cheerfully on.

"Think a little, Policemanji. What is it you have there?

A foreigner only. Who is he that you should wish to die for him? He cannot even know what we are talking."

Ghote reflected dully that this at least was true. Gregory, crouching there just beside him, had not the least notion of what was being plotted against him.

" It is very simple, Policeman. When we have dealt with the American, there is much pay for us. So we would carry you to car and drive to the Bombay road. Soon you would be in hospital and safe. In a few days only you would be at home. You have wife, Policemanji?"

And Ghote found that he was considering the offer. He was not thinking whether he should accept it, but he was turning its terms slowly over in his dulled mind. And on the face of it, they were attractive terms. All he had to do was sacrifice an unknown foreigner, who was quite likely to be killed anyway, and his own chances were automatically doubled.

He touched the bandage round his right arm. It was very heavily soaked now. He must be losing blood at a great rate. His fingers came into contact with the knot.

Gregory tied that, he thought.

" Never. Never."

His defiant shout echoed for a long while round the temple hall. Only when it had completely died away did the dacoits' spokesman reply.

" We can wait," he called.

When Ghote had gathered his strength again a little, he told Gregory the gist of the dacoits' proposal. Gregory did not thank him in words. But the one look he gave him showed he understood what Ghote had done, and what he could so easily have done.

" I guess we can wait too," he said simply.

He nodded towards the running friezes of little carnal figures.

" After all, we have entertainment," he said. " Not that entertainment is quite what they provide," he added after a long, thoughtful pause.

Ghote decided he was not so sure that they could wait. It would take V.V. a good time to reach Panvel and its police post. It would take a rescue party a good while to get back. They could well be too late.

And it was possible that V.V. was not going to the police at all. He might after all have been an India First spy and simply unwilling to unmask himself unnecessarily. He could safely leave the hired dacoits to do their work and creep away himself to report to his immediate superior in that chain of command Colonel Mehta had spoken of. And even if he was merely an obsessed journalist in search of a story, it was quite possible that he would consider getting to Bombay to meet a deadline more urgent than stopping in Panvel to explain things to the police.

For some time Ghote thought about all this. And then he came to the conclusion that after all he and Gregory must not just sit and wait in their little prison, with its compellingly vivid reminders of the joys of life, for death to come almost inevitably. They must make a move themselves.

After a little he told Gregory what he had in mind.

"Okay, go ahead. It may work."

Propping himself near the chamber entrance once more, Ghote called over to the dacoits. They answered quickly enough.

"You are bringing him out, Policemanji?"

"No, I am not," Ghote called back. "But I am going to give you good advice. There is something you do not know. There were not two but three of us in the temple. One of us got away when you ran in."

The effort of calling this out, sentence by sentence, had exhausted him. He shut his eyes and waited listlessly to see what would happen.

The dacoits evidently thought what he had said worth thinking about. He heard them talking together in low voices. Then came their answer.

"Policemanji?"

" Yes?"

"You are lying like the dog you are. We will kill you both."

He could not gather up enough energy to reply. Once more he shut his eyes to everything, to Gregory kneeling watchfully with the revolver resting on his thigh, to the faint sounds coming from their enemy, to the mocking little images of carefree sportiveness all around.

When he opened his eyes next it was to find the dacoits had put out their torch.

" Conserving the power, I guess," Gregory said.

Ghote took a long, deep breath.

" There is something I must tell you," he said.

" What's that?" Gregory answered, a little casually.

Then abruptly he put his face close to Ghote's and looked at him hard.

" Now, listen, feller," he said, " right now you shouldn't be telling anybody anything you don't have to. You're not looking one bit good. You just rest up while you can."

Ghote shook his head with an effort.

" I must tell you now," he said. " You know that at any moment those two out there may rush us. And when our three rounds have gone, that will be that. And I want you to know this. You must know it, in case you die."

" Hell, there's no question of anybody dying. Those guys don't realise we have so little ammunition. They're not going to risk stopping a bullet if they don't have to, and help'll be coming pretty soon. Cheer up. Cheer up."

Ghote sighed a little impatiently.

" You are right, perhaps," he said. " But perhaps you are not. And I am going to tell while I am sure I have enough strength."

" Okay then. Go ahead, if it means a lot to you."

For a few seconds Ghote sat in silence trying to arrange his thoughts. But when he did speak what he had to say came out in an unruly spate which he resented but could not control.

"It is this," he said. " I am not working as a policeman. I have been taken away from the C.I.D. I am working for a Government agency, a security group. It is called the Special Investigations Agency. And Colonel Mehta, the commander, gave me one task before everything else. It is not even to protect you from India First though I have been told to do that. It is to find out just how much your brother discovered on his visit to Trombay. And you do know what he saw there, I am sure of that. That is why you have always refused to answer when I asked about what he told you before you left for Poona. But I had to keep asking. Those were my orders."

For a moment he paused, simply to take breath.

" I wanted for you to know," he went on. " To know I have been trying to trick you into giving me your confidence. All this time I have been lying that this was police matter only."

Gregory Strongbow, kneeling in the entrance of their enforced prison, still keeping an alert watch out towards where the two men with guns waited, chuckled a little.

"You certainly fooled me in the end," he said. " Of course, at the start I pretty well reckoned you must be from whatever the Indian equivalent of the F.B.I. is. I expected to have a spy planted on me, perhaps even a discreet killer. But after all that we'd been through together I'd come to trust you a hundred per cent."

"You were wrong to," Ghote said.

Gregory chuckled again.

"Was I so wrong? You told me the truth finally. You didn't have to, not if you felt your first loyalty was to—what is it?—the Secret Investigation Agency."

"Special Investigations."

"Well, if you felt your first loyalty was to that, you didn't have to say a word. You could have let me die ignorant. And I reckon in any case I'm not going to die."

"It is difficult to know which loyalty is the first," Ghote said wearily. " In so many directions we are tugged."

Gregory did not reply at once. He shifted his position at the chamber mouth a little, and then glanced across at Ghote.

" Yes," he said, " we're tugged in a good many directions, all of us. And I think it's about time I let a different pull take over with me."

" With you ? "

" Heck, I'm just as tugged different ways as you. More even."

" I do not understand."

" No? Well, let me tell you something. All this while that I've been keeping Hector's big secret for him, I've been resenting him dead just as much as I disliked him alive."

" Resenting your brother? Disliking him ? "

Ghote felt his already enfeebled brain suddenly turning topsy-turvy. If there had been one point which he had taken constantly for granted ever since he had first met Gregory on the Poona road and had mistaken this unacademic figure for an American pressman, it was that Gregory was totally loyal to his brother. They had come to India together, bringing with them entwined memories of their family life, brothers friends enough to want to be with one another on a long, exciting holiday. And Hector had met violent death. That had been the picture from the very beginning. And now it had been abruptly and completely reversed.

" Sure I disliked Hector," Gregory said. " He wasn't a very pleasant character. He made a darn fool of himself with all that hysterical anti-Bomb stuff and got into a lot of trouble he purely deserved. And he did it out of spite that he hadn't made a bigger career. Then he ran out on his wife, who is a lovely person, with some damned beatnik girl he'd picked up. And when that blew up in his face, I thought it was just about time to take him out of the way before he did any more harm. So we fixed this good, long vacation in India. And look what mess that got us into, thanks to my kid brother and his poking around."

Ghote simply listened.

"Yes, that's what it was," Gregory went on, "plain poking around where he'd no business to be. And it just so happened that he found out something that was being kept pretty quiet over at Trombay."

He laughed.

"Here comes what you were sent to find out," he said. "It's just this. India not only has the Bomb, in spite of what they all tell you, but she has had it a good long time and what's more has hit on a way of making the things at about a hundredth the cost of any previous type. So she's not only a nominal atom power, but in actual fact ready to knock hell out of practically anybody."

He stopped and allowed himself a long, relaxed chuckle.

"Boy," he said, "when you gave me that stuff on the way out to Elephanta about Indians having a genius for improvisation, I couldn't have agreed with you more. And they can improvise a sight more than running repairs to an old outboard motor."

Ghote forced himself to fight back against growing waves of weakness.

"Gregory," he said. "Thank you for telling."

"Heck, I ought to have told you long ago."

"No," Ghote said, "I did not trust you. I did not even trust you with a simple gun."

He felt himself sliding sideways against the smooth stone of the pillar at his back. He struggled to get his grip on things again.

"I understand a lot more now," he said. "No wonder India First wanted that secret kept. I suppose Hector would not have kept quiet for long."

"He would not," Gregory answered. "It was all I could do to persuade him to keep his mouth shut when we met outside that Victoria Terminus. And no doubt he was haring out to Poona to tell me he'd changed his mind about the promise he gave me. He had that much decency, I guess."

He was silent for a little. When he spoke again, Ghote could hardly hear him because of the murmurous buzz he felt in his head.

" Ganesh," he said, " I've been thinking. If you weren't planted on me by the Government guys, someone was pretty certainly planted on me by India First. Listen, if we do get out of this alive, I want you to question Shakuntala, and question her till she breaks."

" Yes," Ghote said, " I will do it."

As if the words had been a signal, the dacoits' torch beam flicked on again. At Ghote's side the writhing figures of the mithunas sprang back to sensuous life.

Gregory rapidly shifted his stance in the doorway. Leaning tensely forward into the gloom, he found time for one murmured comment.

" Those darn sex-fiends," he said. " Won't they ever leave off?"

After that they listened in silence. Very faint scuffling sounds came from the dark temple hall.

" Damn it, what are they doing?" Gregory exploded at last.

It was impossible to make out. Ghote felt incredibly weary with even making the effort. After a long while he realised that Gregory was talking again. He forced himself to concentrate.

" This ought to do it," the American was saying.

Ghote saw him take something from the inner pocket of his jacket. He strained to see what it was. In the sharp torchlight he eventually made it out. Something the size of a small coin, mostly white with black on it.

Hector Strongbow's C.N.D. button.

Then he saw Gregory toss the little disc carefully forward. It landed out in the hall beyond with a tiny clatter and skittled across the stones of the floor.

Two bursts of shots followed. When the echoes had died away Gregory spoke contentedly.

" I get it," he said. " They're trying to creep up on us. I know where they are now though, and I think I could put a shot pretty near one of them. But I'd like to save it if I can. Listen, Ganesh. Do you think you could call out to them that I've spotted them and I'm ready to shoot. If that scares them back, we've saved a bullet."

" I would try," Ghote whispered.

He breathed deeply. Once. Twice.

He was in real doubt whether he would be able to shout with enough force and conviction. But for Gregory's sake he was determined to try.

A last long breath.

And then he stopped. The two dacoits had begun talking to each other. Urgently and quite loudly. He caught the word " police." And suddenly the torch went out and there was the plain sound of feet running out of the hall.

Ghote gathered his last strength together.

" Do not go, Gregory," he said. " Trap."

Then came total blackness.

CHAPTER XVI

GHOTE OPENED his eyes and pushed himself up on his elbows. For several minutes now he had been feeling that he would be able to cope with things, and he thought that the moment had now come to see whether the curious procession of events of which he had been half-conscious had really taken place.

He looked round a little. It was as he had thought. He was lying on Gregory Strongbow's bed in his room in the Queen's Imperial Grand Hotel. Above him the seven long-bladed fans swept round and round. But about the other events that must have led to his finding himself here he would have to ask.

Gregory was standing by the tall window over which the long brocade curtains had been drawn. He was talking in a low voice to Shakuntala.

" Please," Ghote said, " what is the time?"

Gregory and Shakuntala wheeled round.

"You're okay?" Gregory asked.

"It's nearly midnight," Shakuntala said. "And you're not to worry. Everything has been taken care of."

"It is the same day as when we went to the temple?" Ghote inquired.

"Yes, it's the same day," Gregory said. "A pretty long day, but a pretty good one. According to Dr. Udeshi there's nothing wrong with you that some rest won't put right."

"I feel quite well again," Ghote said.

Gregory grinned.

"Old Udeshi gave strict instructions you weren't to move," he said.

Ghote flopped back on the great mound of pillows behind him.

"Please, do I remember Shakuntala at the temple?" he said.

"You do," Gregory answered. "She was what the dacoits mistook for the police. When they heard her coming, they must have remembered what you told them about V.V. and thought the game was up. Anyway, they lit out pretty quick."

Ghote frowned.

"But what was Shakuntala doing there at all?" he said.

"I was disobeying instructions," Shakuntala replied with a smile. "You know that V.V. came along while I was talking to Mira Jehangir in her car. Well, by that time I was beginning to regret I'd ever started that. She really is pretty awful."

Grinning widely, Gregory gave her a nudge.

"Go on, tell the feller what happened," he said.

"Well, V.V. asked where you two were, and I decided to go with him to show him. When we got to the little lake he told me to wait for him in the car whatever happened. But I began to get worried, and in the end I just disregarded what he'd said and set out to see for myself. Only I got lost."

" Lost in the jungle?" Ghote said anxiously.

" Oh, yes," Shakuntala answered. " I wasn't frightened or anything, because my father was in the Forestry Service and I'm used to jungle. But I tried to be too clever and couldn't find the path again."

" It was a pretty good thing she did," Gregory interrupted. " If we'd had to wait for the police it might have been too late."

" But they came?" Ghote asked. " V.V. did go to them?"

" Yes. We met them later, but I'm afraid they'd be too late to get the dacoits."

" They will pick them up soon," Ghote declared. " The State Police are highly efficient."

Suddenly he sat up straight on the big soft bed.

" The telephone," he said. " I must use the telephone."

" Why? What is this?" Gregory asked with anxiety.

" Kartar Singh," Ghote said. " He told us the truth. I must arrange at once to have him brought to Bombay."

He took the bedside telephone and asked for a number. The necessary explaining and arguing left him feeling a good deal weaker, but eventually he was able to flop back on to the mounded pillows with a sense of duty accomplished.

For some time he lay back while a bearer brought in a meal, under the personal supervision of the manager, who was looking grimly furious and was obviously missing his car, if not his receptionist.

When he had eaten his fill, Gregory looked down at him smilingly.

" You look more your usual self now," he said.

" I feel perfectly better," Ghote declared.

" You're sure? You're certain?"

There seemed to be a note of undue concern in his voice. Ghote put it down to a feeling of emotional loyalty that must have grown up during their ordeal in the temple.

" Really," he said, with a smile, " I am quite my old self again."

" Well, if you really are . . ."

" Yes. What is it?"

" Well, you've got some questions to ask Shakuntala, haven't you?"

The thought of what it was that he had promised Gregory to ask Shakuntala came back into his mind with unpleasant clarity. For a moment he contemplated pleading tiredness, but he felt he could hardly go back so suddenly on his protestations of a moment before, however exaggerated they had been.

He pushed himself up to a sitting position on the high bed.

" Yes," he said, " I have got some questions."

Shakuntala sat down abruptly on the small, cane-seated chair near the foot of the bed. She looked up at Ghote with a suddenly strained expression. There could be no doubt she knew what it was he was going to ask.

" Miss Brown," Ghote began, " you told just now that you took V.V. to the lake near the temple where you knew we had gone. Why was that?"

Shakuntala looked dismayed. This was not the question she had been exactly expecting.

" I wanted him to be there in case he could help you," she said.

" You knew Gregory's life was in danger. Was not V.V. among the most likely ones to be spying on him?"

" No. Well, yes. But——"

She stopped and looked down at her feet.

Suddenly she shook herself as if to break free from a tangle of jungle tendrils that had entrapped her. She looked straight up at Ghote.

" I knew V.V. could not be the India First spy," she said, " because it was me they had set to report on Gregory."

In the far corner of the big, high-ceilinged room Ghote saw Gregory go stiff as a post.

" Yes," Ghote said to Shakuntala, " you were the India First spy. You were always the most likely person, even from the moment that you tried with so much force to persuade Gregory that it was all in the day's work for the dacoits to have waited all morning before deciding to attack one particular car."

He looked down at her implacably. And saw her eyes were flashing with anger.

"Yes," she said, "I was an India First agent. I have worked for India First for a long time. I believed they were right. This country could take its true place in the world if its people were loyal to it as they should be, if they all worked as they should work. But understand this. I found there came a time when I had to choose between India First and something else."

She jumped up suddenly and stood looking intently at the stock-still figure of the American in the far corner of the room.

"I found I had to choose between the country I was born in and a foreigner," she said. "And I found that I could not help myself but choose the foreigner. The man I once thought stood for everything I detested."

Standing gravely in the corner, Gregory Strongbow spoke at last.

"You say you chose me. But you never said a single word to hint to me who or what you were."

"No, I never said a single word. But all the same, from the moment I decided that my allegiance had changed I never did one single thing to help India First. I promise you that."

"But why? Why?" Gregory said.

"I told you. For years I was with India First, heart and soul. Do you think I could change right round in the twinkling of an eye? I think more of myself than that."

Gregory looked across at her with a perturbed frown.

"I do think I see," he said.

"You must see," she replied fiercely. "You must see. All right, I had changed sides. But I still had to be loyal to what I had once believed. I was against India First. Totally, if you like. But I was still with India First in the past."

She looked back at Gregory with utterly concentrated intentness. Ghote guessed that she had probably forgotten that he himself was in the room at all.

Gregory stood in silence. Then he took a pace forward.

" Yes," he said, " I see now why you let me go to find the launch at Sewri and at the same time left that message. You couldn't hound down people you'd been working with until a few days ago. I respect you for that."

And Shakuntala fell on to the edge of the bed in floods of relieved tears.

For minutes Ghote let her weep. But he had not finished yet.

" There is one more thing," he said eventually.

She pushed herself up from the bed and turned to him, brushing the tears away.

" Yes ?"

" You told that from the moment you decided not to be loyal any longer to India First you did nothing to help them. But when was that moment?"

Shakuntala blinked at him from washed-out eyes.

" I can tell you exactly," she said. " It was at the moment you brought Gregory back here after he had been attacked on Marine Drive. I knew then that I could not be loyal to an organisation prepared to do that to a man like Gregory, innocent and in a foreign land."

" But it was you who sent him to that meeting on Marine Drive?"

Shakuntala hung her head.

" Yes, I admit it."

" But you did not know an attack was planned for the Elephanta trip? I thought you were strangely confident that the launch could not be aiming for us."

" Yes," Shakuntala replied, " that was a complete surprise to me. Some other agent must have watched us leave. I was sure no attack had been planned because I had heard nothing."

Ghote nodded.

" And for the attack on Marine Drive," he asked, " you received orders by telephone?"

" Yes."

" Who from?"

" I don't know. Someone high up in the organisation, I think. In the ordinary way you had only one contact above you and one below. Mine were in Poona, because I was there with the Tourist Department. But it was someone else who phoned me here."

" How did you know this man was from India First?"

" There was a code-word for use in emergency."

" I see. And you did not in any way recognise this man?"

" No. It was a man's voice, that's all."

" And as soon as you got your instructions you acted on them?"

" Yes. At once."

" I see," Ghote said.

While he had been asking Shakuntala these last questions, Gregory had come up and rested his broad hands lightly on her shoulders. Now Ghote looked up at him.

" You realise what this means?" he said. " I shall have to see Colonel Mehta immediately."

: :   : :

It was about an hour later that Ghote, after making one telephone call, found himself once more making his way up the interminable flights of neglected stairs that led to Colonel Mehta's eyrie office. He had come by taxi through the now nearly deserted night streets to the back entrance of the huge, old, Gothic office block. Waiting for him there was the chowkidar, an aged Pathan, almost as much a relic of the past as the old building he guarded, wearing a turban and the traditional waistcoat and baggy trousers and armed with a crooked stick. With quavering fingers he had handed Ghote a lamp to light him on his way in the dark, silent building. It was a pathetic enough source of light, a mere tag of wick floating in coconut oil in an earthenware bowl. The little coil of thick, greasy-smelling smoke that it gave

off seemed to add unduly to the stiflingly clammy heat of
the old, still building.

Ghote felt a new onset of weakness as he climbed. He
knew that, like Gregory earlier on, he too should have
obeyed Dr. Udeshi's orders and stayed in bed. He believed
in doing what the doctor told him. But sometimes other
things had a prior claim.

But at last he reached the top of the seemingly unending
series of turning flights and there under the door with the
notice saying simply " Special Investigations Agency " was
a thin line of light.

Ghote stepped forward and knocked.

" Come."

He recognised Colonel Mehta's clipped accent. He
entered, crossed the bare outer office with its embedded
wall-safe, the colonel's sole concession to the need to retain
any documents, and pushed at the slightly open door of the
inner office.

Colonel Mehta was sitting just exactly as Ghote had seen
him before, precise and upright behind the bare table with
its single telephone.

" Well, Inspector," he said briskly, " what's all this
about? I don't like holding interviews in the middle of the
bloody night unless I have to, you know."

" There are special circumstances, Colonel."

" I should damn' well hope so. Let's hear 'em then."

" Very well."

Ghote remained standing in front of the small, bare table,
looking down a little at the spruce, seated figure of the
colonel.

" Colonel, I am near the end of the whole business."

" Near the end? And what precisely do you mean by
that? You've picked up those damned dacoits, I suppose.
Well, I've heard nothing of that. I was supposed to be kept
bloody well informed."

He glared round as if there might be someone in the
bare room to be put immediately under close arrest.

" No," Ghote said, " it is not that. The dacoits have not

been picked up yet. It is that I know who gave them their orders."

"You do, do you, Inspector? I shall believe that when I hear it."

"Very well. Then may I ask how it was that Professor Strongbow was sent to meet an apparently accidental death within minutes of my having informed you, and no one else, that he had in fact seen his brother after the Trombay visit?"

Colonel Mehta did not answer.

He looked up at Ghote from under his bristling eyebrows, steadily and hard. Then he dropped his glance and began fiddling with the button of his trimly fastened jacket. Eventually he looked up again and spoke.

"Let me get this bloody well straight, Inspector," he said, in a voice lacking its former fieriness. "You're saying that I was the only person who knew Professor Strongbow had learnt his brother's secret, and that the orders to kill him went out so quickly that it could only have been me who gave them? Is that it? Have I got it right?"

He sounded almost humble.

"Yes," Ghote answered, "I am saying that the head of Special Investigations Agency is head of India First also. The simple policeman you thought would keep you ahead of any awkward inquiries has found out the truth."

"I see. But why have you come to me with all this? Surely you should have gone higher up? It should have been a visitor from Delhi I was receiving and not a mere police inspector. Unless what you've been telling me is a mere cock-and-bull story?"

"No, it is not," Ghote said. "But who could I go to higher up? You know there was no one. You told me yourself it would be like that. I think no one in Delhi knew about Hector Strongbow's visit to Trombay even. I heard you telling my DSP not to breathe a word about it. Who would believe me then? And if they did, might it not be to another traitor I was talking?"

Colonel Mehta gave a sharp grunt.

" So what have you come here to do then ? " he asked.

" To arrest you, Colonel, on a charge of conspiring to murder Hector Strongbow on or about the fourth of September last."

And Colonel Mehta laughed. A sudden splutter of mirth, as if he could not help it.

Then he slipped the heavy Service revolver from his under-arm holster and pointed it straight at Ghote.

" You bloody incompetent fool," he said.

The shots rang out in the hot stillness of the big, deserted building like a series of minor explosions.

Gregory Strongbow came in through the slightly open door from the outer office.

" Thank you, Gregory," Ghote said. " I knew I could trust your shooting."

He looked down at the body of Colonel Mehta, officer in charge of the rootless Special Investigations Agency, head of the self-centred India First group. It lay sprawled back against the bare wall of the totally bare, recordless little office.

" Unknown assailants have killed another person," he said. " The crime figures will be bad this month."